Twisted Perception

Bedside Books
An imprint of American Book Publishing
P.O. Box 65624
Salt Lake City, UT 84165
www.american-book.com
Printed in the United States of America on acid-free paper.

Twisted Perception

Designed by George Shewchuk, design@american-book.com

Publisher's Note: *This is a work of fiction. Names, characters, places, and incidents either are the product of the author's imagination, or are used fictitiously, and any resemblance to actual persons, living or dead, events, or locales is entirely coincidental.*

ISBN 1-58982-271-4

Avey, Bob, Twisted Perception

Special Sales

Twisted Perception

Bob Avey

Bob Avey

Dedication

For my wife, Kathi

Chapter One

A car horn interrupted the driver's thoughts, and he realized his mind had been elsewhere, reliving a despairing moment, an ugly slice of time in which he'd killed a friend. A tear formed in his eye and rolled down his cheek.

He hoped the night would not hold any more surprises. Enough had already gone wrong. He hesitated, and when he pulled onto the road the reflection of the street lamps off the wet pavement reminded him of a carnival midway, and he fancied being transported to another world where things would not be as they were: life dependent on death.

He tightened his grip on the steering wheel and cursed the troublesome mist that swirled through the air. He could discern no rain falling, though the moisture seemed to be everywhere, a monsoon of molecular proportions emanating from the fabric of the world it coated. His lack of concentration didn't surprise him. He didn't want to be there, driving around town on such a night. The windshield wipers cleared his field of vision, and when he saw the place where he'd found her before, some bar along 31st Street, he slowed the car and pulled in. His actions were not prescient, or even fantastic. He knew where to look. She frequented such places.

He heard a rattling noise and realized it was his ring clattering against the steering wheel as his hands shook. He wanted to blame it on the wine, but he knew better. The drinking had not intoxicated him to the point of being even remotely prepared for the task ahead of him. Beads of sweat ran down his back at the thought of it. There was no getting around what he had to do. She'd come back. And people ought to stay dead when they're put that way.

He thought of Papa. Times like this perpetuated his essence, and he imagined his name—though he didn't speak it, and he did not for a moment pretend to assume his presence. That would be tantamount to disrespect, and disrespecting Papa was not a good idea. He rolled down the car window, letting the cold mist pepper his face as he leaned back in the seat, and waited.

Michelle Baker stepped off the stage and tried to ignore the remnants of the night's audience, the leering faces, each sharing a fantasy they thought their own, and it went through her again, one of those black-hole feelings that sucks you in and tells you you're not getting out, no matter what you do. The doctors called it depression. Michelle called it life, because it had always been that way for her. But there were moments, like that time in Florida, early in the season before the heat set in. A stiff breeze had come off the sea and rolled back the clouds, leaving the moon and stars contrasting against the black sky. Then the dark haired man with rope sandals in his hand slid his arm around her, just as natural as that, and they walked along the beach talking of life as if it were theirs. There had been no darkness then.

Her shift was over. She was going home. She could have her mother pack some clothes and together they could drive down to South Texas, spend a few days at Padre Island.

Lisa, another dancer, a soft little brunette who'd only been there about a month, intentionally brushed against Michelle as she walked past.

Chapter One

"Hey, sweetie," she whispered.

Michelle smiled but said nothing. It came with the territory in these places, the girls loving each other. You learn to hate men so you turn lesbian. The problem with that is after a few weeks, or months, or however long it takes you, you start to hate women too. And where does that leave you? In hell, she guessed.

She didn't even rehearse anymore, worrying over the steps and the music. None of that really mattered. She was a stripper, beginning her act with suggestive clothing and ending with nothing but an idea. It was, though, the boring monotony—the same faces, the same looks and catcalls—that allowed one to detach from it all and exist in such a world. But there were exceptions, those nights when someone would stand out from the crowd, their eyes searching deeper than her nakedness, and that scared her, for she knew the thoughts of such people went beyond fantasy, and they would make them real, given half a chance. She had not seen anyone like that tonight, but the fearful feelings that surrounded those encounters wrapped around her thoughts, and lingered heavy as she said good-bye to the other dancers and stepped outside into the rain.

He sat forward in the car seat and stared in disbelief. She was there all right. There had been no mistake. And when she crossed the parking lot, she saw him as well, her lovely blue eyes piercing the night as if they carried their own source of illumination. She seemed to look right through him, but he knew that was just an act. A smile played across his lips. The parking lot was empty except for the two of them. He'd planned on following her, but it wouldn't be necessary. He did have a bit of luck now and then. He worked his hands into surgical gloves and grabbed the roll of duct tape. He tore off a six- inch piece then ran his hand through the roll, wearing it like a bracelet. Next he retrieved the sock from the floorboard. It was lined with plastic and filled with wet sand.

Opening the car door, he stepped quietly onto the asphalt, sliding the black-handled knife into his back pocket. He did not intend to use it just yet, but he would if he had to. With the torn piece of tape readied in his hand, he came up behind her. She was completely unaware of his presence, and he paused as the sweet scent coming from her hair filled his senses. He wanted to touch her, to take her in his arms and love her, the way he had always loved her. It was then that he saw her the way she had been, laying on her bed, wearing only the top half of her see-through pajamas while she pulled the covers back and shifted ever so slightly. It was not unusual. She often stayed that way after it was over, even getting out of bed on occasion to walk around the room, stopping close where he could see her, watch her through the cracks in the door.

He thought about the small room that had been his prison, where dust particles would dance in the sunlight that showed through the broken window shade, giving an impression of substance to the beams, making it appear as if he could reach out and grab them. But that, like so much else, had been nothing more than an illusion. The dust was not only in the light. It had filled the room. He'd eaten mouthfuls of it with every breath. They were casualties of their own fates, and he thought she must surely understand what he had to do.

He raised the sock, swinging in a high arc to give it more velocity, and when he brought it down against the back of her head, he remembered how the light would catch her pretty necklace as she walked about the room. It was an enlightening moment, for she dropped quite readily to her knees, not unconscious, but dazed to the point of incoherence. He pressed the piece of tape over her mouth then slid the roll from his arm. He pulled her hands behind her and bound them with several revolutions, then tore off another piece and slapped it across her eyes as he brought her to her feet. She offered little resistance and a delightful urge to take her now ran through him, testing his resolve. He pushed the thoughts away and guided her across the parking lot toward the car. Once there, he shoved her into the backseat. The lot was still empty. He started the car and drove away, pulling onto 31st Street.

When he reached Yale Avenue, he turned south, traveling until he found a suitable location, an old house that had lost the fight for survival. It stood in a neighborhood that had been suburban but was now a mixture of banks, retail outlets, and, ironically enough, real estate offices. Acting as a reminder of the house's fate, an industrial trash bin sat in the front yard, boasting the name of some construction company on its side. He thought that a ridiculous notion. What they were up to was anything but constructive.

He pulled her from the car and walked her to the front of the house, pausing briefly to check the door. It wasn't locked. They seldom were. He pushed her inside, his heart pounding with anticipation as he switched on the flashlight he'd doctored for just such occasions. Its dim red glow revealed an old mattress on the floor. Some things were just meant to be. She had begun to struggle, even as he'd pulled her from the car, and he had no choice but to use the sock again. With a small shove she fell onto the mattress.

Kneeling beside her, he removed the tape from her eyes and studied her face, so pretty and yet so lined with fear he hardly recognized it. She could not speak. He'd left the tape on her mouth, but she shook her head and pleaded with every expression she had available. It had been cold in that room, a chilling dampness understood only by those left alone, not for moments, but for eternities in an unforgiving and infinite darkness. He would not go back. She would die first.

Michelle Baker felt the man's warm breath fall across her face, and she thought it like the stale air that might be in a dark room where an electric chair was kept. He was going to kill her. She knew that. But it was not the details of her death that went through her head. She thought of her son, Michael. She could see him in the dirty little yard where he played, and she wondered if his diaper had been changed, and if he was hungry. She was not a good mother. She closed her eyes and prayed for God to forgive her for that, something she did quite often, though it did not show in her life. She regretted that now.

He stroked her hair with the back of his hand, which caused her to squeeze her eyes tightly shut. He kissed her on the cheek and whispered in her ear, "When you wish upon a star, makes no difference who you are." Then he brought the black-handled knife to her chest and put his weight into it, shoving it through her ribcage and into her heart. With that her lies gave way to the truth, and for her penance he laid her throat open, cutting it in the shape of a T. Capital T for Papa Terrance.

Chapter Two

As soon as Detective Kenny Elliot stepped out of his car, he knew he'd slowed, stumbled somewhere along the way, for it had finally caught up with him, and like a twenty-nine-year-old boxer who grows old in the third round of a title fight, he would never be the same. It was what he saw in the vehicle, a late model Mercedes left beside a trash dumpster. It was in the parking lot of the Village at Central Park, a bunch of upscale, newly constructed condominiums just off Peoria Avenue.

Elliot silently cursed Captain Dombrowski for dragging him into this on his day off. It'd been 6:00 a.m. when the phone rang, and Elliot had come out of his sleep in a fit, fighting to rid himself of the bed sheets that trapped his legs and torso like some kind of malignant ivy. He hadn't been sleeping well. It was the dreams; they'd started again. They'd become intense, occurring more frequently and leaving in their wake unsettling thoughts that rambled through his head—burdensome notions that something wasn't quite right in his world, a problem just below the surface that he couldn't quite drag into consciousness.

Elliot had a pretty good idea why Dombrowski had called. Cunningham was on vacation somewhere in Montana and Mendez was out with the flu, but there were other detectives. Obviously, Dombrowski knew there would be more to it than a simple homicide, if "simple" can be used when talking about deliberate death. An informal understanding had begun to develop inside the department. Dombrowski had an instinct about unusual cases, knowing which ones would deviate from the norm, and Elliot had a knack for solving them.

Elliot approached the Mercedes, a knot forming in his gut, his usual calm behavior displaced by his progress like the smooth surface of a pond disrupted by gas bubbles escaping from something vile hidden beneath its depths. An image of Carmen Garcia blossomed in his mind.

Don't do this, Kenny. We can work it out.

He thought about the report. He couldn't write it up indicating the suspect was a ghost, an unseen demon, but as he approached the Mercedes that thought vibrated through his head. Then, as he drew near and confirmed that it was indeed a necklace dangling from the inside mirror, his legs nearly gave way and for a moment his thoughts were in another time and place.

Blood-smeared words flashed through his memory.

Johnnie Boy was here.

Johnnie Alexander and Marcia Barnes were inside the car, both covered in blood, both dead. Then he saw the class ring. The one he'd given to Marcia. She'd worn it suspended from a gold chain around her neck, though it now hung from the rearview mirror of Johnnie's Mustang, where it twisted mockingly in the darkness, catching the light of the moon and sparkling like some distant star.

"Pretty fancy jewelry, huh, Elliot? Hey, man, you okay?"

Snapping back to the present, Elliot looked across the top of the Mercedes to see Sergeant Conley, his forehead wrinkled with concern. Elliot surveyed the condominiums. Several blocks of houses had been torn down to accommodate the construction of the two-story brick villas designed with wrought-iron railings and small balconies to emulate something from the New Orleans

French Quarter. To the north was a park. A sign proclaimed it to be Centennial Park, though it was still thought of as Central Park by those who knew the place. It'd been nice once, playing host to family barbecues and games of badminton on the grass, but the area had deteriorated over the years and had fallen into disrepair, eventually being frequented by those who hid in its uncut bushes and eased their pain with wine and drugs. Recently, for the benefit of the condominiums, the bushes had been trimmed and the grass mowed. They even renamed it. But the shadowy homeless people could still be seen there, sitting in groups around picnic tables, clutching bottles of wine wrapped in brown paper bags.

A small crowd of neighbors had gathered to gawk at the taped-off crime scene. For the homeless it was more of a curiosity, another constant reminder of their own mortality; but for those unaccustomed to such things, like the fresh residents of the newly constructed condos, it was more like a chapter torn from the pages of a horror novel.

Elliot turned back to Sergeant Conley. "Yeah," Elliot said. "I'm fine."

Conley's expression said he wasn't buying it and Elliot wasn't surprised. He was sure he looked as pale and lifeless as the corpse sitting in the car. He backed off a bit then began working his way around the scene, taking pictures to review later. When he came to the passenger side of the car, he lowered the camera and worked his hand into a latex glove, wincing as he opened the door, causing the air inside the car, thick with the scents of urine and blood, to flood his senses.

The victim, a female that Elliot guessed to be about thirty years of age, was in the passenger seat with her head tilted back and her hands in her lap. The deep gash across her throat still looked fresh. The expensive necklace had been removed to keep it from being damaged. Everything about her said money, but through the lens of the camera, the massive diamond on her left hand looked as cold and detached as a severed limb. The necklace that dangled from the rearview mirror matched her earrings.

Johnnie Boy was here.

"Sure is dressed nice," Conley said.

Elliot nodded, noting that her handbag lay undisturbed on the seat beside her, near a smear of blood where it looked like the killer had wiped the knife clean. On the floorboard beneath the brake pedal was a cell phone. Elliot picked it up. It was still on, so he hit redial. The display showed the last call was to the Tulsa Police Department. He started to comment when the sound of an approaching car caught his attention. He knew it would be Beaumont, but he confirmed it, watching the detective pull up. How anyone could keep a car as clean as Beaumont did was a mystery to Elliot. Then again, he suspected that, much like its owner, the car's highly maintained exterior merely masked an embarrassing need for dirty lubricants.

Beaumont climbed out of his car and started toward them, habitually straightening his already perfect tie while he walked around the Mercedes, surveying the scene before he joined Elliot and Conley. "I hope you haven't touched anything," he said.

Elliot shook his head.

He glanced at Conley.

"Not me," Conley said.

Beaumont looked Elliot over, a thin smile crossing his lips.

"What do you think?" He asked. "Do we have a homicide?"

"Looks like it."

Beaumont moved closer to the vehicle, observing the victim. "Looks pretty affluent. By the way, Elliot, where were you last night?"

A wave of regret went through Elliot. He was to have met Beaumont for a beer after work and he'd completely forgotten about it. "Sorry, I guess I fell asleep."

"You must have been dead to the world. I called your house, but you didn't answer."

Conley had walked back to his squad car, where he held the door open, the radio microphone in his hand. When Elliot came over, he tilted his head toward the scene and lowered the mike. "Why'd the captain have to send that jerk?"

Elliot tried to hide his smile. Beaumont, who was already busy dusting for prints, wasn't exactly popular with the patrol officers. He was sharp—real sharp—and he had an impressive way of remembering case details, but he didn't mind letting you know it. "He's pretty good at what he does," Elliot said. "Got an ID on the victim yet?"

Conley nodded. "Name's Lagayle Zimmerman."

Elliot ran the name through his memory, but it didn't register. As he scanned the crime scene, the sounds of traffic on Peoria Avenue wafting through his senses, he noticed two people standing beside another uniformed officer. To Conley, he said, "Any of these people see anything?"

"None that will admit to it," Conley said.

"You question everybody?"

"Yes, sir."

"Who found the body?"

"Some wino," Conley said. "Hang on. I'll get him for you." He signaled for the officer to bring the witnesses over.

The nervous man, who looked about forty, had long, graying hair pulled back in a ponytail. A tattoo of a snake ran up his left arm. The lady reminded Elliot of his second grade school teacher. "I apologize for the wait," he said. "My name's Detective Elliot. I'd like to ask you a few questions."

Conley introduced Bill Morton as the man who discovered the body and Ella Mae Smith as the woman who had called the police. Elliot pulled the man aside first, and after a few steps, he flipped open his notepad. "Mr. Morton, how did you happen to discover the deceased?"

Morton gestured toward the scene. "I was coming up through here, going to the park. The Mercedes was sitting by the dumpster, all crooked-like, so I noticed it right off. When I went past, I saw someone was in the car. She didn't look right, wasn't moving or anything, so I thought I'd better have a look." Morton paused and cleared his throat. "Knew she was dead when I saw all the blood."

Elliot made a notation. "Do you recall what time that was?"

"I don't know, about five thirty, I guess."

"Do you work around here, Mr. Morton?"

"Nah, nothing like that, I was just out getting a little exercise."

Elliot tapped his notepad. Morton was wearing athletic shoes, but the rest of his attire, blue denim jeans and a western shirt, didn't seem to confirm his explanation. "Did you see anyone else nearby?"

"No, but I wasn't really looking."

"Any other cars in the area?"

"Not that I noticed. Except for Mrs. Smith. She pulled in across the way and stopped. She used her phone to call you guys, after I asked her to."

"Why do you suppose she stopped?"

Morton shrugged and reached into his shirt pocket for a pack of cigarettes. He lit up then tossed the match onto the tarmac. "I don't know, Mr. Elliot. Maybe she saw something she didn't like."

Elliot weighed the response. Morton wasn't dressed for a night on the town any more than he was for jogging, but his clothes were free of bloodstains and had no rips or tears. He had no weapons on him, and none were found at the crime scene. It would be nearly impossible to inflict that kind of wound on someone without getting dirty. Of course he could have gotten rid of the weapon, but if he were the killer, why would he leave to ditch the weapon and change clothes, only to return to the scene and call the cops? It didn't seem likely, but Elliot still got the impression Morton wasn't being entirely truthful. "I'd like to ask you to come down to the station with us, Mr. Morton. You're not under arrest. We just want to ask you a few more questions."

A streetwise look of understanding crossed Morton's face. Elliot had seen the look before; Morton had a bit of experience with the police, knew something about their procedures. The last thing he wanted was to go downtown with a bunch of cops, but he figured he had no choice. If he refused it would indicate guilt. If he tried to turn and run, that would be probable cause. He took a draw on his cigarette. "This is exactly why people don't want to get involved. I try to do a good deed and the first thing you know, I'm a suspect."

"Everyone's a suspect, Mr. Morton."

"Yeah? Well, I bet you don't take Mrs. Prissy over there."

"Don't bet on it," Elliot said. "I'd haul the Pope in if I thought he was connected to the case."

Morton shook his head. "You probably would, at that. Yeah, sure, I'll go answer your questions. Not like I got much choice anyway."

After thanking Mr. Morton, Elliot went to the other witness. "Would you mind telling me why you were in the area this morning, Mrs. Smith?"

Ella Mae Smith smiled, and began to speak. "It's Monday. I come down on Mondays and Wednesdays to look after Edna Jones. She gets up with the chickens, if you know what I mean. We're both members of the Presbyterian Church. I've been looking in on older folks who need it for ten years now, not that I wouldn't mind taking a break from it for awhile…taking care of this and worrying about that…but just try and get someone else to do it. Everyone wants to help, so long as they don't have to take responsibility for it. If you want to quiet down a congregation, just ask for volunteers. And Pastor Schaffer can be quite demanding." She paused and shook her head, then continued, "It's not like I didn't know what I was getting myself into. Patricia Letterman, God rest her soul, tried to warn me. She did it for years, you know, until her health started to fail."

"I see," Elliot said. "Could you tell me what caused you to pull up here?"

"Well, it was that car."

"The Mercedes?"

"Yes, sir. Pastor Schaffer has one just like it. Not that he'd park it there. I guess that's what caught my attention. And that strange man lurking about, glancing up and down the sidewalk, all nervous and jittery, like a cat in a room full of dogs."

"You mean Mr. Morton?"

"Yes, sir. I would've just driven on, because I'd figured out by then that it wasn't Pastor Schaffer's car. And that Morton man looked like he was about to leave, too. But then he stopped and pressed his face against the window of that car, like he was trying to get a better look at what was inside. Well, that didn't last long. He backed away from there like he'd touched a hot stove, and I just figured he was going to take off running cause that's what it looked like he wanted to do, but then he saw me."

"Why do you suppose seeing you would bother him?"

"Well for heaven's sake, hon, I don't know. But I can tell you this, when he started toward me, I near lost myself. He scared the wits out of me. I don't know why I showed him my cell phone. I guess I was trying to let him know that I could call for help if I needed to. But that didn't scare him. It seemed to be what he wanted. He started nodding his head and yelling through the glass that someone was inside that car, he thought she might be dead, and would I mind calling the police. Well, let me tell you, I was more than happy to do just that."

"Do you remember what time you made the call?"

"It was before six. That's about the time I usually get here, and I was running a little early."

Elliot closed his notepad and tucked it inside his jacket pocket. "Thank you, Mrs. Smith. That'll be all for now." He stood on the sidewalk for a moment then walked over to the Mercedes, where Beaumont was standing. "You about through here?"

"It's all yours," Beaumont said. Then he surprised Elliot. He put a hand on his shoulder, and with an expression that looked almost personable he said, "You look a little rough around the edges, Elliot. What's bothering you?"

As if on cue, a wind kicked up, a cool and swirling breeze that carried the faint smell of pear blossoms coming from some of the few blooms that had managed to survive the up-and-down temperatures. "It's nothing," Elliot said, "Just a bad case of déjà vu."

Beaumont raised an eyebrow and cocked his head, putting his hands on his hips, an imitation John Wayne in a Park Avenue suit. "Probably not the words you were looking for, but I think I know what you're getting at. The Stillwater murders right? The victims had their throats cut, and as I recall, at least one of them was found like this, in the passenger seat of her car." He paused and rubbed his chin. "That was before your time, too. I must say I'm impressed, old boy."

Elliot wondered how Beaumont knew so much. The Stillwater murders had happened a long time ago, seven years at least, and with no apparent connection to Tulsa. It was a stretch even for a fanatic like Beaumont. Yet he'd brought it up immediately. But Elliot's knowledge of the events hadn't been acquired by studying old case files, as he suspected Beaumont's had. He'd been a little closer to the source, attending classes at Oklahoma State during the murders and reading about them in the *Stillwater Gazette*. "Before your time, as well," he added.

"That it was. Seems there was more to it though, some sort of messages."

"Written in blood," Elliot said. "And the slitting of the throats wasn't like this, a simple cut. They had a pattern, a definite design." Elliot's own words sent a chill through him, but he said nothing more. How could he tell Beaumont the memory that had nearly brought him to his knees hadn't come from Stillwater, but from a time period when he was a high school senior in Porter, Oklahoma?

"Morning, gentlemen."

A team from the medical examiner's office had arrived, and one of them, Donald Carter, had made his way over to them. "Hey, Donnie," Elliot said.

Beaumont gave a curt nod.

Donald Carter slipped on a pair of half-moon glasses and said, "Some crazy weather we're having, huh?"

Elliot smiled and started walking toward the Mercedes while Donald Carter and Detective Beaumont followed. Less than a week ago temperatures had hovered around the high eighties, spawning a tornado that had ripped through the outskirts of town. This morning most thermometers would have to struggle to get above forty: Springtime in Oklahoma. Elliot stopped beside the open passenger door of the vehicle. "How long would you say she's been dead?"

Donnie stepped forward and ducked his head inside the car, for a closer look. He already had his gloves on. He pushed the skin with his finger, observing its elasticity then lifted one of her arms "Several hours. Seven or eight, if I had to guess." He pulled his head back and stood straight. "Looks like she was killed in the driver's seat then somehow maneuvered over to this side."

Elliot nodded. "A hurried attempt to throw us off. The victim was dragged over the console. I think she was killed somewhere else and brought here." He paused, intending to stop there, but before he knew it he was verbalizing his thoughts. "I've got a tip-of-the-iceberg feeling about all this."

The look on Donald Carter's face said he was interested, but one of his team members had called out to him. He turned and walked away.

Beaumont muttered something that Elliot couldn't quite make out, and then he said, "You might be onto something. There are a lot of similarities here, perhaps a little too many. You don't suppose we have a copycat on our hands, do you?"

"Maybe," Elliot said. And again, what he'd only intended to think came out. "Worse yet, maybe not."

Beaumont arched an eyebrow. "Surely you don't think…" He shook his head. "Christ, Elliot, some psycho could've run across it in an old newspaper or something."

Don't do this, Kenny. We can work it out.

"Yeah," Elliot said. "You're probably right." He got some plastic bags from his car and went back to the Mercedes, where he picked up the cell phone and gathered some fibers that looked to be from duct tape. In the glove compartment, he found a book of matches from some bar. For the first time, he hoped Beaumont was right. However, when he slid the necklace off the mirror and dropped it into the bag, he again thought of Marcia Barnes, her blonde hair caked with blood, her petite body riddled with stab wounds.

"You going to be all right?" Beaumont asked.

"Why wouldn't I be?"

Beaumont shrugged. "What's up with that fellow Sergeant Conley took in?"

"His name's Bill Morton. He found the body."

"You think he had something to do with it?"

"I don't know. He's got a record, everything from petty burglary to exposing himself to the sisters at the cathedral over on Boulder, but nothing like this."

"The real cream of society," Beaumont remarked.

Elliot watched the medical examiner's people remove the body.

"How's Molly?" Beaumont asked.

Elliot found that curious as well. Molly worked at the district attorney's office and she and Elliot had been dating, but he hadn't been aware that Beaumont knew that. "She's doing better."

Beaumont nodded. "I know what she's going through. It's tough to lose someone, especially when they're family."

"Not much more we can do here," Elliot said.

Chapter Three

Elliot grabbed a cup of coffee and a bagel from the break room then went to his desk. Beaumont still worried him. He couldn't figure the captain's fondness for Beaumont. Beaumont was sharp on theory, but he was no good in the field. He'd gotten them into trouble a few weeks back. He and Elliot had tracked down a meth lab operator who'd decided to take out the competition, his brother. When the suspect reached for his weapon, Beaumont hesitated just long enough for three of the guy's associates to come rushing out of a back bedroom. Elliot had been forced to act, killing one of the suspects and dropping another. He wound up with a short hospital stay and a reprimand for using excessive force. He didn't mention Beaumont's error in the report.

Tossing the bagel, Elliot picked up the coffee and leaned back in his chair. He sat in a cubicle that served as an office in the bullpen that played host to the homicide squad. To Elliot's left was a computer monitor, and in front of him one of the half walls lined with notes he'd stuck there. There was a five-drawer filing cabinet on his right that served not only as a storage area, but a barrier as well. When he leaned back, the action left him exposed, outside the protective mass of the filing cabinet. Beaumont sat across the aisle in an identical, mirror-imaged cubicle. Elliot glanced over only to see Beaumont leaning back as well, staring at him with a blank look on his face.

Elliot sipped his coffee. Within a few blocks of the department, a victim of murder had been left in the street, but Elliot's thoughts were elsewhere. The small town of Porter was in another lifetime, but from that murky past a cold finger had reached out and touched him. He closed his eyes, conjuring images of Carmen Garcia. The sight of her in that pale yellow dress with her dark eyes sparkling had nearly taken his breath away.

My parents are gone, Kenny. Stay with me tonight.

Nerves crawled in Elliot's gut at the memory. He drained his coffee and crushed the cup. He looked up to see Captain William Dombrowski leaning against the filing cabinet, staring at him. "You got a minute?"

Elliot followed Dombrowski into his office, stopping behind the chairs in front of the desk. Dombrowski gestured for Elliot to sit while he studied him with intense gray eyes.

"What's on your mind, Captain?"

Dombrowski lit a cigar then watched a stream of smoke curl toward the ceiling. "I hear you were pretty shaken up this morning."

"Who told you that?"

"It doesn't matter. I need my cops sharp, impartial. If you've got a problem, I need to know about it."

Elliot didn't like what he was hearing. Dombrowski's concern seemed way out of proportion. "I don't have a problem. Maybe someone else does."

"This isn't the first time I've had complaints about your behavior, and they've all been recent. This isn't like you. What's going on?"

"There's nothing going on."

Dombrowski pushed back from his desk, his chair protesting from the burden of his weight. "Come on, kid. It's me you're talking to."

Elliot rubbed his temples. He and Dombrowski had worked a couple of cases together when they were both detectives. Dombrowski had been captain for less than six months and he was probably just as uncomfortable as Elliot was. Elliot glanced at a bookcase by the wall. Alongside an array of law books sat a hand painted ceramic mug and a plaster imprint of a small hand, things Dombrowski's kid had made him. "I haven't been sleeping well," he said. "Nightmares, that sort of thing."

"Work related?"

Stay with me tonight, Kenny.

"I'm not sure. Probably not."

"Well, I'm a little more inclined to think that it is. You had a close call last month."

"It wasn't that bad."

"Jeez, Elliot. You were shot. There's no shame in being shaken up over that. Maybe you should take some time off."

Earlier that day, Elliot would've jumped at the chance, but a lot had happened since then. "I don't think that would be such a good idea right now."

"All right then, you tell me. If you were in my shoes, what would you do?"

"I'd let me finish the case. You were right to call me in on this one."

Dombrowski puffed on his cigar, adding more smoke to the already stuffy room. "What makes you say that?"

Elliot paused, looking for the right words. "Because nothing about it seems right."

Anyone else might have questioned Elliot's answer, but not Dombrowski. He simply nodded, more of an understanding than an approval. "So, what have you got so far?"

"Not much. But we can rule out robbery. Nothing was taken from her purse, and the jewelry was still there. The victim had a cell phone in her car. Her last call was to the Tulsa Police Department."

"Nine-one-one?"

"No. A direct call."

"Seems odd if she knew she was in trouble."

Elliot nodded. "I checked with dispatch. An unusual call came in around eleven last night. I listened to the tape. It's sketchy, but I think it might have been the victim."

"What did she say?"

"Something like, 'I know who the killer is....' "

Dombrowski arched his eyebrows. "Anything else?"

"After a brief pause, she said, 'Oh, hi, I was just calling...' And that was it."

"Sounds like she got caught."

"Yeah. Her husband's been notified. He's on his way to identify the body. I'll have a talk with him afterward."

"Do you think he had something to do with it?"

To the unaccustomed, such a question might seem premature in its execution, but under typical circumstances the husband is a prime suspect. Elliot shook his head. "It's too early to tell."

Turning his palms over, Dombrowski sighed. "All right, Elliot. You've got the case. But don't make me call you in here again." He puffed out a cloud of smoke and changed the subject. "So how's that restoration project coming along? What was it, some sort of old Chevy?"

"A Studebaker, and don't ask."

"That bad, huh?"

It was a Golden Hawk, a 1957 Studebaker Elliot had purchased from a wheat farmer in Tonkawa after stopping in town to have a look around and visit a few antique shops. He felt a bit ridiculous about it, not having planned on ending up with an automobile, especially one in such dire need of restoration. "Worse. I don't know what came over me. I know more about space travel than I do cars. I just couldn't leave the old buggy there, rotting away in that farmer's field."

Dombrowski grinned. "You'll manage." He stubbed out his cigar. "Now get out of here before I change my mind."

Elliot met Harrison Zimmerman, the victim's husband, at the medical examiner's office. He'd identified the body, taking a quick look, then turning away and nodding. Elliot took him by the arm and guided him outside, where they stood on the sidewalk. "Thanks for coming, Mr. Zimmerman. I know it's unpleasant, but I need to ask you some questions."

Zimmerman nodded. He was a tall, gaunt fellow with neatly trimmed gray hair.

"What do you say we get off the street?" Elliot continued. "Go someplace where we can sit down."

Zimmerman agreed. He suggested they drive across the river and meet at a coffee shop on Cherry Street that he knew of.

Later, when they entered the café, which was patronized by a diverse menagerie of folk, an array of smells filled Elliot's senses and he suddenly began to think of his mother. It was an unusual experience, for he could almost see her sitting in a chair beside one of the small round tables strewn about the floor. She had always loved fancy places. After they were seated, Elliot looked across the table at Zimmerman. "Do you know of anyone who might have wanted to harm your wife?"

Zimmerman averted his eyes, looking first at the floor, then around the room before answering. "No, I can't think of anyone like that."

Elliot sipped his coffee then sat the cup on the table. "Did she exhibit any change of habit that you noticed?"

"She had been acting strangely, leaving the house at night and staying out late."

"She left without you?"

"Yes."

"Do you have any idea where she went on those occasions?"

"Not really, but I have a feeling it was someplace bad."

Elliot thought that a strange answer. "What do you mean by bad?"

Zimmerman frowned. "I have to be honest with you. Things hadn't been going that well between us. In fact, she'd been talking with an attorney."

"Were you still living together?"

"Yes, but we had an argument last night. She was quite angry. I'd never seen her like that before. She stormed out of the house, and…" Zimmerman paused, wiping his eyes.

"Do you remember approximately what time that was?"

"Around eight thirty or nine, I think."

Zimmerman didn't strike Elliot as the shy type, yet he continued to avoid eye contact and he seemed to be answering the questions a little too quickly, as though he'd expected the interview and put some thought into it. "This is just a routine question, Mr. Zimmerman, not designed to upset you, but can you account for your whereabouts during the night while your wife was missing?"

For a moment, Zimmerman seemed to control his visual aversion, looking right at Elliot while he responded with a question, "What exactly are you asking me?"

"I need to know where you were last night, and what you were doing, especially during the hours from ten to midnight."

"I see. Well, my sister had come over earlier. We're fairly close, and she knew Lagayle and I were having problems. I suppose she'd hoped to help patch things up between us. Unfortunately the situation had gotten further out of control than either of us realized. Anyway, I didn't feel up to being alone in the house after all that, so I went home with my sister and stayed the night."

"Your sister was there during the argument?"

"Yes, Mr. Elliot. She was."

"And you went home with her afterward?"

"That's right."

"Did you leave her house at any time after you got there?"

"No. In fact, I left my car at home and rode with my sister."

"What time did you get back home this morning?"

"Around nine, just before you called."

For a moment, Elliot sat in silence, drinking his coffee. Zimmerman's demeanor seemed odd. Elliot didn't trust him, and he was willing to bet he wasn't telling him everything. "What's your sister's name?" he asked, "And how do I get in touch with her?"

"Her name is Kathy. Kathy Chapman."

"Is that her married name?"

Zimmerman reached inside his jacket and pulled out a pen and pad. He jotted something onto a piece of the paper and handed it to Elliot. "Yes. And you can reach her here. Her husband's name is Joseph."

Elliot stuffed the paper into his pocket and pushed back from the table. "Is there anyone else I can talk to who might be able to help us determine where your wife went last night?"

"Not that I can think of. I wish I could be of more help. She had no family, at least none that she told me about."

"What about friends, coworkers?"

"She didn't work. She didn't have to."

"What did she do for entertainment?"

Zimmerman seemed to mull over the question. "I'm afraid she didn't get out much, except at night. There was someone whom she talked with on the phone occasionally, but I'm afraid I don't know who it was. I assume it's whoever she went out with. I didn't approve, but I didn't say anything." After a pause, he added, "I guess I should have."

"What do you do for a living, Mr. Zimmerman?"

"Is that important?"

"It could be."

"I'm in the petroleum industry, Mr. Elliot."

Elliot wiped his mouth with a napkin, then stood and took the tab from the table. "Thank you, Mr. Zimmerman. That'll be all for now."

After finishing the interview, Elliot drove to Wakefield Wrecker Service where the city contracted to store their impounded vehicles. He didn't know what to think about the victim's husband just yet, but one thing was certain: someone out there knew Lagayle Zimmerman. People didn't exist in vacuums. She had to have a circle of friends. And, by Zimmerman's own admission, she'd been going out on him. Elliot entered the office building and went to the counter behind which a middle-aged lady named Rebecca Palmer appeared to be busy filing paperwork. They had met before.

When she saw Elliot, she smiled and said, "Well, if isn't the man of my dreams. Honey, if I was twenty years younger…"

Elliot shook his head and returned her smile. "Becky, you know you're too good for someone like me. I need to see that black Mercedes that was brought in earlier."

"You came all the way out here for that? I'm heartbroken." She picked up the phone and spoke over the intercom. A few seconds later, a young man in overalls appeared. He showed Elliot to the vehicle, then unlocked it and handed him the keys.

"Thanks," Elliot said.

The young man nodded and returned to his duties. Elliot went to the passenger side and opened the door to begin his search. He wasn't sure what he expected to find, but it wasn't the uneasiness that again came over him. He paused for a moment. It was just a car, a bunch of metal and plastic, but being near it definitely made him uncomfortable. He leaned inside and opened the glove compartment, finding it empty. He looked under the passenger seat, and beneath the driver's side; again, nothing. He went around to the trunk and opened it. It looked as clean as the day it had rolled off the showroom floor.

Elliot closed and locked the car doors. He was getting nowhere. He walked back to the office and left the keys with Rebecca Palmer.

Not knowing what else to do, Elliot decided to check out Zimmerman's address, see where he lived, and maybe get a better idea of whom he was dealing with. It didn't take long. Zimmerman's neighborhood turned out to be in the Utica Square area, one of Tulsa's gracefully aging sections. It was a part of town only a chosen few could afford unless they inherited their way in. Elliot followed one of the meandering blacktop roads that wound through a collection of park like settings until he found the one he was looking for. The city was full of modern-day castles purposely made to look old, like an insecure young man who dyes gray streaks into his hair to gain credibility. These houses didn't fall into that category. They were the real deal, the homes of old money.

Zimmerman's place sat on a knoll overlooking a cul-de-sac. Elliot parked on the edge of the roadway close to the end of the circular drive. He got out of the car and walked a few paces to the nearest neighboring house where he climbed a series of stones wedged into the landscape to serve as a stairway. Upon reaching the landing, an oval shaped area made of the same stone, he paused then rang the doorbell. He began to suspect no one was home, but when he turned to leave he saw someone coming up the walk.

"Is there something I can help you with?" the man asked.

He had stopped at the bottom of the stairs, so Elliot descended to meet him. "I was hoping to speak with the owner of the house. Would that be you?"

"I don't believe I've made your acquaintance."

Elliot showed his badge. "Detective Kenneth Elliot. Are you the owner of the house?"

The man took a half step back, as if Elliot had told him he had a bad case of the flu. Elliot was used to the reaction.

"Oh my," he said. "No, I'm not. That would be Stan and Barbara Nelson. I'm their decorator, Shaun. Shaun Miller." After a pause, he added, "They're out of town and wanted me to work while they were away. They left me a key."

"All right," Elliot said. "I understand." He pointed to Zimmerman's place. "Do you know who lives there?"

Shaun Miller nodded rather timidly, like a child forced to rat on his older brother. "Harrison Zimmerman."

"Do you know Mr. Zimmerman?"

"Well, not exactly. I know of him."

"And how is it that you know of him?"

He shrugged with a smirk on his face that insinuated Elliot had asked a question he should've already known the answer to. "He's Zimmerman of Zimmerman-Caldwell Petroleum."

"I see. Do you know if he was home last night?"

"Heavens, no. Why are you asking me all these questions? Something's wrong, isn't it?"

"Why do you say that?"

"Well, you're a detective and…oh, come on, tell me what this is all about."

"Mr. Zimmerman's wife," Elliot said. "She was found dead in her car this morning."

"Oh, Jesus. Not Lagayle." He glanced at Elliot and shook his head. "I don't really know her. I just…"

"You know of her."

"Yes, that's right."

Shaun Miller was timid and nervous, but that was just his nature. Elliot doubted he really knew anything about the case. He handed him one of his cards. "If you think of anything that might be of importance, give me a call."

Elliot went back to his car, where he sat for a moment, and through the window he could see a squirrel walking a wire high above the ground. As Elliot watched the animal move deftly along the phone line, something occurred to him, a source of information that had been right in front of his face all along, and he immediately felt silly for not having realized it earlier. He watched the squirrel jump from the wire to a tree as he called the department. Beaumont answered. Elliot said, "I need a favor."

"Now why does that sound dangerous?"

"I want you to get the victim's cell phone out of evidence and check to see if any numbers are stored in it."

"Sure. I can do that. By the way, Dombrowski left a book on your desk."

"A book?"

"Some sort of car book. And Donald Carter from the medical examiner's office called, looking for you. He said the autopsy turned up something rather interesting."

"Did he say what it was?"

"No, he didn't. Hey, I've got to go. I'll check that phone and get back to you."

Later, when Beaumont called back, he had a list of four numbers. Elliot thanked him, then disconnected. As he drove out of the neighborhood, he dialed the first number. It had been listed in Lagayle's directory under a name that he remembered seeing on the cover of a matchbook he'd found in the victim's car. On the third ring, someone answered. "Yeah?"

"Is this Gemini?" Elliot asked.

"Who wants to know?"

"I'm looking for someone. Perhaps you could help?"

"How did you get this number?"

"Her name's Lagayle Zimmerman," Elliot said.

Moments later, the voice said, "Look, darlin', a lot of people come and go around here, if you know what I mean. If you want, I can make an announcement. Maybe your friend's here, maybe she's not."

"Why don't you give me your address so I can come and see for myself?"

After a pause, during which Elliot could hear talking in the background, the connection he'd made was intentionally severed.

Chapter Four

Elliot sat at his desk, flipping through the pages of the copy of *Hemming's Motor News* Dombrowski had left for him. He'd called all the numbers from Lagayle Zimmerman's address book. She'd listed them under initials: MJ was Miss Jackson, her hairdresser; MD, Mary Ann Davenport, who knew Lagayle but hadn't seen her in a couple of months; and another woman, RJ, who wasn't home. Elliot left a message with RJ saying he had some important information regarding Lagayle Zimmerman, and would she please call him back.

Donald Carter wasn't around and with the time closing in on 1:00 p.m., Elliot decided to take a break. He'd agreed to meet Molly for lunch, so he left the office and drove to a restaurant off Yale Avenue, where he noticed her dark green SUV parked just behind the building. She saw him when he came in and waved to gain his attention. Elliot reached the booth where she was seated and slid into the seat across from her. "Hey, Molly."

Reaching across the table, she took his hand, a smile turning the corners of her mouth. Elliot always felt a little uneasy with Molly. She was intelligent, witty, and complicated enough to keep any man interested, and Elliot wondered why he wasn't falling for her.

They had met six months ago at a firearms conference in Dallas, finding one another in the crowd and immediately hitting it off. Elliot could find no fault with Molly Preston. He liked her and he liked being around her. But there was something holding them back. He suspected she felt it too. All the ingredients were there but the relationship just wasn't going anywhere. It didn't bother Elliot at first, but now it hung over him like a dark cloud. He figured there was just too much emotional baggage between the two of them.

"Nightmares again?" she asked.

Her intuition amazed Elliot. He nodded.

"Have you given any more thought to what we talked about?"

It was Elliot's time to be intuitive. "You mean about my visiting your friend, the shrink?"

"My friend, the psychologist."

"Whatever."

"She's good at what she does, and very well respected."

"Yeah, I know. And yes, I've given thought to it. A lot of thought, actually."

"And?"

"I don't know, Molly. It's not that I doubt her abilities, it's just that…"

"You're afraid. You feel your problem is too deeply personal to be laid out on the table and analyzed."

"Maybe you should be a psychologist."

She smiled. "Maybe I should. Care to give me a try?"

"No, thanks."

A hint of sadness flashed across Molly's face, as if Elliot's last comment meant more than it should have. "You don't know what you're missing."

Elliot wanted to change the subject. "Detective Beaumont asked about you."

A look that Elliot couldn't quite read crossed her face, but she said nothing. "I didn't know you two were acquainted."

"We live in the same building, but of course you already knew that. We bump into one another now and then."

"He expressed his condolences. Said he knows what you're going through."

She nodded, biting her lip.

"How's your father taking it?"

"Not well," she said. "He depended on Mom for everything. He's lost without her."

Elliot didn't know what to say. He had no experience in family matters, nothing to draw on, and he should've kept quiet as he'd intended, but he didn't. "I never knew my father."

Concern filtered through Molly's eyes. "What?"

Elliot shook his head. "I'm sorry. I don't know why I said that."

She squeezed Elliot's hand. "You carry around a lot of pain, Kenny. I see it in your eyes, feel it in your touch. Why won't you let me in, let me help?"

"You have helped. More than you know."

The waiter appeared and quickly took their order, seeming to sense that they were engaged in a discussion and didn't want to be bothered. "I'd like to think so," Molly said, "but you know as well as I do you're just trying to be nice."

With that the conversation seemed to falter and when the food arrived they ate a quiet lunch and left the restaurant. Once outside, Elliot walked Molly to her car. For a moment they stood silently, then she pressed against Elliot and he felt her lips touch his. "I could easily love you," she said.

"But you don't."

She frowned. "Kenny, sometimes I think you're the most decent man I've ever met, but other times you scare me. Why are you so distant, so hard to know?"

"I thought women liked that sort of thing, a bit of mystery."

She released her grip and started to pull away, but Elliot gently brought her back. "I do care about you, Molly. Don't give up on us, not yet." He pulled her closer, but before they could embrace in another kiss, the sound of his cell phone ringing jarred them back to reality. Elliot took a step back and brought the phone to his ear. "Yeah?"

After a brief silence, a soft feminine voice said, "This is Rachael Johnson. You left a message for me."

Chapter Five

Elliot left Molly standing beside her car. She'd said she understood, but Elliot wasn't so sure, and as he wove his car through the streets of Tulsa, he began to wonder where his nearly five years as a cop had gone; good times and bad times, all just as lost. He guessed living each day like it was no different than the one before carried that kind of price.

Rachael Johnson had agreed to a meeting. He hadn't told her much. He wanted to see the look on her face when he gave her the information.

Elliot wheeled the car to a stop at a hamburger stand near 15th and Peoria where Rachael Johnson told him she worked. She'd said her supervisor didn't like employees having visitors while they worked and didn't think he would be receptive to Elliot showing up. However, when Elliot walked in and showed his badge, the manager nodded and pointed him toward the kitchen. The blonde with the trapped look on her face turned out to be Rachael Johnson.

Giving the manager a look somewhere between *I dare you to say anything*, and *please help me*, she left the kitchen and came into the lobby.

Elliot opened the restaurant door and held it. "Would you mind stepping outside for a moment?" he asked.

He'd left the car parked beneath the canopy of a large oak tree that overshadowed the lot, and he and Ms. Johnson stood in its shade. "What's this all about?" she asked.

Elliot stepped off a small rock ledge and onto a grassy area beside the sidewalk. Rachael followed. She was rather ordinary in appearance, wearing a greasy smock over jeans and a faded blue shirt. Her blonde hair was twisted into a bun with strands hanging, rather disheveled, on either side of her face. Elliot had to admit she wasn't what he'd expected. The victim's taste in clothing and jewelry had been top notch. It seemed odd that she would have friends so far outside her social status. "Do you know Lagayle Zimmerman?" he asked.

A flicker of worry crossed her face. "Yes, I do."

"When was the last time you saw her?"

Again, her expression communicated concern. "It was just last night."

"Could you tell me where you were and approximately what time that was?"

"She stopped by the house, around ten o'clock, I think."

"Does she come by often?"

"Not really. In fact, she surprised me. I hadn't seen her in a couple of weeks."

"How long did she stay?"

She shrugged. "Just a few minutes. What's this all about, anyway?"

The restaurant manager pushed open the door to his business and stuck his head out. He didn't say anything, but lingered for a moment before ducking back inside. Rachael looked away briefly, and it was then that Elliot realized he was a bit mesmerized by her. It was her eyes. They were deep, and though he'd never considered blue eyes mysterious, something about hers certainly was. When she turned back, he said, "Lagayle Zimmerman is dead. She was found in her car this morning."

Rachael Johnson looked ill. She backed against the tree then slid to the ground. "Oh, God," she said. "How?"

Elliot hesitated for a moment before answering. "Her throat was cut."

Rachael covered her mouth with her hand. "She'd been fighting with her husband. I asked her to stay, but she wouldn't listen."

"Was she going home when she left you?"

"She said she was."

"Did you hear from her again after she left?"

She shook her head.

"Do you think her husband had something to do with her death?"

Rachael took a deep breath, letting it out slowly before speaking. "I don't know. I don't like him, and I didn't want her to marry him. He's powerful and domineering."

Elliot thought of the tall man with the hollow face he'd met earlier. He could think of a lot of words to describe Harrison Zimmerman, but powerful and domineering were not among them.

"But whether he's capable of something like murder," she continued, "I'm not sure. He just gives me the creeps, that's all."

Elliot made a notation. Creeps he could go with. "Is it possible she went someplace other than her home?"

"I don't know, I guess so."

"How long had you known her?"

Ms. Johnson paused. Elliot couldn't determine if she was thinking over her answer, or if the death of her friend was closing in on her. He leaned toward the latter.

"Not long really. About a year, I guess. She used to work here until she got married."

"Do you know how she met Harrison Zimmerman?"

"She said she met him at a party. It was only three months ago: they got married right away."

Elliot jotted down the address and contact information for Rachael then handed her one of his cards. "Thanks for your help. If you think of anything else, would you call me?"

"Sure," she said. She got to her feet, tucked the card away inside the pocket of her smock and started toward the restaurant. Before going inside, she turned back. "You know, I probably shouldn't say this, but I always thought there was something a little strange about Lagayle."

"Like what?" Elliot asked.

"I don't know. It was one of those things you can't quite put your finger on. She was just different. Sometimes being around her made me uncomfortable."

"Uncomfortable?"

She nodded. "I don't know any other way to describe it. But she was a wonderful person. I really liked her."

After that, Rachael turned away and disappeared into the restaurant. The address she'd given Elliot was less than three blocks from where the body had been found. He decided to drive by and check it out.

Chapter Six

Rachael Johnson's house, a rather large and badly maintained two-story wood-frame, sat on the corner, fronted by a numbered street running east and west, with a named street going north and south on the side. It was part of a mature neighborhood that had managed to survive intact. One of the neighbors, an elderly gentleman wearing khaki pants with a matching shirt, stood in his front yard watching as Elliot approached Rachael's place. Several concrete steps led from the sidewalk to the property level. The house, like many others in the area, had been constructed on a hill; a pile of dirt raising the property a few feet above street level. Elliot climbed the stairs, traversed a short sidewalk and went up a couple more steps that led to a wooden porch. Reaching the door, he knocked, wondering if anyone else did, in fact, live there. It was then that the neighbor spoke up.

"She won't come to the door, not with Rachael being gone."

Elliot stepped down from the porch then walked to the chain link fence separating the properties. He showed his badge. "Who might that be?"

The man cautiously inspected Elliot's credentials. "Mrs. Johnson, of course. Rachael's mother."

"What about her father?"

The man shrugged and shook his head.

Elliot tucked his badge inside his jacket. "I wonder if I might get some information from you Mr. ..."

"Eagon," the man said, "John Eagon. Don't know much, but you're welcome to try."

"Did you happen to see or hear anything unusual around here last night?"

John Eagon rubbed his chin. "Well, if I lived a little further southeast, I'd have to say yes, but since I don't, I guess the answer would have to be not really."

Elliot smiled. The man was a crusty old sort. "Would you mind telling me exactly what you did see?"

He nodded, leaning closer. "Rachael's fancy little friend came to see her."

"Driving a Mercedes?"

"That's the one."

"Was she alone?"

"That she was, and crying too."

"Are you sure?"

"Oh, yeah. I heard her. You asked me what I heard."

"Anything else?"

"She didn't stay long," he said. "Came trotting out about ten minutes after she got here. That's when her boyfriend showed up."

"Boyfriend?"

"Looked that way to me. Jumped in her car with her, started kissing her."

"How did he get here? Did he drive up after she did?"

He shook his head. "Didn't see any other cars. He just sort of showed up. It's not unusual. There's no shortage of strange goings-on around here anymore. Wasn't always like that though."

"Did you get a good look at him?"

"Nah. It was kind of dark."

"Was he tall, short, thin, heavyset?"

John Eagon scratched his head. "He wasn't what I would call big...about my height, and kind of slender."

Elliot immediately thought of Bill Morton. The description fit. And his story had seemed less than honest. But there was a problem with that theory. Why would Lagayle Zimmerman hang around with someone like Morton? He wasn't the boyfriend type, unless you happened to be a bottle of wine.

"What happened after that?" Elliot asked.

Eagon shook his head. "Looked like they were getting ready to get serious, if you know what I mean. So I went inside. I peeked out a few minutes later and the car was gone."

"What time was that?"

"About ten thirty, I guess."

Elliot wrote down what Eagon told him. It appeared as though Lagayle had known her killer, if indeed that was who John Eagon saw. On the other hand, with the park being nearby, anyone could easily have come from there.

After questioning John Eagon, Elliot called the medical examiner's office and spoke to Donald Carter. Carter thought it best that Elliot come and see for himself what had been discovered during the autopsy.

The examiner's office was on the west side of the river, so it took Elliot a few minutes to get there. When he arrived, he entered the building and made his way to the area where Donald Carter worked. When he got there he saw the body of Lagayle Zimmerman lying on the worktable, her red hair spilling over the sides. As Elliot walked over, Carter looked up from his work and grinned. "Hey, Elliot."

"You have something to show me?"

"Sure do," he said. "But I don't think you're going to like it." He raised the sheet covering the body. "Your victim. He's not a she."

"What are you talking about?"

Carter took a piece of rubber tubing and snipped it in half with a pair of surgical scissors. "He had a sex change."

Unable to resist, Elliot looked the body over, noticing the breasts, the feminine shape. "She looks real enough."

Carter shrugged. "Implants and hormone treatments. You see it all down here."

"How long ago was it done?"

Carter thought for a moment. "The scars are well healed. At least a year, maybe more."

Near a metal table that held various pieces of medical equipment, as well as Carter's half-eaten sandwich, Elliot found a chair and sat. The day was quickly turning into one that would be remembered because forgetting it wouldn't be easy. "Anything else?"

"There were no signs of molestation, and no semen. Her alcohol level was pretty high. She'd been drinking."

"Where would a person go to have such an operation?"

Carter grinned and shook his head. "Forget it, Elliot. You'd make an ugly broad."

"Is it easy to arrange?"

Carter walked over and picked up his sandwich. "Not really," he said, taking a bite. "The candidate would have to undergo a psychological evaluation, get it approved."

"Are there any particular clinics in town that cater to that sort of thing?"

"Not that I'm aware of. But I've never had cause to research the matter. You might try the American Medical Association or the County Health Department. They'd be good places to start."

Elliot left the medical examiner's office with a lot more on his mind than he'd come in with, and he'd already had enough to think about. He had some ground to cover, and there was one certain stop that he shoved to the head of the list. He needed to pay Harrison Zimmerman another visit. Perhaps he hadn't been lying, but at the very least he'd been withholding information. Either way, Elliot didn't appreciate it. However, he had only taken a few steps when he ran into Rachael Johnson.

"Detective Elliot. I was just at your office. The receptionist said I might find you here."

Elliot wondered why she'd come in person instead of calling. It must have showed in his expression because she answered his unspoken question.

"I had an appointment downtown," she said. "And since I was here anyway…"

Rachael was dressed differently too, wearing a wool suit and perfume. "What can I do for you?" Elliot asked.

"After we talked," she said. "I did remember something. Something Lagayle told me. It didn't seem like anything at the time. I guess that's why I forgot about it." She paused, fussing with her purse. "Mind if I smoke?"

Before Elliot could answer, she lit up, tilting her head to blow the smoke away while her eyes rolled to look at him. "She said she thought someone was following her."

That caught Elliot's attention. "Did she have any idea who it might be?"

Rachael shook her head. "She thought she was being stalked, if you know what I mean. I guess she was right, huh?"

Elliot decided not to tell Rachael that her instincts about Lagayle being different had been right. "We haven't determined that," he said.

Rachael nodded. "I have to be going or I'll be late. Call me if you have any more questions."

With that she walked away, trailing a faint smell of perfume mixed with cigarette smoke.

Elliot watched her for a moment, then found his car and drove to Zimmerman's house. When he arrived and began ringing the bell, he imagined a refined man in butler attire asking him if he was expected, but Zimmerman answered the door himself.

Upon seeing Elliot, his face soured. "Detective. I thought we'd taken care of everything."

"I'm sure you hoped as much," Elliot said. "Unfortunately a few things are left unanswered. May I come in?"

Zimmerman sighed and stepped aside. "If you must."

Elliot followed him into the house and through a high-ceilinged foyer, then up a small staircase to a room lined with shelves. Zimmerman called it the library. They sat more or less across from one another in wingback chairs of green leather placed at angles beside a heavy table. In front of them, a medieval-style fireplace dominated the room. After a moment, Zimmerman raised his eyebrows, as if in question.

"When we talked earlier," Elliot said, "you left out a few details. Some pretty important ones, I'd say." After his words had settled, Elliot added, "That doesn't look good, Mr. Zimmerman."

Zimmerman put his hands together in the shape of a steeple. "I take it you are referring to…"

"The sex operation," Elliot finished.

Zimmerman looked at the floor, nodding his bowed head.

"I need some answers."

Taking a deep breath, Zimmerman straightened in his chair. "What do you want to know?"

"Why you didn't tell us, for starters."

"I suppose I'd simply hoped it would just go away," Zimmerman said. "Wishful thinking, I'm sure. But try to understand, something like this can be quite embarrassing to someone in my position."

"Are you saying you didn't know about it when you married her?"

"I'm an old man, Detective. When I met Lagayle, I was looking for companionship. We slept in separate bedrooms."

"What was it that tipped you off?"

"She started staying out late, making excuses. I thought she was having an affair."

"So you confronted her with it and the truth came out, she told you everything?"

The expression on Zimmerman's face said it all. He was hiding something, and he suspected Elliot could tell. "Not exactly," he said.

Elliot then recalled what Rachael Johnson had said about Lagayle being followed, and it all fell into place.

"You hired a private investigator to tail her, didn't you?"

He said nothing.

"I will find out, one way or the other," Elliot said. "It would be better if I heard it from you."

Zimmerman frowned. "Very well then. Yes. Yes, I did."

Elliot picked up an antique-looking figurine from the table beside his chair and began to examine it. He found it an area of focus to control his anger. Zimmerman, it seemed, had withheld quite a bit. He sat the figurine back on the table. "Do suppose your PI would have any information concerning the murder of your wife?"

"I don't see how," Zimmerman said. "He only worked on it for a few days. Then he dropped off some pictures, told me what he knew, and said he was finished. He seemed quite agitated. Said he wanted no further part of it. Perhaps he was threatened or something."

Elliot studied Zimmerman's face, but discerned nothing from it. If he was lying, he was doing a good job of it. "Who would have threatened him?"

"I'm sure I don't know. Someone from her world, I would assume."

Elliot leaned back in his chair. He knew a little about PIs and it wasn't like them to turn down money. "What did your investigator find?"

"What's that?"

"You said that before he quit the case, he told you what he knew."

"So I did. Yes, I wanted to know what Lagayle was up to. After following her, he was able to tell me."

"And?"

Zimmerman closed his eyes and rubbed his temples. "He said she'd been frequenting clubs. You know, the type that would cater to people like her."

"You mentioned pictures. Could I see them?"

Zimmerman stood and walked to the west wall, where he grasped the corner of an oil painting and pulled it away from the wall, exposing a wall safe. Opening it, he pulled out several items. "You might as well keep them," he said, after coming back and handing Elliot several five-by-seven shots. "I have no use for them now."

The first few photos were not the best quality—typical work from a nervous PI—and they featured only Lagayle either going into, or coming out of different places. However, the last photo was different. Examining it, Elliot could again make out the likeness of Lagayle Zimmerman, with a man, his face obscured by shadows. "Do you have any idea who this other person is?" Elliot asked.

"No. I don't."

"Do you know why he, or anyone else, would have wanted to harm your wife?"

Zimmerman sat down, wiping his eyes. "I haven't a clue."

"I'll need the name of the investigator."

"He specifically asked me not to tell anyone about his involvement."

"That's not an option. Murder is serious business, Mr. Zimmerman. I need the name."

Zimmerman hesitated then pulled open a small drawer from the table between the chairs. He took a business card from the drawer and handed it to Elliot. "The man's name is Sykes," he said. "Bernard Sykes. I believe he goes by Bernie."

Elliot read the card then tucked it inside his pocket and gathered up the photos. "How did you happen to run across Mr. Sykes?"

Zimmerman shrugged. "He specializes in divorce cases and came highly recommended."

Elliot rose from his chair. "Thanks for your cooperation, Mr. Zimmerman. Don't bother getting up. I can find my way out. I'll be in touch."

Chapter Seven

Bernie Sykes, Private Investigator, kept a small office in a run-down area not far from downtown. He wasn't happy to see Elliot.

Sykes looked too big for his clothes and he was perspiring, although it wasn't that warm. He could have been tough once, but now he was soft and overweight. He shifted uncomfortably in his chair. "What can I do for you, Detective?"

Elliot sat in a wooden swivel chair that took up the space between the desk and the door. "I need some information on Lagayle Zimmerman."

A look came over Sykes's face, like that of someone who'd just walked into a dentist's office. "I doubt I could tell you anything you don't already know."

"Why did you quit the case?"

"Hey, I gave the old man what he wanted, found out what his wife was up to. The case was over. I didn't quit."

"That's not how Zimmerman made it sound. He said you were scared. You know what? I tend to agree with him."

"I guess that's your prerogative."

"You don't look like someone who would frighten easily. Did someone lean on you?"

"It's like I told you. I did what I was supposed to do. The job's over."

"About that information," Elliot said. "Care to share your findings with me?"

"I don't have to show you anything. I know my rights."

Elliot showed the photographs he'd gotten from Zimmerman. "Recognize these?"

"Sure I do. It's my work. So what?"

"Where were they taken?"

"Downtown, a place called Gemini."

"Who's the clown with Lagayle?"

Bernie shook his head. "I don't know, honest. I couldn't find anything on him."

Elliot considered Sykes's answer. The story of the murder hadn't hit the newswires. They'd asked the media to hold off. "Would it make any difference if I told you Lagayle Zimmerman was dead?"

Sykes pulled a handkerchief from his pocket and wiped his forehead. "I'm sorry to hear that."

"Sorry, but not surprised, right?"

"Hey. What're you trying to say? I didn't do nothin'."

"I can get a court order, if that's how you want it. Haul your whole office downtown."

"Hey, I'm running a respectable business here. I got bills to pay. Why are you rousting me? I haven't done anything."

"All right," Elliot said. "Have it your way." He started to stand.

"Hold on a minute. You don't have to do that. Come on, you look like a decent guy." He leaned forward, motioning for Elliot to do the same. "What if I was to tell you I didn't quit the case for the same reasons you think I did? I'm not saying that's how it was, I'm saying, what if."

"I'm listening."

"What if I was to tell you it was the old man, that maybe he said some things I didn't like?"

"Like what?"

"Like maybe he asked if I knew of anyone who could help him with a special problem."

Silence dropped over the room. Elliot knew perfectly well what Sykes was saying, but he wanted to be sure. As if to confirm his statement, Sykes nodded slowly.

"Are you saying Zimmerman had his wife killed?"

"Hey. I'm not saying anything. And if you try to bring me in on it, I'll deny it. You can tear through my files if that makes you feel better, but you won't find anything. I ain't been in business this long 'cause I'm stupid."

"Anything else you care not to tell me?"

Sykes wiped his forehead again. "That Zimmerman broad ain't what she seems."

"Yeah. I know about that. Question is, how did you find out?"

"I got my ways."

"I'll bet you do," Elliot said. "Now how about a name?"

"Name? What do you mean, name?"

"I have a feeling you dug up quite a bit on the victim. Zimmerman doesn't seem like the type to off his wife simply because she was having an affair. But to find out he was married to a man, that might do it. And something tells me his wife wasn't using the name Lagayle before."

Bernie Sykes shook his head then scribbled something onto a notepad. When he finished, he tore it off the page and slid it across the desk.

Elliot picked up the paper. It read: Larry J. Segal.

"You didn't get that from me."

"Yeah. Now how did you find out about Lagayle's gender?"

"Someone at the club told me." He paused. "I shouldn't have to tell you this, but when you been on the streets for as long as I have you get a feeling about these things. I could tell this was a bad deal. Sure I need money, but not that bad. So I dropped the case."

"What can you tell me about Segal?"

"Nothing. Nobody would talk about it. Every time I'd bring up that name, they'd clam up, back away." He shook his head. "I'm telling you it's a bad deal."

"Do you think Zimmerman had his wife killed, found someone to do it?"

"I don't know. I wouldn't put it past him."

Elliot nodded. "Thanks, I owe you one."

"Yeah, I'll believe that when I see it," Sykes said. And as Elliot was leaving, he added, "I'd be careful if I was you. This case has got crazy written all over it."

After leaving the PI's office, Elliot placed a call to the department to run a check on Larry Segal. Sure enough, Segal had been picked up nine years ago on a drug charge. It wasn't entirely luck; Elliot had a feeling something might show up. As it turned out, Larry Segal was the only child of William and Mallory Segal.

Segal's last known address was in an apartment complex on South Harvard Avenue. Elliot read the name of the apartments embossed on a brass plate bolted to a wall of brick, then confirmed it against his notes. On the right, he saw a row of mailboxes with names above and addresses below. When he found one labeled Mallory Segal, he wrote down the number and followed a sidewalk to the apartment.

Mallory Segal, a short lady with gray hair chopped into a pageboy, led Elliot into the living area and asked him to have a seat. The furniture was antique, and if Elliot hadn't known better he'd have thought he'd entered an 1890s home where Victorian clutter was the style. As his eyes adjusted to the darkness, he was able to identify the clutter; the shelves, the tables, and every other surface was crammed with dolls and doll furniture. There was even a tiny dining table with doll chairs and place settings.

"Could I get you something?" she asked, "perhaps a cup of tea?"

Elliot shook his head. "No thank you. I have something to tell you. It might be better if you were sitting down." When she complied, Elliot continued. "I have some bad news. It's about your son, Larry." He paused. It was never easy. "He was found in his car this morning. Your son is dead, Mrs. Segal."

Her face lost its expression, but she said nothing.

"I'm sorry, Mrs. Segal, but I need to ask you some questions. Does the name Lagayle Zimmerman mean anything to you?"

She smiled, her eyes becoming distant. "Do you like my little friends?" She gestured toward her dolls.

"Yes," Elliot said. "They're very nice. Do you know of anyone who might have wanted to harm Lagayle?"

She picked up one of the dolls, a fragile ceramic bride. This is one of my favorites, Mr....?"

"Elliot."

"Yes. That's a nice name. My husband's no longer with us, Mr. Elliot. My little friends are all I have." She stood and began twirling around, as if dancing with the doll. "I don't know anyone named Lagayle."

"How about your son, Larry?" Elliot asked, "Could you tell me about him?"

She spun around, eyes gleaming, and snatched up a couple of photos from the table and sat on the sofa beside Elliot. "This is when he got his first bicycle. It scared me so to see him ride it. And this is Larry with his father. He did love his father." A tear ran down her cheek. "My boy's been gone a long time, Mr. Elliot."

"Did he ever call or come to visit?"

Mallory Segal looked at the floor, the doll and the pictures she'd been holding sliding from her hands.

Elliot caught the ceramic doll before it hit the floor. He placed the doll on the sofa then picked up the pictures, placing them beside the doll.

"Someone called," she said, "someone I didn't know."

Elliot paused, thinking about Lagayle and Harrison Zimmerman and their relationship. "Did Larry ever tell you what he was doing, or who his friends were?"

She didn't answer.

"This is important, Mrs. Segal. Did Larry mention anything about being in trouble?"

She nodded.

"Tell me what he said, Mrs. Segal. I'm sorry to put you through this, but I have to know."

"His friend found out," she said.

"What friend?"

"He found out that Larry was…different."

"Was the friend Harrison Zimmerman?"

Mallory Segal began to cry.

Elliot put his arm around her. "It's all right. You've told me enough."

Elliot didn't have the heart to torture Mrs. Segal any further. He stood, thanked her for her help and commented on how nice her collection was, then let himself out.

Elliot paused for a moment in front of the apartment complex where Mallory Segal lived, watching the traffic squeeze up and down the narrow, crowded lanes of Harvard Avenue. The case appeared to be heading in a different direction than he'd previously anticipated. He didn't want to think he was happy about that, but he couldn't deny being somewhat relieved. However, when he closed his eyes he could still see the necklace dangling from the rearview mirror of the victim's car. He recalled the matchbook he'd found in the Mercedes, and the name that was printed on it: Club Gemini. The photograph Bernie Sykes had snapped of Lagayle Zimmerman had been taken there. And someone from the club had known Lagayle's secret. Sykes had told Elliot that much, but he hadn't known the man in the photo with Lagayle. For lack of a better idea, Elliot figured Club Gemini would be his next stop.

The building in front of Elliot, an aging two-story structure of red brick, held a look of abandonment. Elliot began to wonder if he'd been led astray. Rust, combined with inactivity and a padlock, secured the first door he came to. It looked as if it hadn't been used in twenty years. He found no other entrances along the south wall facing the street and nothing on the west side, but on the east end a couple of metal overhead doors were positioned about five feet above the driveway. It was a dock designed to accommodate the loading of trucks. The building had been used as a warehouse at one time.

After examining the overhead doors, which were locked, Elliot jumped down from the dock and walked to the back of the warehouse. A concrete retaining wall ran behind the structure, leaving a walkway about four feet wide between the building and the wall. Elliot recalled the snapshot of Lagayle standing beside a shadowy figure, and he recognized the area as the place where the photo had been taken. He started down the path, and as he neared the halfway point, he noticed a greenish glow reflecting off the concrete wall. A few steps more led him to the source of the strange light, a neon sign hanging above the entrance. The sign blinked out the name: Club Gemini.

Elliot pushed the buzzer. A few moments later the door creaked open slightly. Elliot showed his badge and pushed the door open as he stepped inside.

A man with a black moustache and a stocky build stood in the darkness. "Is there something I can do for you?"

"I'm looking for the manager," Elliot said.

The man examined Elliot's badge then pointed to the rear of the room. The place reminded Elliot of a cave and the expansive darkness, with cool, damp air pumping out of gray conduits suspended from the ceiling, intensified the sensation. As his eyes adjusted to the darkness, Elliot began to see details. In the middle of the chasm-like room was a dining area with tables covered with white tablecloths. The tables were gathered around three circular stages decorated with running lights ready for the night's entertainment. Near the back of the room, a large and well-stocked mahogany bar skirted the wall. To the right of the bar Elliot saw a small hallway leading to a door labeled Manager. As he neared the office, he noticed the outside wall had been outfitted with a one-way glass, and before he got to the door it opened and a tall, emaciated man stepped out. "May I help you?" he asked.

Elliot identified himself.

The man stepped forward, extending his hand. "Charles Metcalf," he said. "How may I be of service?"

His somber demeanor and all-black clothing reminded Elliot of an undertaker in an Old West movie. His skin was wet to the touch as they shook hands. "I'd like to ask you a few questions," Elliot said, wiping his hand on the back of his pant leg so Metcalf wouldn't notice. "Do you know Lagayle Zimmerman?"

The look on Metcalf's face implied that he wanted to lie, but it also said he was worried about trying it with a cop. He stroked his chin. "The name rings a bell, but I can't place it. Then again, people come and go around here. It's hard to keep up with everyone."

"She was also known as Larry Segal," Elliot added.

Metcalf gave Elliot a curious look, as if he'd said something offensive. He shook his head.

Elliot opened the brown envelope he carried and pulled out the photos Harrison Zimmerman had given him. He showed them to Metcalf. "Do any of these people ring your bell?"

He leaned forward to examine the photos, a look of worry invading his face. He shook his head. "I don't think so. But I can't be sure."

"Come on, the pictures were taken outside your club."

"Yes," he said, "it appears they were."

Elliot stuck a business card into the front pocket of Metcalf's dinner jacket. "Let me know when your memory improves. It would be in your best interest." Elliot turned away and walked back into the interior of the club. As he walked past the tables, strobe lights began to flash, followed by an array of rapidly moving lights of varying colors that were thrown about the room by large black spheres rotating overhead. The impression of countermovement caused by the lightshow made Elliot dizzy, and as he reached for the support of a chair someone touched his arm. He spoke with an English accent. "The pictures, mate. Could I have a look at them?"

Several other people came over and gathered around. Some of them were dressed as women, but they were all male. Apparently, the performers and crew were preparing for the night's performance. Elliot placed the photos atop one of the tables and spread them across it. "I know her all right," the Englishman said. "I've seen the bloke, too."

"Do you know who he is?" Elliot asked.

"Can't say I do. I saw him though, right here in this club not more than two days ago. What do you want with him?"

"I need to talk to him, that's all. What can you tell me about Lagayle Zimmerman?"

The Englishman shrugged. "She used to hang out here. Then she had a go at being straight. Didn't work out though, husband found out her little secret."

"Speaking of her husband," Elliot said. "Did he ever come in here?"

"Not bloody likely."

Laughter rippled across the small crowd. "What was Lagayle doing here with Mr. Anonymous?" Elliot asked.

"Don't know, mate. He was hitting on her though. That's for sure." He glanced around. "We all saw him, but we kept our distance."

"Why's that?"

"We know trouble when we see it."

Elliot nodded. It appeared gender was not the only thing faded and blurred within the confines of Club Gemini. He looked toward Metcalf's office. In places where the air was caught by the lights, it looked milky blue from cigarette smoke. Lagayle and the unknown man had been in the club. Whether that meant anything or not, Elliot wasn't sure. He asked the Englishman to let him know if he saw the strange man again, then made his way across the room and walked out.

Outside it had started to rain again, a cold downpour that sent the street people scampering for any alcove or corner that might offer some protection. What threatened Elliot was not the weather, but a feeling of hopelessness and desperation waiting like an open pit in the darkness. He couldn't give in to it. He'd been down that road before, and falling in was a hell of a lot easier than climbing out. He made his way to his car, and as he slid the key into the door lock, he caught a faint whiff of perfume, and a strong sensation that he was being watched came over him. He scanned the area but saw no one in the immediate vicinity. He looked inside the car. It was empty. He opened the door and climbed inside, then picked up the mike and radioed in that he was calling it a night.

Chapter Eight

After leaving Club Gemini, Elliot called Molly but she didn't answer. He took a deep breath and relaxed, glad the workday was over. The action allowed him to realize how tired he was. He turned onto the expressway, and a few minutes later he exited, going east on 91st Street until he reached his neighborhood. The peace and quiet it offered made him thankful. He hoped it would always be that way.

Inside the house, he checked for phone messages then took a shower. Later, he fixed himself a sandwich and watched television, but soon he sank into the cushions of the couch and somewhere between consciousness and sleep he began to relive snapshots of time.

Elliot jerked awake and looked at the clock on the fireplace mantel. It was eight p.m. He'd dozed off and begun to dream again. He couldn't go on fighting sleep forever; he had to do something. He went into the garage and flipped on the light, looking around for some tools. When he had what he needed, he sat on a creeper and began removing the bolts holding the front bumper to the Studebaker. The bumper was badly rusted and he'd read in *Hemmings Motor News*, the book Dombrowski had given him, about a place where he could send it and have it re-chromed. After about twenty minutes, however, he realized his mind wasn't on the project. He put the tools away and went back inside to call Molly again. When she answered, he said, "Hey, Molly."

"I was hoping you'd call," she said. "It's been one of those days."

"You can say that again."

"Are you all right?"

"I've been better."

After a long pause, she said, "You don't sound like yourself. What happened to that tough cop I know?"

"He's still around somewhere."

"Why don't you come over for awhile? We'll talk."

Molly lived downtown in a remodeled condominium. Elliot had no trouble getting in; the doorman was used to seeing him come and go. Elliot strode across the plush lobby and boarded the elevator as the doorman gave him a salute. When he reached the tenth floor, he got off and made his way to Molly's door. He rang the bell, and though his hands were steady, he felt like he was holding the handle of a running lawnmower. He had an urge to walk away, but before he could, Molly opened the door. She smiled, and after letting Elliot in she left the room, disappearing down the hallway that led to her bedroom. A sitcom played on the large screen television that dominated the living area, the message light on the telephone next to the sofa blinked, and in the kitchen the microwave oven announced the end of its programmed cycle.

Elliot closed the door behind him, and as he walked across the marble foyer, his footsteps echoing in the high-ceilinged emptiness, the thought that Molly must be lonely living alone as she did went through his mind. Perhaps he was merely projecting the vacuum of his own life onto hers, though the places they called home were nothing alike. Molly's condo, with its rounded corners, indirect lighting, and just the right shades of beige and moss green, looked as if it had been cut and pasted from the pages of a fashion magazine. High above the city, its expansive windows offered a view of a world much different from the one he knew.

A few minutes later, Molly returned wearing a bathrobe. She sat Elliot on the sofa then went into the kitchen. When she returned, she switched off the television and slipped a glass of wine into Elliot's hand. "So, what's the trouble?" she asked.

Elliot shook his head. "If there was any, I can't seem to remember it now."

She smiled and snuggled close. "You're not getting off the hook that easily. You were upset when you called. I'm worried about you."

Elliot sank back into the sofa and took a long sip of the wine. It had a bite to it, but it was soothing just the same. "I haven't been myself lately, that's for sure."

"Have you ever thought about doing something else for a living?"

Elliot considered her question. While it was true that he'd toyed with the idea of being an attorney when he was younger, police work had so intrigued him that the idea now seemed completely unattractive. "Not really," he said.

"Well, maybe you should."

"What would I do?"

She studied his face. "I don't think you realize the impact you have on others, Kenny. You could do just about anything you wanted."

Elliot wasn't sure how to respond to that, so he didn't. Instead he let a question slip out. "Do you ever wonder about your past?"

Molly's face showed concern. "I guess we all do now and then."

"What if it involved things you didn't understand and didn't want to remember?"

Molly reached for the bottle of wine on the side table and refilled Elliot's glass. "Do you want to talk about it?"

Elliot took another sip. If the wine was intended to relieve his anxiety, it had done so.

She smiled. "Okay, Mr. Detective. I want you to tell me what's bothering you."

"Molly the psychologist again?"

She leaned closer, playing with his hair.

"All right," he said, "but you'll probably think I'm nuts."

"So, what's new?"

Elliot studied Molly's face and suddenly his guarded secret didn't seem so imposing. "I have this crazy dream," he said.

"A dream, that's what this is all about?"

"Well," Elliot said, "it's a particularly bad one. I had it all the time when I was young. Eventually it began to occur less frequently, until it was gone altogether."

"If the dream has stopped, why does it still bother you?"

Elliot rubbed his forehead. It was wet with perspiration. "It's happening again," he said. "And it's come back with a vengeance."

"What do you mean?"

"It happens every night. I'm afraid to sleep. It's beginning to affect my work."

Molly pushed her hair back. "When I was a little girl it always helped me when I told somebody about it. You know how dreams are, all in your head. When you try to explain them, put them into words, they don't make sense anymore. It's like you expose them for what they really are, a bunch of nonsense."

Elliot thought about that for a moment, then began to speak. "In the dream, I'm driving down this country road in the middle of the night. No one else is around; the road is completely deserted except for me. It's exhilarating and I press the accelerator to the floor, feeling the car surge with power. But it's not my car. It's Johnnie's Mustang."

"Who's Johnnie?"

"Johnnie Alexander, a friend of mine from high school."

"You said you were alone at first. Did that change?"

"I meant no other cars were on the road. I'm not alone, but it isn't Johnnie who's with me. It's his girlfriend, Marcia."

"Go on," Molly urged.

Elliot wondered if her curiosity had evolved into an interrogation, but he kept talking, letting it out, as if the memories had been bottled up long enough and had to come out. "I look at her long, tanned legs glowing in the moonlight that flows into the car through the windshield, and I become aroused. Marcia sees this and moves closer, putting her arm around me and sliding the other hand beneath my shirt. I find a secluded area and bring the car to a stop. I pull her close and our lips meet. It's like fire inside me. But then Marcia pulls away and looks at something, the worst look of fear I've ever seen covering her face. I turn to look and I see someone outside the car, peering through the window, watching us. I can't really see who it is, only their eyes. Then the figure begins to back away and I see that it's Marcia."

"Wait a minute," Molly said. "Is this the same girl that was in the car with you?"

"Yeah, only now she's outside, floating above the ground, wearing a sheer gown that clings to her curves, her feet crossed as if fastened to a crucifix. Her arms are outstretched and she's calling to me, but no sound comes out. She's crying, but her tears are droplets of blood streaking down her face like war paint."

Molly sipped her wine. "That's a pretty wild dream, Kenny."

Elliot couldn't tell if she was amazed, or if she just didn't believe him. "There's more," he said. "I look back to see who's in the car with me and it's no longer Marcia. It's Carmen Garcia, my high school girlfriend. Suddenly, I'm out of the car and walking through the woods toward a car. It's the Mustang."

"The same one you were driving?"

"That's right, but now I'm walking toward it, coming from behind the vehicle. I'm angry with Johnnie and I mean to confront him, set things straight."

"What kind of things?" Molly asked.

"We had a good football team that year. But after Johnnie got involved with Marcia, he spent all his time with her. The team suffered because of it."

"What happens after that?"

"Carmen is following me as I approach the Mustang. She's pleading with me to stop. She keeps saying, 'Don't do this, Kenny. We can work it out.' Then, as I near the car, I see that something is smeared across the back window. It's words, written in blood, and I read it as I go by. The message reads *Johnnie Boy was here*. It frightens me, but then I see my class ring on a chain hanging from the rearview mirror of Johnnie's car and I become angry again. I go to the driver's side and yank the door open. What I see there sends a chill up my spine: Johnnie Alexander, my friend and the best quarterback to ever play at Porter High, is slumped over the steering wheel with blood dripping from the side of his head. And when I look at the passenger seat, I see Marcia Barnes. She's covered in blood, much of it still seeping out of the holes in her torso."

"Jesus, Kenny. You don't suppose the dream is based on actual events, do you?"

Elliot wondered if that was a question, or an accusation. "I don't know," he said. "I guess that's why it bothers me so much."

Molly's face looked ashen.

Elliot thought for a moment then said, "Marcia and I did go out several times, parking in a car I'd borrowed. And once we did see someone looking through the window at us."

"Anything else?"

"Yeah," Elliot said. "Johnnie and Marcia were found dead in his car. It was the same area where we all went to park."

"Well, it's no wonder you dream about it. You were traumatized, seeing something like that."

"Well, you see, that's just it. I wasn't there, or at least I wasn't supposed to have been."

"What are you saying, Kenny?"

"Carmen Garcia testified that I'd spent the night with her, never leaving her house during the night. Chief Johnson didn't seem to have a problem with that, in fact he seemed relieved, glad I was no longer a suspect."

Molly's face grew serious. "Were you there?"

"I'm not sure. The image of my friends lying dead in the front seat of Johnnie's car is so real in my mind, yet everything else about that night is a blur."

"I'm sure an event like that would have been widely publicized, especially in a small town. You probably picked up the details through the media."

"Yeah," Elliot said. "I've wondered about that. You're probably right."

"Could you tell me more about this Marcia Barnes?"

"She was gorgeous," Elliot said, "petite and shapely with long blonde hair and deep blue eyes. Every boy in school wanted her."

"Including you?"

"No, not really. I know it sounds crazy, but I was head over heels in love with Carmen. Looking back, it seems ridiculous what I did, but cocky teenagers don't always behave rationally. I only dated Marcia to anger Johnnie. I had no idea my actions would inflict so much pain on everyone." As Elliot spoke, tears welled up inside of him, but he held them back. "I've never regretted anything so much in my life."

"Does anybody else know about this?"

"No," Elliot said. "It's been my secret until now."

Molly took a deep breath, letting it out slowly. "Look at the time," she said.

Elliot felt unsure of himself, like a child who'd just copped to a dirty deed while caught up in the throes of childhood confusion. He began to wonder if he'd made a mistake.

Chapter Nine

The melody still played inside his head when Mama shuffled into the room, stooping to keep a low profile while throwing evasive glances here and there, as if that might afford them some measure of protection should Papa actually be there, hiding in some dimly lit corner. "Just look at you," she said, shaking her head. "My poor baby. You can't go around like this. What if he saw you?"

In troubled times, Mama's eyes seethed with changing emotion, so much so that he never knew which to lock onto. He couldn't anyway. The changes were too fleeting, a dark thundercloud of emotions as black as oil, churning and roiling, as if made of clay and forced into hideous and distorted shapes by angry and unseen hands. "But you told me I could play," he said. "You promised."

She began to cry. "That was a long time ago. Things have changed. Just look at you."

What could he do except agree with her? She was right, after all. Things had changed. He had changed. While she watched without seeing, he obediently took off the nice clothes, folded them neatly and hid them beneath the mattress.

"Hurry," she said. "You must hurry."

He slipped back into the rags that he usually wore and took his place in the corner, holding his hands over his ears while she closed the door and locked it. He sat there for hours, waiting for the food Mama would hide and bring to him later. But the food never came. He could hear them, laughing while they watched television, the smell of buttered popcorn wafting through the air.

At some point, he drifted into sleep, only to be awakened by the sound of the jewelry box. It played a tune when opened, the tune that ran through his head like a broken record. But as painful as the sweet melody was, it paled in comparison to the carnal noises that would follow. He dared not make a sound. Now was the worst time to be heard. He held his breath as he got down on his stomach, using the slightest of movements to crawl on his belly across the floor, praying he would not disturb the rotting boards. When he reached the door, he put his face close, straining to look through the cracks. As his eyes adjusted he could see Papa slipping beneath the covers, like an evil gopher burrowing just below the surface of the soil, breathing heavily as he moved about, touching her while she giggled with satisfaction. She didn't always like it, but sometimes she did.

Suddenly, he snapped back to the present, realizing with disgust what he'd been doing. He got out of bed and broke the reverie. He had to stop living in the past. It was nonproductive. Now was now, and it belonged to him. Less than twenty-four hours ago he had triumphed over her most recent appearance, but she could make a comeback. It was unlikely but not out of the question; it had happened before. And he'd been lulled into complacency, having her nearly catch him off guard. He couldn't allow it to happen like that again. From here on out, there would be no rest. He had to be vigilant.

He got dressed and grabbed the canvas bag that held the black-handled knife and other tools then walked silently down the hallway. When he reached the door, he quietly opened it and stepped out into the darkness. She would not catch him napping again.

Chapter Ten

Elliot awoke early the next morning, hungry and determined to spend less time worrying about his own problems and more on applying himself to the case. He made a breakfast of scrambled eggs, sausage, and hash brown potatoes, and stuffed himself. He didn't eat that way often, and he had to admit he didn't feel guilty about it. In fact, he enjoyed it immensely.

After breakfast, he checked in at the department then drove to Joyce Roth's office, the attorney Lagayle Zimmerman had consulted about divorce proceedings. Joyce Roth's office was on 31st Street, not far from Harrison Zimmerman's neighborhood. She greeted Elliot with a smile and pointed to an overstuffed chair that looked like it belonged in someone's living room. "Have a seat," she said. She sat at her desk.

"What can I do for you, Detective?"

Elliot put a lot of stock in first impressions, and Joyce Roth made a good one. Her office was neat and organized, and she wore feminine business attire that made the same statement. "I'd like to talk to you about one of your clients, Lagayle Zimmerman. I understand she'd consulted with you about a divorce from her husband, Harrison Zimmerman."

The paper had now run the story and Joyce Roth glanced at the morning edition. "I'm sorry to hear about her death. And yes, we talked a few times."

"Then I'll get right to the point," Elliot said. "Did Lagayle Zimmerman tell you anything that might help us solve her murder?"

"We never actually met, only talked on the phone a few times."

"Did she ever say anything that gave you cause to suspect she was in danger?"

Ms. Roth seemed to consider the question, looking off into space and tapping a yellow pencil against her desk. "This is off the record, Detective. Most of what she communicated was confusion, but she did tell me she was afraid of her husband. But you have to understand, most of my clients say the same thing."

"What do you know about Harrison Zimmerman?"

"Just that he's a prominent business man."

"Has your firm ever represented him, or his company?"

She smiled, aware of where Elliot's line of questioning was going. "Not that I'm aware of." She looked at her watch. "I wish I could be of more help, but I have a meeting to attend. Is that all?"

After leaving Joyce Roth's office, Elliot was unsure of his next actions. Checking up on someone like Harrison Zimmerman would be difficult. He wondered why he'd ever thought Lagayle Zimmerman's murder was connected to the Porter and Stillwater killings. There were very few similarities. But he knew the answer. It was the necklace, nothing more. He was still reliving the details of his first encounter with Joyce Roth when he climbed into his car and picked up the mike to answer a call. It was Captain Dombrowski.

Elliot wasn't there to witness Dombrowski's expression, but he could tell from the sound of his voice that if he could see him, his face would look as heavy as cement. "What's up?" he asked.

"It's happened again," Dombrowski said. "There's been another killing."

Dombrowski's words sent a feeling of helplessness running through Elliot. He laid down the mike and drove to the location, an empty house scheduled for demolition, somewhere off Yale Avenue. It was a wood-frame, probably built in the 1950s. An enormous trash dumpster sat on the front lawn.

The uniformed officers at the scene looked like soldiers, unwilling sentries guarding a death house. The foreman of the construction crew had discovered the body during a final walk-through of the property, something he always did before tearing down a former dwelling. He often found people hiding in the old houses, but never anything like this. He had never before found a dead body.

Elliot climbed the steps and entered the neglected house and what he saw inside ripped a chasm in his chest. Every cop's life becomes a part of his dreams, but Elliot's nightmares had just invaded his waking moments. The victim couldn't have been more than eighteen years old. Her face was unmolested, but that was much more than Elliot could say for the rest of her. She'd been stabbed thirty or forty times. And her throat was cut, with the marks leaving behind a hideous crimson-colored T. Once again visions of Marcia Barnes invaded Elliot's thoughts. He had to fight to regain control.

Elliot glanced at Detective Beaumont then stepped closer to the body. The victim was lying on an old mattress. She'd been staged with her hands on her thighs so it looked as if she were holding her legs apart.

Beaumont spoke, his voice startling Elliot. "Take a look at that," he said, pointing to the wall. "Looks like you got your blood writing. I guess you were right, but I sure don't know how the hell you knew."

Elliot had already seen it, a message written on the wall above the body, and as he read the scribbled words the same cold shiver went through him as it had nine years earlier when he'd first read that blood-smeared inscription on the back window of Johnnie's

Mustang. And whether the memories were real or imagined, he was powerless to stop their painful flow. The message, written in the victim's blood, said: *In your stead, I take the heat of moist breath against my neck.* The content was different, but there was no doubt in Elliot's mind that the same hand had drafted the writings.

Johnnie Boy was here.

Chapter Eleven

In the department break room, Elliot stared at the bulletin board without focusing on any one item. Dombrowski had called him while he and Beaumont were still at the crime scene of Michelle Baker, the latest victim. The captain wanted to discuss some things, said it was urgent.

Elliot went to the counter and poured two cups of coffee, then picked up a couple of doughnuts someone had brought in. After that he went into Dombrowski's office.

Placing one of the cups and a doughnut on the captain's desk, Elliot leaned back in a chair and sipped his coffee, its heat soothing his nerves. Dombrowski smoked a cigar, puffing like a locomotive. His face was flushed, the tendons in his neck bulging.

"What's up?" Elliot asked.

"Beaumont told me about the blood writing on the wall. I'm not sure what to think about it."

Yeah, Elliot thought. *I bet Beaumont's given you an earful all right.*

"The connection to the Oklahoma State murders is obvious," Elliot said. "I plan to go to Stillwater and talk it over with the sheriff there."

Dombrowski drummed his fingers against the top of his desk. "We need to have a heart-to-heart discussion. We need to talk about Porter."

Elliot couldn't believe what he was hearing. He found it odd the captain would bring up Porter instead of Stillwater, until he glanced at a notepad on Dombrowski's desk where he saw written the name of Molly Preston.

He had been betrayed.

Apparently his talk with Molly was more than just a little chat between friends. It'd been arranged, and it had Beaumont written all over it. "I'm not sure I know what you mean, Captain."

Dombrowski's lips tightened into a straight line. "Beaumont did a little checking of his own. You were more than just an innocent bystander, you were a murder suspect."

Elliot rubbed his forehead. "That's not exactly true."

"Maybe you ought to tell me just what went on there."

"There's not much to tell. It was a long time ago, back when I was in high school. A couple of people I knew were found dead in their car parked outside of town one night. The chief of police questioned me about it."

"Why would he do that?"

"Porter's a small town. He questioned everybody who knew the victims."

"So, what happened?"

"The case was ruled a murder-suicide."

Dombrowski was silent for a moment, his probing eyes intense enough to run a chill through Elliot. "Did you have anything to do with it?"

Elliot hoped his face didn't reflect that he wasn't sure about that night, and he was surprised at how fast the answer came out. "No, I didn't. I know the chief of police in Porter. If you want, I could have him call you, talk to you about it."

"That won't be necessary. You were what, eighteen at the time?"

"A senior in high school."

"I guess it must have been pretty rough on you."

Elliot thought of Carmen Garcia. *Don't do this, Kenny.* "You've no idea, sir."

Dombrowski sighed. "Sorry to put you through it again, but Major Sullivan's giving me a lot of grief. He's all excited about it."

"Back-to-back murders would tend to do that."

"Yeah," Dombrowski said. "Anything on Bill Morton?"

"He did some time a while back."

"What was he in for?"

"Burglary."

Dombrowski sipped his coffee. "Anything lately?"

"Not unless you count drunk and disorderly."

"What about Zimmerman?"

"His alibi checks out," Elliot said. "But I don't trust him."

"What have you got on him so far?"

"He's in the oil business. Runs Zimmerman-Caldwell Petroleum. He holds an influential amount of stock in several banks. He's also into real estate. And here's a kicker for you. He's one of the investors behind the Village at Central Park, the condos where his wife's body was found. Everything seems to be pointing his way."

"You don't sound convinced," Dombrowski said. "What is it, his alibi?"

"Not really. Even if Zimmerman didn't do it himself, someone in his position could certainly find a way to have it done."

"That thought crossed my mind too."

"I had a talk with Bernie Sykes," Elliot said, "a local PI Zimmerman hired."

Elliot sipped his coffee. Something Harrison Zimmerman said had him thinking, and he didn't like where it was going. Zimmerman had assumed someone from his wife's world shook down Bernie Sykes. Elliot had been to one club, but it stood to reason Lagayle Zimmerman would have frequented other places the general public never knew existed. She didn't wake up one morning bored and deciding to be female. She'd lived a major portion of her life as a male and she'd obviously been unhappy with it. Perhaps she'd tried to make a break from her problems by entering into a straight marriage only to have them catch up with her, taking revenge for her departure.

"Why did Zimmerman hire an investigator?" Dombrowski asked.

"To tail his wife, find out what she was up to. But there's more to it than that. He asked Sykes if he knew of anyone who could help him with a little problem. He wasn't specific, but Sykes didn't like it. He got nervous and quit the case."

Dombrowski relit his cigar. "Sounds pretty convincing to me."

"I know," Elliot said. "But Sykes doesn't want to get involved, says he'll deny telling me about it. He's already gotten rid of the paperwork. It'd be tough."

Dombrowski blew air across his teeth. "Sounds like we've got ourselves two unrelated killings."

Elliot nodded, but he wasn't sure he agreed. The captain's logic made perfect sense. Lagayle's throat had not been cut in the shape of a T, there was no message written in blood, and her body wasn't staged. On top of that, she didn't fit the profile of blonde hair and blue eyes.

"Something about it still bothers me, though," Dombrowski added.

"It bothers me too," Elliot said. "Like, why would the killer resurface after all these years, and why here and not Stillwater?"

"Let's not forget about Porter."

Elliot wondered if he saw a hint of accusation in the captain's face. *Yeah,* he thought, *let's not forget about that.*

"And I'm not so sure," Dombrowski continued, "that the killer has waited to resurface."

The captain's eyes were flat, the color of lead. Elliot wondered what was coming next. "Sir?"

Dombrowski shook his head. "Just thinking out loud."

"Well," Elliot said, "it looks like we had the same idea. I did a little checking of my own, using hair and eye color, and the rest. Seems our boy's been busier than we thought. I don't have the details with me but there's been at least three other similar murders in the Tulsa area, the first in 1999."

"Why didn't we pick up on it?" Dombrowski asked.

Elliot was pretty sure the captain already knew the answer, but he detailed it anyway. "They were botched attempts, more or less. But all of the victims fit the profile."

"What does that tell you?"

"Our killer's delusional," Elliot said, "that's why he does what he does. He's not that organized and things can go wrong, causing him to cut the job short, unable to finish to his satisfaction."

Dombrowski's expression remained flat, unreadable. "Sounds like you know what you're talking about."

"I've done a little reading on the subject," Elliot said.

Dombrowski stared off into space.

Elliot had seen the captain in a lot of moods, but he'd never seen him at a loss for words. However, the same weighty stillness had crept over Elliot, too. It was as if the verbalization of the facts had somehow made them more real.

"I have more leads," Elliot said as he stood to leave. "I'll keep you informed."

Dombrowski nodded, but Elliot could tell by the captain's expression that he was more than worried about the way things were going.

Chapter Twelve

Elliot left Dombrowski's office suspecting he'd lost something valuable—the captain's complete trust. He'd seen looks of uncertainty flicker through Dombrowski's eyes on occasion, but never before had he witnessed his expression reflecting such a measure of doubt.

The next stop on Elliot's list was Michelle Baker's mother, Amy Harris. The neighborhood where Ms. Baker lived had been a good area at one time. Part of it—the deep interior that was protected by enough money to muster up a reasonable amount of social insecticide—still was. But Michelle Baker had lived with her mother on the periphery, where urban blight was a kind description. Some of the houses appeared empty, with doors and windows boarded shut, though Elliot suspected a few of them were lairs for heroine and cocaine users.

Most of the other dwellings just lacked pride of ownership, with window dressings hanging loose or broken, and wood sidings that screamed for a coat of paint. Defunct automobiles, some with missing wheels and perched on blocks, decorated the curbsides, and kids with a mixture of fear and contempt in their eyes roamed in gangs. As was usually the case, though, a few of the houses clung to their dignity; gingerbread anachronisms, neatly maintained and fastened to manicured lawns, homes to grandmas and grandpas with Pekingese and Pomeranian companions.

Such was not the case with Michelle Baker's house. In that yard, a couple of toddlers scrambled about, clutching baby bottles and wearing diapers that hung nearly to the ground.

Elliot found an empty spot and pulled to the curbside. Some of the older kids had gathered in one of the yards, gesturing and getting vocal. They quieted and backed away as Elliot climbed out of the car and let his jacket fall open to expose his shoulder holster. As he opened the small gate and started toward the house, a window curtain moved and Elliot slid his hand around the grip of the Glock. As he stepped onto the porch, the door slowly opened and a lady peeked out. "Is there something I can help you with?"

"Are you Amy Harris?" Elliot asked.

Her eyes darted back and forth. "Well, maybe I am, and maybe I ain't."

"I'm Detective Kenneth Elliot. I called earlier about your daughter, Michelle Baker."

The lady hesitated then stepped aside. "Yeah, I'm Amy Harris."

Foul odors invaded Elliot's senses when he went inside the house. Dirty dishes filled the sink and most of the countertops in the kitchen, and food stained the floor.

"Can I get you anything?" she asked.

Elliot shook his head. "This shouldn't take long," he said.

She moved some items from a chair. "Have a seat."

Elliot didn't want to, but he sat in the chair Amy Harris had cleared for him. Moments later, a dark-skinned boy who looked about thirteen walked into the room wearing baggy pants that hung low, exposing his underwear; he wore no shirt. He paused briefly when he saw Elliot then went outside.

Amy Harris had already been informed of her daughter's death so Elliot was spared the unpleasant task. "Ms. Harris, I'm sorry, but I have to talk to you about your daughter."

She frowned. "Yeah, I figured as much. And don't call me Ms. Harris. Nobody calls me that. I don't like it, makes me feel old."

Elliot thought about that for a moment. Ms. Harris certainly didn't seem to be grieving. "I'll try to keep that in mind."

"And while we're on the subject, I'll tell you something else, Mr. Law and Order. Maybe it'll save you some time. I don't know where Michelle was, and I don't know where she'd been. She was a grown woman, and I didn't keep tabs on her."

Elliot stared at Ms. Harris. He didn't care for her attitude, and his body language must have told her that. She stopped talking, forced a smile, and sat in a chair. She was about four feet away from Elliot, and even at that distance the strong smell of alcohol on her breath was hard to take. The day had yet to reach its midpoint and Ms. Harris was well on her way to being drunk. It would've been nice to think it was the grief, but Elliot suspected her present condition was not that unusual. "I don't appreciate your insolence, Ms. Harris. And it won't get me out of here any faster. I have a job to do, and I fully intend to carry it out. Now, who was the young man that just walked through the room?"

She paused, a puzzled look crossing her face, then said, "Oh, that's just Darrell."

"Is he related to you?"

"Yeah, he's my son. I sent him out to watch the babies."

Elliot nodded. She was talking about the children he'd seen in the front yard. "Are they your children?"

"No. They're not mine. One of them was Michelle's. I'm baby sittin' the other."

"I see. Well, I need some answers. Maybe Darrell knows more about Michelle's activities."

"He don't know nothing. Look, I'm sorry, okay? Can we have a truce? I saw Michelle before she went to work that day."

"Do you mean Sunday?"

"Yeah, that's what I mean. She was here. She was going on about taking a vacation, or some crap. Wanted me to drop everything and drive to Padre Island with her. Can you imagine that? Don't know why she wanted to do something like that. Ain't nothing down there but sand and water. I guess it's too late for that now anyway, ain't it?" She shook her head. "I told her not to go working in those strip clubs. Do you think she listened to me? I can tell you right now she didn't. And I'm not trying to be smart aleck or anything, but I know you're going to ask me anyway, so I'm going to tell you. Michelle didn't have a clue where her no-account husband was, and I don't know either."

"You're quite perceptive, Ms. Harris. Could you tell me his name?"

"Yeah, I can tell you. It's Bill Baker. Can you believe that? She shook her head and snapped her fingers, as if mimicking a blues singer. "Won't you come home Bill Baker, won't you come home?"

Elliot smiled. "I think that's Bill Bailey...in the song, anyway."

"Yeah, whatever. I still don't know where he is."

"What about his parents? Do they live around here?"

She wagged her finger. "I asked Michelle that very same question. Never got no answer, 'cause she didn't know. She didn't know nothing about nothing. Hell, for all she knew he and his whole freakin' family could've been ax murderers or some crap like that." She paused before continuing: "And no, I don't think he had anything to do with it. The little twerp wouldn't have the nerve. Besides, he hasn't showed his face around here in six months." She shook her head. "No. It was those sleazy clubs she worked at that got her killed."

"Could you tell me the name of the place where she worked?" Elliot asked.

"Well, she didn't just work at one of them. But I'm pretty sure she was at the Starlight that night, the one over on 31st Street."

"Was your daughter dating anyone in particular, Ms. Harris?"

"Heck if I know. She always had some guy or another hanging around. Like I said, I gave up trying to keep tabs on her. And I still wish you wouldn't call me that. My name's Amy."

Elliot stood. "That'll be all for now," he said. "Thanks for your help." He took a final look around the room, which was littered and stacked with more things than he would've thought possible. He felt sorry for Michelle Baker. She hadn't had much of a life, but as sad as it was, it was hers, and she didn't deserve to have it taken from her. He thought about asking Ms. Harris if she'd noticed anyone unusual hanging around, but he remembered what he'd already seen outside and changed his mind. Instead he said, "One more thing, Amy. Pour yourself a cup of hot coffee and try to stay sober for awhile."

Elliot found the Starlight Club on 31st Street like Amy Harris said he would. As he neared the entrance, he read the sign on the marquee that proclaimed the establishment to be a gentlemen's club. He paused, contemplating the origin of the root word, *gentle.* It had been another term for someone above the common people, a person belonging to a family of high social station, of noble or aristocratic birth. Somehow he didn't think he would find anyone like that inside the club.

A man named Lance Bossier ran the club. "I've got to hand it to you guys," he said, "you sure are thorough."

Elliot stuffed the badge back into his pocket. "What makes you say that?"

He shrugged. "I just got through talking to a cop."

Elliot didn't like the sound of that. "Is that right," he said. "What was the officer's name?"

"I'm not good with names. Hell, around here nobody uses their real ones anyway. He was a fancy talker, though, dressed real sharp. Said he was a detective, just like you."

Elliot suspected the club manager was referring to Beaumont, but he had to confirm it. "Did he wink his left eye while he talked, like a reflex action?"

"That's the one."

"I apologize for the inconvenience," Elliot said, "doubling up on you like this, but what can you tell me about the night Michelle Baker disappeared?"

"Just another night," the club manger said, "like all the rest. I was here but I didn't see anything out of the ordinary. She didn't come to work the next day, but that's not unusual in this business. I didn't know anything was wrong until one of the girls called her house today and talked to her mother." He paused then continued, "I sure hated to hear she was dead. She was a good kid. If I ever get my hands on the guy who did this, you cops won't have to worry about putting him away. You can count on that."

"Do you have any idea who it might have been?" Elliot asked. "Ex-lover, disgruntled boyfriend, unhappy customer?"

Lance Bossier shook his head. "If it was anybody else, I'd say any of the above, but not Michelle. She was a real sweetheart. Everybody liked her."

"Who else was on duty that night?"

"Just about everybody. Most of the girls are in the back. You can talk to them if you want. Doubt you'll get much out of them though."

Elliot followed Lance Bossier to the rear of the room where the manger stopped and knocked on the wall before continuing through a curtained doorway. On the other side of the curtain was a crude dressing room with mirrors and vanity tables where the dancers changed into their costumes. Three of the dancers were there, putting on makeup. Lance Bossier introduced Elliot before he went back through the curtain, leaving Elliot alone with the dancers. "I guess you know why I'm here," Elliot said. "If there's any information you could give me, anything at all, I would appreciate it."

One of the dancers got up and walked over, stopping about one foot away from Elliot. She smiled. "You're a tall one, aren't you? You're even taller than old Lance." She put her feet together, as if standing at attention and stuck out her hand. "I'm Tami."

Even wearing her pink-feathered high heels, she stood about five foot four inches from the ground. Elliot shook her hand. She was flirty to the point of being comical, but Elliot suspected it was nothing more than an occupational hazard. "Nice to meet you," he said. "Were you here Sunday night?"

"Sure," she said, rolling her eyes. "But you already knew that, didn't you."

"What do you mean?"

"You came to the club that night. I saw you."

Elliot shook his head. "You must have me confused with someone else. I've never been here before."

"Are you sure? You look awfully familiar. And I always remember the cute ones."

Elliot pulled out his notebook. Tami's comments didn't surprise him all that much. Others often came up to him, asking if he was from here, or from there. People found him familiar. He guessed he had that kind of face. "What can you tell me about Michelle?"

"She was one of the few girls I got along with around here. I'm going to miss her."

"Did she have any enemies?"

She shrugged. "She was really popular with the guys. Some of the girls get ticked off about that."

"Can you recall anything unusual happening that night, something out of the ordinary, customers behaving out of character?"

She turned away and walked to one of the dressing areas where she sat. Elliot followed her. She stuck out her lips, as if pouting, and began to apply lipstick, a dark purple color that matched her nails. "Do you like to watch movies, Mr. Elliot?"

"Sure I do. What does that have to do with Michelle?"

She smiled at her reflection in the mirror, moving her head back and forth, quite pleased with what she saw there. "I like the old ones, you know, with Rock Hudson, Marlon Brando, that sort of thing." Sorting through a small suitcase, like an overnight kit, she took out a few items and began to apply false eyelashes. "My mother would go to the video store when she got in the mood and rent dozens of tapes. She'd fix popcorn and we'd sit and watch movies all night. I used to fall asleep in class the next day, but it was worth it. You know, like quality time spent together. Happy times like that don't come along too often, so you have to grab them when you can."

Tami's reminiscing caught Elliot off guard, and for a moment he began to recall his own childhood. "Your mother," he said. "She sounds a lot like mine."

Tami stopped what she was doing and smiled. "That's sweet."

Elliot forced himself back into the present, focusing on the case. "These old movies you mentioned, do they have anything to do with Michelle Baker?"

She paused for a moment, as if thinking over the question. "I don't know," she said. "But there was this guy who was in the club that night."

"Someone who drew your attention?"

She nodded. "Do you know James Dean, Mr. Elliot?"

"You mean the actor?"

"Yeah, that's the one."

Elliot didn't know if this was going anywhere, but he decided to go along with it. "I'm familiar with his work."

"Well, like I was saying, I like old movies. I have quite a collection of things I've picked up over the years at garage sales, flea markets, and that sort of thing. You know, like memorabilia, posters, and stuff like that."

Elliot tried to imagine how movie posters would fit in to all of this, but he couldn't. He wanted to hear more. "Please go on," he said.

"Well, like I was saying, there was this guy. He came in alone and sat by himself." She paused and shrugged. "Nothing unusual about that. Guys do that all the time."

Elliot tapped his pencil against his notepad, a habit he was trying to break, and when he became aware of it he stopped. "What was it about him that caught your attention?"

"James Dean."

"Come again?"

She held an eyebrow pencil in one hand and an eyelash curler in the other, and she moved them up and down together as if she were a band director trying to add emphasis. "He didn't just look like James Dean, he *was* James Dean."

Elliot began to wonder if he was dealing with a stable individual. "I see. And how is this important?"

She pursed her lips. "I don't know. Like I said, I remember the cute ones."

Elliot closed his notepad and went to the next dancer. He questioned them all, getting pieces of information here and there, but nothing of much interest. It wasn't their fault. It'd been business as usual at the Starlight Club. Elliot pushed through the curtain and walked into the club area where the day's action had already begun. One of the dancers was moving about the stage, stripping to the beat of some hip-hop recording. Elliot thanked Lance Bossier, the club manger for his help and headed for the door. As he was leaving, he heard Tami say, "See you around, Mr. Elliot? I always remember the cute ones."

As Elliot walked across the parking lot outside the club, with Tami's insistence about seeing him running through his mind, he caught a glimpse of something out of the corner of his eye.

Chapter Thirteen

Elliot threw himself, back first, onto the hood of his car just as another vehicle slammed into it. The impact shoved the car sideways, nearly knocking Elliot off the hood. Reaching over his shoulder, he found a handhold in the gap between the windshield and the hood, which kept him from sliding onto the other car. In the same instant, his free hand closed around the handle of the Glock, pulling the weapon just as the other vehicle shot backward then straightened.

The driver of the vehicle reacted quickly, tearing out of the parking lot before Elliot's weapon cleared the holster. Elliot fired three shots, taking out the car's back window and busting a taillight. The vehicle squealed onto the roadway.

Elliot rolled off the hood and jumped inside his car, then stabbed the key into the ignition. When the car came to life, he dropped it into gear and mashed the accelerator pedal to the floor. The guy had a good start on him, but he could still see him weaving in and out of traffic, going south on Yale Avenue. Elliot followed, turning on the siren and pulling the portable light from beneath the seat, sticking it on the dashboard. Up ahead, the vehicle slammed into another car, but kept going. The driver was putting distance between them in a hurry. Elliot began to wish he hadn't used the light. Instead of getting out of the way, the other drivers had become frightened, stopping where they were, causing a traffic jam. Within seconds he'd lost sight of the other vehicle.

Elliot released the tension on the brake pedal, letting the car roll forward until it touched the rear bumper of the car in front of him. The driver looked in his mirror but didn't turn around. With solid contact made, Elliot eased down on the accelerator, shoving the other car forward. He then changed gears and repeated the process in reverse. When he had clearance, he threw it in drive and cut hard to his left, climbing halfway onto the center median before regaining momentum. However, as he glanced in his rearview mirror he saw a commotion of traffic a couple of blocks behind his present position, and he realized what had happened. The car he was pursuing was heading in the other direction.

When Elliot reached 36th Street, he headed east just long enough to turn into St. Andrew's Church, where he did a turnabout. After that, he hopped back onto 36th then shot north on Yale. His gamble paid off. When he reached 21st, he saw the other vehicle. He swerved around a couple of cars, jockeying for position, the maneuver landing him three or four cars behind his attacker. As soon as another gap opened in the traffic, Elliot pressed the accelerator and shot through the opening. He was now right behind the other vehicle.

The driver made a move of his own, slamming on the brakes. Elliot cut to the right, managing to miss everything except the rear quarter panel on the passenger side. The driver used the opportunity of Elliot's lack of focus to his advantage. He fishtailed, knocking Elliot's car off course, then turned, going full bore onto a side street leading into a residential neighborhood. Elliot followed.

He searched the neighborhood but he'd lost sight of the guy. Elliot left the area and pulled back onto Yale Avenue. On more of a hunch than anything else, he sped north, and it wasn't long until he again found the other car, just barely catching sight of its taillights as it turned east onto Pine. He stomped the accelerator, gaining on his adversary, but suddenly the smell of an overheating engine filled the car's interior. Elliot knew what the problem was. The radiator had been damaged in the collision and was leaking coolant. It wouldn't last much longer.

The driver turned north again when he reached Mingo Road. Elliot followed, but his vehicle was becoming sluggish, and again the driver had evaded him. Elliot contemplated pulling over and calling for help. He passed an area where school buses were stored, then drove by several buildings owned by American Airlines. When he reached the intersection of 44th Street North and Mingo he had a bit of luck. Sitting in the parking lot of an abandoned school was the vehicle he had been chasing.

Elliot went through the intersection and drove into the lot, parking just behind the vehicle. It appeared to be empty. He decided to shut down his car. It would be awhile before he could get the overheated car started again, but it wouldn't make it much further in its present condition anyway. When he turned the key to the off position, the engine sputtered for a few seconds, pre-igniting on its own heat, then stopped, leaving only the hiss of steam to show for its efforts.

Elliot climbed out of the car. He knew he should call for backup, but the way things had been going he decided not to. The traffic in this part of town was minimal, giving a deserted feel to the area. It all seemed a little too easy, and Elliot began to wonder if he'd been led into a trap. Even though the driver had lost him several times, it seemed as though he had wanted Elliot to stay with him.

Elliot stooped and looked beneath the vehicle. No one was hiding there. He pulled his service weapon and cautiously walked toward the car, edging up to the window and peering through. It was empty. Across the street to his right, and also immediately behind him, he saw patches of weeds thick enough to offer someone natural cover if they chose to hide there. But he saw no movement. To his left was the schoolyard, and beyond that an open area that was the old baseball field. Only unkempt grass played there now.

It seemed as though the driver of the vehicle had simply vanished, but Elliot suspected he was still in the area. There were plenty of places to hide, but his gut feeling was that the driver was in the schoolhouse. The school had been around awhile, with several additions built through the years. The addition in front of Elliot had a natural rock entrance, but just a few feet up, the yellow metal structure it masked jutted out in defiance. It was a gymnasium. Big blue letters proclaimed the building to be the home of the Wildcats. Elliot started toward it, stepping onto a sidewalk lined with outdoor lights, but when he tried the glass doors he found them to be locked. To his right were two side entrances located about fifty feet apart. He began to walk toward the nearest entrance, but he'd only taken a few steps when he heard a sound coming from above. He jerked his head in that direction, swinging the Glock upward. It was only a squirrel, jumping from limb to limb in one of the oak trees that formed a canopy over the yard. Elliot tried both sets of doors. They were locked.

When he reached the corner of the building, Elliot eased around it and walked across the yard. He was now standing in front of the original structure, the old schoolhouse. It looked a bit like the Alamo, except it was made of red brick. At the apex of the arch above the main entrance a cement block embedded in the bricks read: 19 Mingo 30. As if later designers were bent on destroying the ambiance of the antique structure, a gaudy white metal awning had been constructed to offer protection from the rain for students as they filed into the place. But it was another in-bad-taste addition that caught Elliot's attention. Two rather large and elongated windows had been built just below the arch to give light to the second story and one of them, the one to the north, had been turned into a doorway. A brown metal stairway led to the unusual entrance. The whole thing looked like a bad afterthought, but the glass to the door had been broken, leaving nothing but the white frame—and it was that which interested Elliot.

He climbed the stairs, then ducked through the doorway and stepped inside the school. Broken glass littered the red tile floor of the hallway. Elliot didn't know how long the glass had been there, but something about the way it shined against the dusty floor made him suspect the breakage was recent. He'd brought a flashlight from the car and he switched it on, shining the light up and down the hall. He didn't see anyone and he noticed that the dust along the floor had not been disturbed except for the shards of glass. The idea of a trap—a deliberate setup—again went through his thoughts, but he couldn't reconcile himself to the notion of walking away and leaving the building unsearched.

Elliot had another choice to make. The hallway offered three different directions: straight-ahead, to the left, or to the right. He chose straight ahead simply because it was the path to the closest classroom. He walked forward, the hair on his neck standing on end as the sound of glass crunching against his shoes and the floor echoed loudly in the empty expanse. When Elliot reached the door, he turned the brass knob, and when he pulled it open something came at him, falling toward him like the scathing blade of a horse soldier, a Knight Templar bent on guarding his treasure.

The mop handle crashed to the floor as Elliot took a step back, taking a deep breath to calm his nerves. It was not a classroom, but a closet for supplies. Elliot scolded himself for letting such an innocuous event scare the wits out of him. He continued his journey, the hallway darkening as he put distance between himself and the windows lining the front portion of the building. He stopped more than once, listening to the imagined sounds of someone sneaking up behind him, only to turn around and see nothing.

When Elliot came to a double doorway, he stopped and looked into the darkness of an auditorium. He hesitated then walked slowly down the slanted aisle, looking between rows of folding seats. Upon reaching the last row, he paused to consider the stage hidden behind a heavy curtain, like in an old-fashioned theatre. Elliot imagined walking up to the booth, a circular glassed-in cage beneath a triangular marquee, and purchasing tickets for a weekend matinee, like he and Carmen had done when they were young.

A set of stairs led to the stage. Elliot went up, one step at a time then ducked behind the curtain, his flashlight penetrating only a small portion of the black void at which it was pointed. An old piano sat near the front of the stage. Toward the back was a podium surrounded by stacks of boxes. Elliot searched the area but found nothing. Pushing the curtain aside, he went down the small set of stairs and walked back up the aisle, returning to the hallway outside the auditorium where he continued, walking deeper into the school.

When he came to another room, Elliot held the flashlight in his teeth and pulled the heavy wooden door open. He wedged his foot against it then transferred the flashlight back to his hand, holding both the flashlight and his weapon in front of him while he stepped inside. As the door closed behind him, it became much darker. Elliot grabbed a small chair and stuck it in the opening, propping the door open. He saw no one in the room, but it wasn't empty. A wooden teacher's desk, numerous smaller student desks, and a large green chalkboard occupied the classroom. It looked as if the students had stepped away only briefly for recess and would, in a few moments, return from the schoolyard. Elliot walked to the front of the room and looked behind the teacher's desk. He wondered what had happened to the children who had roamed the hallways throughout the years, and suddenly the loneliness and abandonment of the place saddened him. Lesson notes were still written across the chalkboard. It seemed wasteful for the old school to sit there, unused and unoccupied, like a castle without its king and court.

Elliot's reverie didn't last long. He heard a noise coming from behind, and he turned and ran for the door, arriving just in time to see it slam shut, blocking the opening like a rock slab sealing a tomb. Someone had closed the door, locking him inside. He twisted the knob and pushed. It moved only slightly, less than an inch. Whoever had closed it had also blocked it. To make matters worse, the culprit was standing just outside. Elliot could not see him through the small gap between the door and doorjamb, but he knew he was there just the same. He could feel his presence. It had to be the driver of the hit-and-run vehicle.

Elliot called out but received no reply. He could picture the man standing there, grinning; pleased with his victory.

After a long silence, the man finally answered, and when he spoke he sounded mechanical, like a robot, an android from some science fiction film. Elliot wondered if he'd undergone throat surgery that had left him disabled, needing an artificial device with which to speak.

"When you dance with darkness," his captor said, "you wear her essence. She blackens you like the night."

Elliot tried to discern the meaning of the words but nothing came to mind. "Do I know you?" he asked.

Again the android voice took awhile to answer. "You could say that, though I doubt you would recognize me."

"Why are you doing this?"

He made a clicking noise. "When the time comes, you're always around, lurking like a dog in heat. You're connected, a harbinger of her vengeance."

"Why don't you open the door?" Elliot asked. "I want to see you, talk face to face."

He laughed. "You'd like that, wouldn't you? Your disguise might fool your friends, but I know who you are, football stud."

Elliot considered his captor's words, something that finally made a little sense, and he began to wonder if this was someone from his past, perhaps from Porter. "So you know who I am. You have the advantage of me."

"And I fully intend to keep it. I saw you that night, embracing the dead. You took her in your arms and kissed her. You should have left the little tramp alone. It would have made all our lives easier."

Elliot heard footsteps that grew softer as they continued. The man was leaving. "Are you still there?" Elliot received no answer, for his jailer was gone. But he'd left something behind to replace his machine-like words. It was an odor—the strong odor of gasoline.

Chapter Fourteen

Elliot backed away from the door, expecting to hear the sound of petroleum igniting, but it never came. Moments later, he eased back to the door and shoved it outward, peering through the gap. He saw no flames, but he could still smell the fumes. He suspected his captor was toying with him, trying to prolong the moment of victory, milking it for all it was worth. Elliot called out, "You still out there, Slick?" Nothing. He tried again. "You seem like an interesting guy. Let's talk football. Come on, you've piqued my curiosity."

And then it came, the hollow rumble of rapid combustion, the fire sucking in oxygen. Elliot shined his flashlight to the top of the door, hoping to find a window, the kind designed for ventilation. No such luck. He considered blasting his way out. Not enough time. He had no idea what was blocking the door, and the walls in buildings of this vintage were constructed too well to even think about shooting enough holes to escape. The flashlight batteries were about to go, the light beginning to dim. Elliot shined it around the room, saw a door in the corner and ran to it. It was just a closet.

Tears blurred Elliot's vision as the smoke and fumes trickled into the room. At the thought of ventilation, he looked up and saw dingy tiles suspended on aluminum tracks. The ceiling had been lowered to accommodate lighting and to make room for air conditioning and heating ducts.

Elliot climbed onto the teacher's desk. Not high enough. He couldn't reach the tiles. He jumped down, found a student desk, and threw it on top of the teacher's. Climbing back up, he tore away the tiles, dropping them to the floor. With that done, he grabbed one of the twisted wires that held the ceiling tile tracks and tried to pull himself up, but the wire wouldn't hold his weight. It was all he could do to maintain his balance. He was actually thankful for that; a busted ankle would not be good right now. He climbed down and lined the desk up with an overhead vent, then shoved the desk to the wall behind the teacher's area. The wall would be altered, with holes cut into it to allow the ductwork to be installed. He climbed back up and tore away more tiles. He was right. He tugged at the metal pipes; they were sturdy, installed well. Taking the Glock by its barrel, he used it as a hammer, knocking loose a portion of the ductwork. He pulled it down and grabbed the piece running through the wall. When it gave way and fell, Elliot pulled himself through the hole where it had been.

Balancing himself on the wall, Elliot pounded the tiles loose on the other side and dropped to the floor. He was now in the next classroom. The air felt like sandpaper in his lungs. He ran to the door. It was hot, but he had no other choice. He shoved it open and ran to his left, away from the larger flames, and deeper into the school building. He suspected he would find more windows in the back of the building. The light filtering through the smoke said he was right. He ran, ignoring everything but freedom. When he reached the glass, he lowered his shoulder and dove into it, tucking and rolling as he saw the ground coming.

Elliot got to his feet, bruised and bleeding in a few places, but feeling no sharp pains; nothing seemed to be broken. He made his way to the front of the schoolyard where he'd left his car. The other vehicle was gone. He climbed into the car and used his radio to call in. The dispatcher put him through to Dombrowski.

Elliot didn't tell the captain all the things his attacker had said about football and kissing dead people, only that he'd tried to kill him. Even with that, Dombrowski hadn't taken him seriously, acting as if Elliot were trying to make a big deal about nothing. Letting his imagination run away with him was how Dombrowski put it. The hit-and-run vehicle turned out to be a stolen car, reported missing two days ago. No big surprise there. Somehow, Elliot had managed to convince Dombrowski he needed another car in a hurry, and that Stillwater would be his next stop. He always kept a change of clothes in a locker at the department, and after cleaning up he left the downtown area and headed onto Highway 412 going west.

About an hour later, Elliot pulled into Stillwater. He intended to go straight to the police department but followed an urge to take another route instead, driving through the campus of Oklahoma State University to relive some memories of his days there as a student. He didn't know he would find one that would act as a key, opening doors that had been closed a long time. It happened in front of Eskimo Joe's Restaurant. As soon as Elliot saw the place, he knew that it was there, while eating dinner with a friend, he'd again seen those eyes, the same eyes that had looked through the car window at him and Marcia that night. He'd looked up from the table and across the restaurant and it was there, in a crowd of people, that he'd seen…someone. He couldn't put a face with his memory. The eyes were all he remembered.

Elliot left the campus area and drove to the intersection of 7th and Lewis. There he found the municipal building, a new, sand-colored structure that housed the police station.

The young man extended his hand. "Dan Wallingford. What can I do for you?"

"We've had a couple murders in Tulsa," Elliot said. "I'm the investigating officer."

The young man nodded, a puzzled look crossing his face.

"I believe at least one of them is connected to the student murders that occurred here several years ago."

The officer raised his eyebrows. "Are you serious?"

"Yes," Elliot said. "I was hoping to talk to the officer in charge of that investigation."

Dan Wallingford paused, rubbing his chin as if to allow saneness a chance to catch up to the conversation before he answered. "That'd be Phil Malone."

"Is he available?"

"Not really," the officer said. "He retired last year. But you could probably find him at home. About five miles out of town on 177 there's an old white house on the west side of the road. Two red wagon wheels mark the driveway. You can't miss it."

As Elliot was leaving, Wallingford said, "Wait a minute. You don't want to just drive up to Malone's place and hop out. He's a little spooky. I've heard he'll take a shot at you if he doesn't know you. I'll give a call and warn him that you're coming."

The distance turned out to be more like six miles, but the wagon wheels were there, along with a mailbox marked Malone. Elliot pulled into the gravel driveway and drove across a cattle guard, stopping beside an old green pickup truck at the end of the drive. He honked the horn a couple of times then climbed out.

Phil Malone stood about five foot six, resembling James Cagney in his later years. He led Elliot to a room in the back of the house that served as an office, and motioned for him to sit down while he perched himself behind a massive desk that looked as if it would swallow him, had his chair not been so high. Frowning, he gestured toward the walls covered with newspaper clippings of police cases, including several recent events. "As you can see, I try to keep up with police matters. Just in case I'm needed."

"Well, Mr. Malone, I do need your help."

"Call me Phil."

Elliot glanced at the clippings on the wall. "What do you think about my theory that your killer could be the same man I'm looking for?"

"I don't know," he said. "What makes you think it's the same guy?"

Elliot remembered reading about the Stillwater murders in the campus newspaper. "The murder shares a lot of similarities. Throat cut in the same manner, the blood writing, that sort of thing."

"Sure sounds like it could be," he said. "Folks around here don't pay me much mind anymore, think I'm crazy. But I know a few things."

"I'd like to go over any leads you might have, and your list of suspects, if you have one."

Malone frowned. "I'm afraid I don't have much. That whole mess was the most frustrating case I was ever involved in. Ruined my career and nearly ruined me as well."

Elliot felt bad for Phil Malone. "I'm sorry to hear that."

Malone placed his hands on the desk. "No fingerprints, no witnesses, nothing. Just three young women cheated out of their lives: two college coeds and one high school senior." He shook his head. "Folks demanded justice and I couldn't give it to them, didn't have squat to go on."

Elliot wondered if the number three had any significance. There had been two in Tulsa, if Lagayle Zimmerman counted. "I understand how you feel," he said. "We're having the same problem." A vision of Marcia Barnes suddenly invaded Elliot's thoughts. "Tell me something, Phil. Did the victims fit any type of profile?" Elliot already knew they did, but he wanted to be sure, and maybe there was something else he didn't know.

Malone stared at Elliot for a moment, then got up and walked to a bookshelf. He pulled out a large three-ring binder. "Like I said, I don't have much. But what I do have is yours." He flipped through a few pages then turned the notebook toward Elliot. What Elliot saw rattled his nerves. They were eight-by-ten photographs of the Stillwater victims. Elliot had to turn the page to see the third one. The pictures were hard to look at, but it wasn't their graphic nature that shocked him; it was the fact that he could slide the photo of Michele Baker into the mix and it would fit right in.

Malone wiped his forehead. "No matter how many times I look at them it still gives me the shivers. It started seven years ago. Of course you already know that." He pointed to the first picture. "Christine Wakefield. According to the few that knew her, she was somewhat of a loner. Had a habit of taking late night walks alone across the campus. She was found just like you see her."

The body was leaning against a tree, naked from the waist down and staged, with her hands holding her legs apart, just like Michelle Baker. Also like Michelle, she wore thick red lipstick and heavy eye shadow. A piece of notebook paper had been pinned to her chest, upon which was written in blood: *Hush now. From your death, I arose.*

Phil Malone tapped his finger against the second picture. "This one happened six months later. Her name's Tracy Harper, a high school student. She liked to dress up all provocative-like and drive around the campus trying to pick up college boys. She was found in the front seat of her car, on the passenger side."

Elliot swallowed a lump in his throat. It was all he could do to not see Marcia Barnes in the picture. This time the message was scrawled across the passenger window of the victim's car. It read: *I walk in your silence.*

"We thought she was the last one," Malone said, "Then almost two years later he struck again." He turned the page to the last picture. "Megan Phillips," he said, "cheerleader, popular girl. She went home on the weekends, leaving Friday afternoon and returning Sunday evening. She didn't make it home this time. Found in her car, just like Tracy Harper."

The writing on the window read: *Cry not from your grave.*

Malone closed the book. "To answer your question, Detective, yes the victims most definitely fit a profile. They were all young, between the ages of sixteen and nineteen, petite, none of them weighing over 115 pounds, and they all had blonde hair and blue eyes. And of course, they were all killed in the same manner."

Elliot took a deep breath, letting it out slowly. Again it was obvious Lagayle Zimmerman did not fit in. "Looks like we're dealing with the same killer all right."

Malone shook his head. "Then God help you, Detective. I've got a scanner and a color printer. I'll give you some copies."

"Thanks," Elliot said. "You must have questioned a lot of people. Do you have a list of suspects?"

Malone pulled a spiral notebook from the desk. He examined it for a moment then said, "Old Gus Haringer, now there was an odd sort if I ever saw one."

"Was?" Elliot asked.

Malone nodded. "Two weeks ago he got up and ate breakfast, put on his Sunday-best suit, then sat down on a bench in his backyard garden and died of a heart attack, like he knew his time was up or something."

"Why did you suspect him?"

"Strange fellow," Malone said, "worked as a janitor at the university until they opened his tool chest one day and found it chock-full of things stolen from the girls' locker room; bras and panties mostly."

"What made you rule him out?"

"Bad back for one thing. It was all Gus could do to lift a twenty-five pound feed bag. His doctor confirmed the injury, but I'd already noticed it."

Elliot nodded. The bodies had been staged, often moved to different locations to get the desired effect. With a bad back, lifting 115 pounds of dead weight would be next to impossible.

"Besides that," Malone added, "I questioned him good. Old Gus was nutty all right, but he was no killer."

"Were there any others?" Elliot asked.

Malone shrugged. "Well they really don't deserve to be called suspects, but I got some names. Both were students at the time. William Lathrop was one of them. He was Megan Phillips's boyfriend and the last one to see her alive, except for the killer that is. Anyway he had an alibi—spent the weekend at the lake with a bunch of his frat buddies. Last I heard, he'd moved up north, working for some engineering firm in Maine. Then there was Conrad Winters. He'd dated Christine Wakefield a couple of times. She broke it off. He wrote a nasty letter saying he'd get even with her some day. But he was also able to account for his whereabouts during the time of the murder of Christine, and he'd already graduated when Megan was killed. He went to dental school and has an office in Tulsa." Malone shook his head. "Not squat to go on. Didn't have it then and I don't have it now. I wish to dickens I could be of more help."

"You're not the first cop to leave the force with an unsolved case," Elliot said. "It's obvious you put a lot of work into it. You did the best you could."

"Thanks. That means a lot coming from a fellow police officer." He paused and scratched his head. "I probably shouldn't even bring this up, but there was one other suspect."

Elliot nodded. "Go on."

"Well, first off, my list has an order to it, from most likely to least likely. To be honest, I don't even know why I put this guy on the list. I guess there was just something about him I didn't like."

"There must have been a reason, other than your not liking the guy."

Malone nodded. "He was always hanging around the clubs off campus. By the time I figured out what he was up to it was too late."

"What exactly was he doing?"

"Selling drugs," Malone said. "He was into exotic stuff, like ecstasy."

"Did you ever bring him in for questioning?"

Malone shook his head. "I never got the chance. He went and got himself killed. Ran head-on into a tree."

Elliot wasn't exactly sure why he asked the next question. It just sort of came out. "Do you suppose the crash could have been intentional?"

Malone gave Elliot a curious look. "No," he said. "That's one part I am sure about. The skid marks, impact of the crash, the car's direction, all indicated accident. I've seen my share of twisted metal. Nobody planned that one."

Elliot thought for a moment, the names of suspects and victims running through his head. "What was the suspect's name?" he asked.

Malone flipped through his notes. "I've got it here somewhere. Yeah, here it is. Segal, his name was Segal. Larry J. Segal."

Elliot felt the blood run from his head. *My boy's been gone a long time, Mr. Elliot.* Lagayle Zimmerman had just jumped back into the picture. "Who identified the body?"

"Wasn't much left to identify. We didn't even know who to contact, so we called the university. They gave us the name of his mother. She came out. She wasn't much help but she did recognize some of the jewelry. Based on her testimony, and the fact that it was his car, we made our decision." He paused then continued, "What's left of the car is still collecting weeds down at Palechek's Salvage, if you want to have a look at it. I've got some errands to run, and I'll be going in that direction anyway. I can show you, if you want."

Elliot followed Malone and his old pickup truck down Perkins Road to Palechek's Salvage Yard. Malone led Elliot through a maze of rusted metal to the rear of the yard, where the burned out remains of a 1982 Oldsmobile Cutlass occupied a piece of ground. "There she sits," he said.

Elliot walked around the car, taking his time, trying to visualize the collision. He stopped near the front on the passenger side.

"Looks like the major portion of the impact occurred here," he said.

Malone nodded. "That's what we figured, too. Then it caught fire."

"Perhaps you're right," Elliot said, "Maybe Larry Segal didn't plan the crash. Maybe he just took advantage of an opportunity."

Malone shook his head. "I'm not sure I follow what you're saying."

"Let's just say you might want to check and see if you had any unsolved missing persons reports during that time. I don't know whose charred body you pulled out of this car, Mr. Malone, but it wasn't Larry Segal's. He's dead all right, but he died in Tulsa. We've got his body lying on a slab in the morgue."

Chapter Fifteen

Elliot met Dombrowski at a restaurant on Elm Street in Broken Arrow. The captain lived on the east side of south Tulsa, so it wasn't out of his way. He'd called Elliot on his cell phone while Elliot was on his way home and still on the highway, halfway between Stillwater and Tulsa and asked to meet him there. Elliot didn't mind. A lot had happened and he wanted to give the captain an update anyway. By the time Dombrowski got there, he'd been off work for a couple of hours and he came in casual, wearing a Hard Rock Cafe T-shirt and a St. Louis Cardinals baseball cap. Elliot wasn't used to seeing the captain dressed that way, and he had to admit it made him feel more at ease and relaxed around him. Elliot tore open a couple of sugar packets and dumped them into his coffee, then added cream. Watching this, Dombrowski shook his head. He'd always told Elliot if he didn't like coffee black then he didn't like coffee. Elliot thought he was probably right.

Dombrowski forced a smile. He looked tense. "So how did it go in Stillwater?" He asked.

Elliot sipped his coffee then sat the cup down and spread the color printouts across the table. He'd dropped by the office before coming to the restaurant and picked up the photograph of Michelle Baker. He laid it on the table as well, a perfect match.

Dombrowski showed his disgust. He studied the layout for a moment then nodded. "I still don't see the connection to Lagayle Zimmerman though."

Elliot and Dombrowski sat in silence for a moment, sipping their coffee and staring at one another like a couple of gamecocks in a standoff. Elliot finally broke the tension and spoke. "You might change your mind after you hear what else I found."

Dombrowski raised his eyebrows. "Let's have it."

"Larry Segal, also know as Lagayle Zimmerman, was in Stillwater during the murders that took place there."

Dombrowski considered that then said, "That's interesting all right, but it doesn't really mean anything."

"It gets better. Segal was dealing drugs. He was also a suspect in the murders."

"So what happened?"

"According to the officer in charge of the investigation, Segal was involved in an automobile accident, ran himself into a tree and burned to death in Stillwater five years ago."

Dombrowski's face went blank.

Elliot waited a moment, allowing Dombrowski time to think about what he'd said before he continued. "Kind of puts a new spin on things, doesn't it?"

Dombrowski looked preoccupied, as if he was thinking through the information, sorting it out. "Yeah," he said.

A notion went through Elliot's mind, one he didn't intend to verbalize, but somehow it busted out anyway. "By the way," he said. "You can call off the dogs now."

Dombrowski's startled appearance indicated he couldn't believe it either. He studied Elliot, as if he were a new recruit he'd just met. "What the hell's that supposed to mean?"

Elliot shook his head. The waitress appeared, making her rounds, and Elliot waited until she'd filled their coffee cups and went on to the next table. "Just thinking out loud I guess."

Dombrowski sipped his coffee, watching as Elliot again doctored his. "So," he said. "What's Segal's connection to all of this?"

Elliot sat his cup on the table. "My guess is he and the killer go way back, old friends if you will."

"Are you saying they worked together?"

"No. Nothing like that. Just acquaintances. Segal probably had his suspicions but nothing ever fell into place until a couple of nights ago."

Dombrowski grinned. "I read this book once where there were two killers. One serial killer with a definite MO, and one who followed him around, cleaning up afterward, like a guardian angel. It's an interesting theory. But I'm not sure it's a good one. Don't get me wrong. I'm no psychologist, but I know a little about the behavior patterns of serial killers. And they don't typically step outside their MO."

"I know that," Elliot said. "But this one's different. I guess he forgot to read the psych books, and doesn't know how to act."

"Come on. I admit there appears to be some kind of connection, but there has to be another explanation. Besides, I thought we'd agreed Harrison Zimmerman was our prime suspect for the murder of his wife."

"I know how it looks," Elliot said, "but Zimmerman has money and money has connections. He didn't get where he is by being ignorant. He would've hired a pro, someone with enough experience to make it look like an accident or a robbery gone bad. He certainly wouldn't have them leave the body in his own backyard, making it look like he had something to do with it. And then there's the phone call Lagayle made. She didn't say 'someone is trying to kill me.' She said 'I know who the killer is.' It didn't sound like she was talking about her own killer. Someone she knew surprised her. I'd say whoever that was also killed her. Zimmerman wanted his wife out of the way, but he didn't kill her. Someone beat him to it. Lagayle Zimmerman wasn't killed for who she was. She was killed for what she knew—the identity of the killer."

Elliot paused, wanting to tell Dombrowski no one wished all of this were only in his mind more than he did. "It's not the first time he's done something like this," he continued. "He killed Johnnie Alexander, and Johnnie did nothing more than be at the wrong place at the right time. It could've been me in the car with Marcia that night."

Dombrowski leaned back in his chair. "Pardon me for changing the subject, but about this guy who tried to run you down earlier. Do you have any idea what might have instigated such a thing?"

"My guess is he was trying to kill me," Elliot said. "And you didn't change the subject at all, Captain."

"What are you trying to say, that the killer was driving the car and tried to take you out?"

"Yeah, that's pretty much it."

"Why would he want to do that?"

"Because he doesn't like what I'm doing."

"And what exactly are you doing?"

Elliot sipped his coffee. Dombrowski was acting strangely. He suspected the captain's conversation with Molly Preston, coupled with what Beaumont had been telling him, was working overtime on his mind. "My job, Captain."

Dombrowski paused briefly then continued. "I'm sorry, Elliot. But it seems you were the only one who saw this person, and the only one to witness the car chase."

Elliot couldn't believe what he was hearing, but then it dawned on him. "What you mean is, your boy didn't see it."

"Why don't you just go ahead and say what's on your mind, Elliot."

Elliot took the napkin from his lap and threw it on the booth cushion, then stood and pulled a five-dollar bill from his pocket and tossed it on the table. "Your boy's been following me around, Captain. He even got to the Starlight Club before I did. That's why he didn't see anything. I guess he got a little ahead of himself. With the department being in a crunch to get things done, it looks to me like Detective Beaumont could spend his time a little more wisely."

"So now you're trying to tell me how to run the department?"

Elliot took a step toward Dombrowski then stopped himself. "Maybe somebody should," he said. After that he turned and walked away. He pushed through the door, stepped outside, and found his car. He didn't wait around to let Dombrowski catch up with him. He was too angry. He had to put distance between them.

A few blocks down the road, Elliot grabbed his cell phone and called Molly. She didn't answer. He left a message then pressed harder on the accelerator pedal. He was hot. Perhaps it was lack of sleep, or stress, but whatever the cause, anger boiled inside of him. He needed to find Beaumont. He knew what he was up to, so he knew where to look. He visited a few bars and a few beers later, he caught up with him at a place called Daddy's, a club housed in a run-down structure that had once been a convenience store. As if it were an expression of the owner's heart, light-blocking paint as black as asphalt covered the glass of the expansive windows. The door had been painted too.

Elliot pushed through the door and stepped inside, having to fight the smile that tried to form on his lips when he spotted Beaumont, standing near the back of the room beside a cigarette machine. Elliot figured he'd been seen as well, but Beaumont was doing a good job of keeping his expression in check. A small thing for which to be thankful, but little things count in bad situations. Elliot showed the bouncer his badge and continued on.

Elliot had worked vice for a year before moving to homicide but out of the four people who surrounded Beaumont, he recognized only one: Gordon Tremain. Gordy, when it came to menacing behavior, was like a small dog, more of an irritation than a threat. But he had a way with punks, getting them to do his work for him. As for the other three, one appeared to be another no-threat, a boyish kid for this area, while the second one could go either way. But the last one, a skinny guy with hollow eyes and one hand tucked inside the vest area of a black overcoat, had Elliot's attention.

Elliot stopped at the bar and ordered a beer, then walked over, stopping just behind Could-Be. He took a drink then smiled. "Gordy, my man."

Gordy looked as if he might drop to the floor in the clutches of a convulsive fit. "Bury me on a bed of roses," he said.

Elliot kept Hollow-Eyes in visual range. "It's good to see you too, Mr. Tremain. But I thought we had an understanding. You're not to deal anymore."

Gordy's head twitched. "Wa...word on the street is you bought the ticket, man, else I wouldn't be here, honest."

Elliot figured Gordy must've heard of his taking a bullet. "Sorry to disappoint you," he said. But as soon as he got the words out, an uneasy feeling crawled along his spine. Perhaps it was something about the way Gordon Tremain was behaving, or just his imagination, but Elliot suspected the situation had already begun to deteriorate before his arrival, and was now poised on the brink of disaster. Holding true to form, Could-Be pulled a knife, a butterfly that in his hands looked as if it'd do more harm to the user than its intended recipient. It was not a convincing move, just a miscalculated show of hardware. Elliot grabbed the man's wrist and twisted until the weapon fell from his hand, hitting the floor. But Could-Be's action was only a prelude to the real problem, and from the corner of his eye Elliot saw Hollow-Eyes pull his hand from beneath the black overcoat. Years of learned reflex took over. Elliot un-holstered the Glock and fired.

Chapter Sixteen

A deliberate silence rolled over the crowd as Hollow-Eyes slid to the floor, leaving a bloody trail along the wall. He wouldn't die, but he'd probably wish he could. Elliot had managed to pull the shot. Could-Be made another move for the knife and Elliot swung around, bringing the Glock to rest on the bridge of the man's nose. "Time to face the truth," he said, pressing the gun harder into his forehead. "And the truth is I don't have all that much to lose anymore, and this kind of dying just doesn't scare me."

Could-Be held his head still but rolled questioning eyes toward Gordy. Gordy scooped up the knife and shuffled over to Hollow-Eyes, taking the gun from beside his accomplice. He edged back, placed the weapons on the table, and backed away. Could-Be's legs wilted and he slumped into a chair.

Beaumont stood frozen in shock, his eyes as big as baseballs.

Elliot held his badge over his head, high in the air for people to see. "Your bust," he said.

Beaumont blinked and swallowed. "You're crazy. I can't be a party to this."

"Too late. You already are."

He shook his head.

Elliot glanced at the weapons on the table. "I could give the gun back to your nervous friend here and fade back into the night."

Beaumont took a step forward. "No," he said. "But I can't take the heat for this."

"Then we walk."

"We can't just leave. A man's been shot."

"Your bust then."

Beaumont put his hand to his head as if to reach in and pull out the right decision. "Let's get out of here," he said.

Still holding his unfinished beer, Elliot asked the bartender to call for some medical help then he holstered the Glock and took Beaumont by the arm, walking him outside. They kept going, neither of them speaking until they were well away from the club. Elliot stopped abruptly and grabbed Beaumont by the lapel, backing him into a wall. He searched him until he found what he was looking for, a bag of white powder. He pulled it from Beaumont's pocket and held it to his face. "You weren't busting. You were selling."

Beaumont's eyes widened. "You can't prove that. You can't prove a thing."

"Maybe not," Elliot said.

"What about Dombrowski?"

"Maybe I won't tell him. It's not my style. But I need a little cooperation. Besides, he thinks the world of you. It'd kill him if he knew you were dirty."

"What do you want from me?"

Elliot backed away, releasing his hold on Beaumont. He actually felt sorry for him. Holding the beer in front of him he said, "Even small monkeys have sharp teeth, Beaumont. But big nasty ones like you're dealing will drag a person down, leaving them in the gutter." He tossed the bag of cocaine to the ground at Beaumont's feet. "You're in over your head, kid. I know Gordon Tremain. He plays for keeps. The situation was out of control back there, and I just saved your ass."

Beaumont bent over and picked up the cocaine, sticking it inside his pocket. "What would you know about it anyway?"

"Probably nothing," Elliot said, "except for watching my mother slowly kill herself with a needle. It got so she couldn't do anything for herself, always depending on me. Then she didn't wake up at all one morning. It took me three days to get up enough courage to go out and tell someone what had happened. I was nine years old."

"Well, maybe that explains it then," Beaumont said. "You know what they say about boys without fathers."

Elliot took a step forward. "What are you getting at?"

"I'm talking about murder. Terrible thing, especially when it happens in small towns. They were friends of yours, weren't they? But you didn't stick around. You got yourself a football scholarship to Oklahoma State and left it all behind. But guess what? It began to happen in Stillwater. Three young girls, if I'm not mistaken. Then, just as they'd started, the killings at the University suddenly stopped. Interestingly enough, that happened right around the time you graduated and moved to Tulsa. And again the killings didn't stop, they merely changed location. Kind of like you did."

Elliot wondered why he'd wasted a private part of his life on such a worthless individual. Perhaps he'd thought there was hope for him, but as Beaumont finished his statement, Elliot's right hand doubled into a fist and rose quickly from its lowered position to connect hard with Beaumont's chin. He stumbled back and fell to the ground, nearly unconscious but still able to speak. "Keep away from me you psycho freak."

Beaumont's words hit home, for Elliot realized Beaumont saw him as others in his world did. What had started out as nothing more than a good poker face had evolved into a better-than-life facade that his peers knew as Kenny Elliot, while the real Elliot stood in the corner and tried to cope with the multitude of fears and anxieties behind the mask. Standing over Beaumont, he said, "Stay out of my affairs, kid. Don't make me tell you twice." He left

Beaumont lying on the sidewalk. He wasn't happy about what he'd done, but Beaumont hadn't left him any choice.

Elliot found his car and began to drive. He had no idea where he was going. A few minutes later, he called Molly. This time she answered. "It's good to hear your voice," she said.

A heavy silence followed while Elliot worked up his answer. "I don't know what Judas said, but I suspect it was something like that."

"What are you talking about?" She asked.

"Don't play dumb with me, kid. When you start dealing in friends, you've lost your soul. Let me put it to you straight. I'll get out of this somehow, get back on my feet. You might want to consider a new venue. I'm good at what I do. Everybody's got something to hide and I'll find it. I'll drag you through the mud, Molly." With that he disconnected and threw the cell phone on the floorboard.

The emptiness closed around Elliot like the jaws of a trap. He drove until he found a suitable location to relieve his anxiety. He pulled into an out-of-the-way local dive, parking behind the building so he wouldn't be seen. He needed to cool off. He didn't want to be bothered, but he soon realized it might or might not happen. Someone else was in the parking lot with him. He heard a car door slam, and footsteps, but he didn't look up. He locked his car, went inside, and found the loneliest seat he could, a booth in a dark corner of the room. He slid in, facing the wall. He didn't want to talk to anyone, and he didn't want anyone talking to him. When the waitress appeared, Elliot told himself to just keep his head down, but he didn't. She spoke and he looked up. She was pretty, with wide blue eyes. Elliot wondered about her hair. He thought it looked blonde.

Chapter Seventeen

In his car, he lowered the sun visor behind which he kept a photograph to remind him of what she had been and in so doing he caught a glimpse of himself in the vanity mirror. It was unnerving. The sight of their own image doesn't shock most people, even when it's bad, but seeing something entirely wrong, well that's a different story. She was to blame for that. As if it might gain her attention or offer insight, he stroked the surface of the photograph, and along with an array of jumbled emotions a disturbing memory ran through his head. He'd been awakened during the night, knowing from the sick feeling in his gut what it was. He'd gone outside where he'd heard somewhere in the distance the sound of breaking glass followed by laughter: Just a pack of kids, delinquents abusing their privilege of freedom as if it were nothing more than a worn-out emotion, cheap and easily given. They could not be more wrong. But they were not the problem. She'd come back. He had no doubt about that, but like a terrified homeowner creeping through the darkness to check out a noise in the night, he was powerless against a pressing need to confirm it.

It was not a ritual he cherished. She scared the hell out of him, and as he knelt before her, the moisture from the damp earth seeping into his pant legs, he began to tremble. He could not understand why she wanted such a life back, but she always did, and he had no more than placed the fresh cut roses onto the ground when…

"What have you got there, sweetie, picture of your girlfriend? Must've dumped you, the way you've got her all wadded up like that, like you're trying to squeeze the life out of her. Bet you'd like to, huh?"

Jerked back to the present, he took a moment to gather himself. He'd blanked out again. He hated that sensation, losing pieces of time. But he was back now, and inside some bar. He opened his hand and watched the photograph uncurl then he straightened it and stuck it in his pocket.

Posing as a waitress, she put a beer in front of him, and he paid her with a twenty, wanting her to make change so he could get a better look. His run of luck was still holding out. Even considering her sudden propensity for tenacious behavior, her being there was almost too much to accept. Indeed it was like wishing upon a star, and having it come true.

She caught him watching her as she handed him his change and her lips quivered into a smile. Her apprehension didn't stem from his attention. She was quite used to garnering the stares of men. She was trying to hide the fear that crawled alongside her recognition of who sat in the booth in front of her.

"Are you all right?" she asked.

He blinked, nearly knocking over his beer. Had she actually spoken to him? Yes, he thought she had. This was a new development. He wondered if she might actually sit beside him, and they could be together for a short time, maybe even hold hands while they talked about old times. It seemed plausible, but then he caught himself. Remember Papa's words, he scolded under his breath. It was just one of her tricks. In spite of himself and his warning, he smiled at her. "The beauty of your eyes is quite incomprehensible," he said. "I never could get over it." He studied the ball cap she wore. "What have you done with your hair?"

She stepped closer, taking off the cap and letting her long blonde hair spill from beneath, its softness falling across his arm. His pulse quickened. Even a relationship as non-symbiotic—and yet arguably just the opposite—as theirs had its limits, and she was testing it, stepping over the boundaries. Every ounce of common sense he had screamed for him to walk away and leave this uncanny happening alone, but a part of him, a part that had been left unnourished and starving for answers couldn't let go. He'd dreamed of such an encounter. To let it slip away now would be a sin. They had never had the chance to talk and they had so much to talk about.

And then, as if she'd read his mind and decided to let him off the hook, she spoke again. "He lived in our house and he made sounds like a man. He wore pieces of my pride hung on his trophy belt like bloody scalps."

"Why did Mother allow it?" he asked.

"Maybe you should have something to eat with that," the waitress said, but what he heard was, "Mother was a shadow, not in the sense that she followed anything around, but rather as a non-distinct being, existing from the corners of our eyes as she slunk about the house. I was surprised to see her when on occasion she'd sit with us at the table and beckon with her shadow hand for me to join her. She seldom spoke and when she did the venal bastard mounted his assault, a strident coughing of visceral threats and accusations. I couldn't blame her for being afraid."

"It hasn't done well for me either," he said. "Even among strangers I'm a stranger. My sanity has cost me my insanity, for no longer can I hide in it. Some have reached out in genuine gesture, but a leper cannot be touched or helped."

She nodded. "He was a throwback, living in the wrong time. His demeanor, his clothes and even his speech gave witness. I hated his hair, always cut wrong and always shining from a fresh dose of tonic, the cheap alcohol-based variety found in barbershops that cater to old men. His angry spider eyes float in the darkness of my night."

"He growled like a demented dog."

The waitress' forehead wrinkled, part curiosity and part concern as she kept silent, only listening, but he heard her say, "At least you were spared the demands of his cleanliness, the house smelling of furniture oils, and everything in its place."

"But I could hear and see the clock, clinging like ivy to the wall and breaking the monotony with its tedious ticking."

"I used to imagine that the dust constantly driven from the house hid behind the walls, caked thick and providing the exiled roaches a place to live with acres of musty tunnels."

Again Papa's words rang through, "'Even angels take out the garbage.'" Ralph quoted. "Which means," he continued, "they also tweeze unwanted hairs and shave the tops of their toes. Love, like blue denim jeans and memories, is meant to fade. Just you remember, cats hate the water, but they'll run through the rain to get to you."

"When Papa smiled," she said, "It was a slow, sadistic process, his lips curling, exposing unnaturally large teeth with gaps between them like tombstones in a cemetery. He was an undertaker with a false air of Baptist minister laced about. He destroyed everything, even the marker I'd made from ice cream sticks to put over my pet's grave. I used to dream you would break free and rescue me, come out of your room and creep into his exile where you could put the blade to him, plunging it deep into his chest, and make him see the color of life and the dingy gray of death."

He shook his head. He couldn't believe how much they had in common. They stared into one another's eyes for a moment then she turned and walked away. He was truly saddened. He couldn't deny their kinship, and yet he had to overcome it. She had defiled Papa, disrespected him in his name.

And then she turned back and said, "I wanted to set you free, but I couldn't, for I knew Papa snaked through every inch of you, like the invasive roots of a mint plant twisting through the fertile soil of a garden."

Her abusive words blackened her lips as she spoke. Papa was right. She was designed to torment.

Chapter Eighteen

Elliot sat in a lawn chair on his front porch, holding a cup of coffee that had turned cold, and watching the sun crawl over the eastern horizon. He'd been there for hours, trying to convince himself to move ahead and stop avoiding the obvious. It was time he got to the root of the problem. He threw the brown-colored contents of the cup onto the lawn, then went inside and showered. He had a trip to make.

When Elliot reached Coweta, he picked up Highway 51B and his heart began to sink. It was just a stretch of road that led to a town—a place like many others, where people acted out their lives—but it was his hometown of Porter, and it harbored a past he'd always thought best to leave alone.

It didn't take long to get there; the trip was a little over thirty miles, but as he entered the outskirts of town he realized it was another world and he thought of turning around and heading back to the city. Charlie Johnson, Porter's chief of police, had always held a high opinion of Elliot, even looking out for him when he needed it. But a lot had happened since then and Elliot had no idea how Charlie felt about him now. Facing him would not be easy.

And then there was Carmen. Her presence had never really left Elliot, and again seeing the familiar streets and houses where they created those memories intensified his emotions, like removing tarnish from antique silver or brushing the dust from a piece of crystal art. He was still in love with her.

Elliot pulled into a parking space in front of the Porter municipal office, an old WPA structure made of native stone, and slowly climbed out of the car, readying himself for the confrontation. As he neared the entrance, the sudden sound of barking made him pause on the sidewalk. He stared at the large oak tree in front of the building, remembering.

A dog had been baying outside his window that day. He was hungry, but the only thing that filled the house was death. It was Charlie Johnson who saw him walking alongside the road and stopped to pick him up. Later, he helped arrange for foster care.

Elliot walked the few paces left to reach the building and went inside, opening the first door on the right, the office of the Porter Police Department. Charlie Johnson wasn't there, and a middle-aged lady who came to the counter told Elliot he might catch him at home.

Charlie lived a couple of blocks away. Elliot left his car parked at the municipal building and walked. The old house peeked from behind several massive oak trees that dominated the yard. Charlie kept it looking neat and tidy, with a fresh coat of yellow paint for the clapboard siding each spring, and white for the trim. Two wicker rocking chairs sat on the front porch on either side of the white French doors, and an American flag, hanging from one of the wooden porch supports, waved in the breeze—a perfect picture from the heartland.

Elliot knocked on the door and a few seconds later he stood face to face with Porter's chief of police. Grinning, the old police officer stepped outside. He'd put on some weight, his well-curved belly making it nearly impossible to see his belt, but other than that he looked like the same old Charlie Johnson.

Studying Elliot, he said, "Well if my eyes don't deceive me it's Kenny "Bulldog" Elliot."

Elliot smiled. It was a nickname he'd picked up in high school. "How you doing, Charlie?"

They went inside where Johnson sat on a Victorian couch, Elliot on a rocking chair. Charlie's expression said he still couldn't believe Elliot was there. "You know, to be honest, I never thought I'd see you again."

Charlie seemed happy Elliot was there, but his statement sounded as if he didn't think he ought to be. "It's been awhile," Elliot said, "seems like a lifetime."

"So what have you been up to?" Johnson asked, meaning, *what do you want?* Charlie was never one for small talk.

Elliot pulled out the leather case that held his badge and handed it to Johnson.

Charlie leaned forward, placing his forearms on his knees, and examined the badge. He looked both pleased and worried. "Never figured you for a cop. Strange things do happen, I guess." He handed the badge back to Elliot. "So what is it exactly that brings you here?"

"You've probably heard about the murders in Tulsa?"

Johnson nodded, a grave look crossing his face.

"I'm the investigating officer."

Johnson drew his hand across his forehead to wipe away the beads of perspiration that had formed there. Standing, he said, "I could use some coffee. Want a cup?"

Johnson went into the kitchen and came back carrying cups with matching saucers. He handed one filled with black coffee to Elliot. Elliot thought of Dombrowski and didn't mention cream or sugar.

"I need to get ready," Johnson said. "But don't leave, I'll just be a minute; make yourself at home." He took a sip of his coffee then took it with him down the hallway toward the back of the house.

Several minutes later, Elliot took his cup into the kitchen and rinsed it out, placing it in the sink. Johnson was still gone. Elliot had been in Charlie's house before, but never beyond the living room or the kitchen, and as he walked past the hallway he noticed an open door leading into a back room. He recalled a small addition that protruded from the back of the house. He and his friends had always wondered about it. Unable to resist, he quietly walked down the hallway, going through the doorway into the addition.

The small room was clean and bare of furniture except for a twin bed and a chest of drawers, and it could've used a coat of paint to cover various places along the walls where pictures had once been. Over the chest was such a spot, triangular in shape as though some kind of sports pennant had once hung there. Following an instinct to explore further, Elliot opened the closet door and poked his head in for a look. It was empty, no clothes hanging on the bar, no shoes on the floor. But something was on the top shelf and when Elliot stretched to see he found a football. He pulled it down and when he flipped it around he saw that it had words on it. A name written with a black marker read: Johnnie Alexander.

Elliot sat on the bed, closing his eyes and gripping the football, close to his chest the way Coach Sims had taught, and in his mind he saw Johnnie walking toward him across the field. It'd been a rough game and Johnnie was dirty, his shoulder pads showing through rips in his jersey. "Who's the kid?" Elliot asked.

Johnnie shook his head. "I've seen him at a couple of the games." Pausing Johnnie looked around to see if the kid was still there, but he wasn't. "He wanted my autograph."

After that Johnnie and Elliot autographed a few cheap footballs and tossed them into the crowd on game days.

Elliot put the football back in the closet where he'd found it and left the room, returning to his chair in the living area. Dressed in his uniform, Charlie came into the room and sat on the couch. He stared at Elliot for a moment then said, "Tell me something, Kenny. How does Porter figure into your investigation?"

It took Elliot a moment to answer. He had to force the words out. "I think the killings in Tulsa might be connected..." He paused then continued, "connected to the deaths of Johnnie and Marcia. I was hoping you could tell me a little about the old case."

Johnson nodded but said nothing.

Elliot had known this wasn't going to be easy. To relieve the tension, he said, "We can talk about it later, if you want."

Johnson sighed. "Do you reckon that'll change anything?" He got up and walked to the window, pushing the curtain aside so he could look through the glass.

"Were there any suspects?" Elliot asked.

"I think you know the answer to that."

"Any *other* suspects?"

"Not really."

"How about fingerprints?"

Johnson shook his head. "Just Johnnie's and Marcia's."

"Evidence?"

"Other than the knife on the floorboard and the gun in Johnnie's hand, no. The ground was dry and hard, so there were no footprints and no additional tire tracks. Johnnie had Marcia's blood all over him."

Elliot thought for a moment. "Which hand was Johnnie holding the gun in?"

A curious look crossed Johnson's face. "His right one, why?"

"Johnnie was left-handed."

Johnson rubbed his chin. "Of course that occurred to me, but what other conclusion was I to draw from the facts?"

Elliot retrieved the photograph of Michelle Baker, the one that showed the blood writing on the wall, and handed it to Johnson.

As Charlie examined the photo, the color drained from his face. When he looked back at Elliot, he was pale and gray. "For God's sake, Kenny, don't do this. Just leave it alone."

"I can't do that," Elliot said. "It's my job."

Charlie shook his head. "How long have you been a cop?"

"About five years."

"Are you any good?"

"Some people seem to think so."

Charlie nodded. "Well, I'd love to stay and chat, but I need to get going."

They walked outside, stopping on the porch, and Elliot waited while Charlie locked the doors. When he'd finished, Charlie turned to Elliot, grabbing his shoulder with his hand. "Some things are better off left alone, son. I shouldn't have to tell you that." He shook his head. "You almost got arrested for those murders and now you're investigating them? The world does go around. You know plenty of folks around here thought you were guilty, most of them banking on the trouble you'd already caused. I was under a lot of pressure to put you away."

"I got off to a rocky start, but I was turning things around."

"Yeah," Johnson said. "Football did wonders for you...that and Carmen Garcia. She did you a favor, coming forward like that."

"I know."

"Then don't cause her efforts to be in vain, son. You start digging, you might not like what you find."

"You're trying to make a point. Why don't you just come out with it?"

Charlie's face softened. He looked apologetic and spoke softly, "There's nothing left in Porter for you, Kenny. It'd be best for all of us if you went on back to Tulsa where you belong and left us out of your investigation."

Charlie's insinuations angered Elliot, but they also hurt. Part of him, the part he'd been running away from all those years, felt Charlie was right. Walking out of Charlie's yard, he said, "I'll leave when I've found what I came for."

"And what might that be?" Charlie asked.

Answers, Elliot thought, but said nothing. As he walked back to the municipal building, a car driving along the road slowed to a near stop, and when Elliot turned, he saw that the driver was Carmen Garcia. She had a child, a young boy with her. She raised her hand—almost a mechanical movement—and slowly waved, but the look on her face was one of shock. Elliot returned the gesture but kept on walking. He didn't know what else to do.

Elliot didn't stop at the municipal building. He kept going, following the narrow blacktop road along an old but familiar path. He wasn't sure what was going through his mind as he stepped off the road and into the waist-high weeds, walking toward the remnants of the house on Dixieland Avenue where he once lived, and where his mother spent the final years of her life. Obscured by weeds and tree branches, the home site, with its sagging roof and rotting lumber, looked like something out of a twisted Norman Rockwell collection. Not the wholesome vignettes we all know and love, but the others, the ones he kept hidden beneath his bed, inspired by nightmares and knowledge of a world that was not so right.

Elliot kept moving forward, and when he pushed open the door and stepped inside he had to brace himself as his knees grew weak. Placing his hand against the wall, he dealt as best he could with the menagerie of memories that flooded his senses. He loved and missed her, but he had to tell himself over and over that it was the drugs and not his mother that locked him inside that room, letting him go hungry all those nights while he buried his head beneath his pillow to muffle the sounds of her satisfied customers.

It was then that he recalled Maggie, someone who'd befriended his mother and him, stopping by now and then, bringing food and an occasional comic book for Elliot to read. He hadn't known it at the time, but later he came to realize that Maggie wasn't in full command of her faculties, which was probably why she was the only one, other than Charlie Johnson, who dared visit them. Elliot turned and left the dank, depressing atmosphere, stepping outside and going back to Main Street where he got in his car and headed for Tulsa.

About four miles up the highway, though, Elliot spotted a sign marking the turnoff for Alexander's Orchard, and it dawned on him that he was doing exactly what he'd promised himself he wouldn't do. He turned off the highway and started down the old road, pulling to the side and parking when he recognized the area. Alexander's property appeared to be unmolested by progress, but not by time. Because of the distance and the lay of the land, he couldn't see the house, but part of the old orchard was still there, overgrown and unattended. He crossed the road and crawled through the fence to enter the property. The orchard seemed permeated with a sense of hopelessness, and the aroma of fermenting fruit tainted the air like the smell of cheap wine as he walked among the peach trees, stumbling occasionally on the soggy ground. Finding the tree he was looking for, he paused, breathing in the sweetened air as the moment took him back.

"I don't like it here, Kenny. Let's go."

"This is one of my favorite places," he said, showing her the tree.

Marcia had smiled at the fresh carvings of affection he'd put there. "But what if he comes?"

"Who?" Elliot asked.

"Old Man Alexander. I don't like him. He scares me."

"He's not so bad," Elliot said, "Just a little weird."

She had pulled him close, whispering in Elliot's ear. "Sometimes at night, I see someone walking along the road by my house. I think he watches me through my window."

A metallic click brought Elliot back to the present and he turned to find himself looking down the barrel of a shotgun.

Chapter Nineteen

"You got no right coming around here, boy."

Elliot stared into the face of the man holding the gun. It was Marshall Alexander, owner of the property. As Mr. Alexander's quivering finger embraced the trigger, Elliot couldn't decide if he shook more from age, or from anger. The barrel of the shotgun looped back and forth, tracing out a rough figure eight in the air.

"Mr. Alexander," he said. "It's me, Kenny."

Keeping his eye on Elliot, he turned his head and spat tobacco juice onto the ground. "You think I don't know that? I ain't likely to forget the one that killed my Johnnie."

Elliot shook his head. "It wasn't me, Mr. Alexander. You have to believe that."

Marshall Alexander jammed the barrel of the shotgun into Elliot's head. "You're lying. I tried to tell Johnnie not to hang around with the likes of you. You, the football stud, and that little blonde-headed tramp. But he wouldn't listen."

Elliot took a step back, thinking about the driver of the vehicle that had tried to run him down in Tulsa. Speaking in his mechanical voice, the assailant had said pretty much the same thing just before he torched the place. Elliot tried to imagine Marshall Alexander doing those things, but he could not. "Why don't you put down the gun before you do something we'll both regret?"

The old man's gaze held Elliot's like a steel trap. He spat again then repositioned the shotgun. Speaking with a raspy conviction he said, "Now you're going to pay for what you did."

Elliot's heart pounded in his chest. Then he heard a car coming to a stop along the roadway, and as he turned to see what had made the commotion, he saw someone walking toward them. It was Chief Johnson.

"Don't do it, Marshall," Johnson said.

Marshall Alexander didn't even blink. "Stay out of this, Charlie. I'm warning you."

Charlie stepped closer. Pulling his .38 he said, "Don't make me use force, Marshall. Ain't neither of us wants that. Now you get on back to the house. I'll take care of this."

Finally the old man lowered the shotgun. "Yeah, I just bet you will. Just like you always do; sweep it under the carpet and hope it all goes away."

"Don't push your luck, Marshall. You get on back to the house like I told you. Don't make me run you in."

Marshall Alexander's eyes widened, and his face flushed. He opened his mouth to speak but changed his mind and turned and walked away.

Charlie holstered his weapon. As he was leaving he said, "Don't say I didn't warn you, Kenny. People around here got long memories."

Elliot watched Johnson drive away. In the eerie quiet that followed, it seemed he had never been there at all. Elliot crawled back through the fence and went to his car. His business in Porter wasn't finished, not by a long shot. He drove back to town and parked in front of Brazleton's garage.

Nick Brazleton's father had worked on cars for a living when that occupation wasn't known for its pay scale. Elliot guessed that was why he and Nick hit it off, growing up in the same low-rent fashion in the same part of town. He would always stop by Elliot's house and they'd walk to school together, coming home the same way. He was a friend, and one of the few people who had stood behind Elliot when everyone else had written him off.

The old white building that reminded Elliot of a train depot hadn't changed much. Above the front door, the same hand-painted sign read: BRAZLETON'S AUTO SHOP. A couple of elderly gentlemen sat on a park bench in front of the shop beside a soft drink vending machine. Elliot nodded to them as he walked through the open doorway leading to the office. What he saw there ran a chill through him. Missing from the office walls were the foldout pictures of pinup girls, and faded calendars with caricatures of dogs playing card games. Instead, tacked to the office walls where grease-smeared pink and yellow business receipts should have been, was a curious collection of items, meandering across the wall like yellowed newsprint ivy. There were clippings and photographs, but mostly it was the assortment of memorabilia from their childhood that sent Elliot's senses reeling. It was a shrine dedicated to a past that already wouldn't die.

Surrounding Elliot was every Porter football accomplishment he'd ever made. There was even a crayon sign from a tree house they'd built and the pellet gun with a handmade stock he had given to Nick. Memories shot through Elliot, both in and out of sequence, like a kaleidoscope of rapidly firing flashbulbs. He sat down in an old swivel chair behind the desk, putting his hand over his eyes. But between the cracks of his fingers, the writing on a worn piece of notebook paper burned through. Pinned to the wall and standing out from the neighboring clutter was Marcia's poem. She'd shown it to Elliot the day she and Johnnie took their last ride.

Do you know the Sandman?
He lives.
Like the mannequin,
in the window,
in the emptiness it grows.
A town without life,
deals in death.

Elliot had thought the poem was just Marcia's rambling, but it made a little more sense to him now. Marcia, the mannequin in the window, had suspected someone was watching her a little more intently than she was comfortable with. The question was this: who was the Sandman?

A noise startled Elliot and he turned to see someone coming into the office.

"Something I can help you with?"

The man standing in front of Elliot didn't look the part, but he knew it was Nick Brazleton. From beneath a dirty baseball cap, his hair hung to his shoulders. Aged grease stained the overalls he wore, and a two- or three-day growth of beard, like that of the derelicts on skid row, covered his face. As soon as Elliot stood, Nick recognized him. His face lit up. "Hey, old buddy." He threw his arms around Elliot in a bear hug then released him and took a step back. "Yeah," he said, flashing a white-toothed grin. "It's you all right. About time, don't you think?"

Elliot didn't know what to say.

Nick raised his cap and scratched his head then motioned for Elliot to follow him into the garage area.

Inside the bay, Elliot thought of Nick's father, his head always stuck under the hood of some car, looking like the dinner of the metal beast with his legs dangling from its mouth. Elliot couldn't remember him being any other way, except when he'd take a break to yell at his son.

Nick walked over to an old refrigerator sitting in the corner of the garage and jerked open the door, reaching inside. "Here," he said, hurling a missile at Elliot.

Reflexively, Elliot snatched the soft drink can from the air then popped it open with a spray.

Nick laughed. "Still got those great hands."

Elliot was quite fond of Nick, but for reasons he'd never understood, he was always worried by him. Marcia had said he was like a storm cloud, waiting to unleash its fury. But she was always saying stuff like that.

Nick pushed aside some tools and climbed onto a workbench to sit down, his legs hanging over the edge like those of a child sitting on a large sofa. "Man, it's good to see you again, Kenny. We had some times, didn't we? We were some team, too, except you and Johnnie deserved all the credit."

"That's not true," Elliot said. "You did your part."

He didn't seem to hear but kept on talking. "Want to know something else? Coach Sims told me it was you that made Johnnie look so good."

Again Elliot protested, but Nick raised his hand for silence. "Honest-to-God truth, man. That's what he said."

Elliot took a drink of his soda. Eric Sims had come to Porter when Elliot was in the ninth grade. He was a good coach, but more than that, he'd been a father figure and a positive role model for mixed up kids like Nick and Elliot. His guidance earned Elliot a scholarship. "How is Coach Sims?"

Nick shook his head. "He moved back to Florida a couple of years ago. Said he had kin there." He paused before continuing. "We had some moments though, didn't we? Remember the Hulbert game? Two minutes on the clock and fourth down. Of course, you and Johnnie were fighting again. But I convinced him to give you the ball anyway, because I could tell by look in your eyes they weren't stopping you. You meant to score. And you did, too, using me like a bridge over troubled water. Never did tell you how much that hurt, did I? Still got the scar on my back. But hey, we won, didn't we?"

"Won a lot of games that year," Elliot said. "We had a good team."

"Yeah. They didn't call you Bulldog for nothing."

"Cut it out, Nick."

"Hey, don't get me wrong. For a low-rent kid like me, you were a good friend to have. Half the kids in school were scared to death of you, and those that weren't thought twice about crossing you."

"It's not something I'm proud of."

"I'm not trying to criticize you," Nick said. "You had good reason. If anyone understands that, I do. You know how my dad was."

"At least you had a father."

Nick smiled. "So do you, somewhere out there."

"I guess so. I asked Mom about him once."

"No kidding?"

Elliot nodded. "She told me he was nothing more than just another John. And she'd be damned if she could remember which one."

"Jeez, Kenny. That's the saddest thing I've ever heard. Guess that's why we got along so well. Nobody ever cared much about either of us." He paused, his expression darkening. "Except you always had Carmen."

"Yeah. I blew the hell out of that one, didn't I?"

"You worked at it, buddy, worked real hard." Then Nick said, "That girl loves you, Kenny. She always thought you'd come back, waited a long time."

Elliot studied Nick's face, remembering something Nick had told him long ago. It seemed to conflict with what he was hearing now. "Do you think I should go and see her?"

"It might be a little late for that."

"Is she married?"

"You got it."

Changing the subject, Nick gestured around the garage. "I always said I'd never end up like this, doing what my father did. I guess down deep, though, I always knew I would." He smiled. "It doesn't look like you've done much better. I take it you never made it to law school?"

Elliot shook his head, and after a brief silence they both laughed. Nick climbed down from the workbench then came over and hugged Elliot again. This time Elliot returned the embrace.

"I've missed you, Kenny. I miss Johnnie, too, and the things we did."

"Yeah," Elliot said. "I know."

"It was Marcia. Everything changed after she showed up. Like you and Johnnie didn't have enough to fight about. And you were both too stubborn to sit down and talk about it." He turned away, fishing through a toolbox behind him, and when he turned back he held not a wrench or screwdriver, but a large black-handled knife.

Elliot watched nervously as Nick examined the weapon, testing the sharpness with his thumb. "You know," he said, pushing the bill of his cap up with the blade, "if the truth be known, your world was the most shattered. At least that's what I think. Always figured it'd be you and Carmen all the way to wedding bells. On second thought, maybe you ought to go and see her."

"I thought you said she was married?"

"I did, but it's kind of like temperature, it should be the same but it isn't, not always."

"What's that supposed to mean?"

"You know, like when you set your thermostat to seventy-two degrees. Well, when it's a hundred and two outside that setting feels pretty good, maybe even a little warm, but in the middle of January that same seventy-two feels cold, might even put on a sweater. I even put a couple of thermometers in different rooms once just to check it out. Sure enough, seventy-two was seventy-two. But if you're cold, you're cold, and you just have to go with what you feel. Know what I mean?"

"Not really," Elliot said.

Nick shrugged and tossed the knife back into the toolbox. "She's going through a divorce." He walked over to a car and started to work on it.

"Whose idea was it?"

"They never did get along," he muttered from beneath the hood of the car.

"What's his name?" Elliot asked.

Nick worked in silence for a moment, allowing no sounds except for the dull clatter of tools against greasy metal then he came out from under the hood, holding what looked to be the severed head of Medusa. "I guess you remember Anthony Davenport?"

"You've got to be kidding," Elliot said. The thought of Carmen being with Davenport put a knot in his stomach. Davenport wasn't one of the rich kids, but he wanted to be, hanging with them at school, pretending to be a socialite.

Elliot thought about asking Nick how he'd managed to collect the paraphernalia decorating his office—and more importantly why—but he didn't. After all, how much worse was Nick's fixation with the past than his running away from it?

"There's something else you need to know," Nick said, his face growing serious. "I mean about Carmen."

Nick's actions told Elliot he was building up to something. Nick didn't drop bombshells. He dragged them in and placed them beside you. "What is it, Nick?"

He shook his head. "Somebody's coming."

Nick laid the part on the workbench and wiped his hands with a rag. Seconds later, a man came walking into the shop. As Nick went over to greet the customer, Elliot pulled the knife from the toolbox and began to examine it. It was high quality, about ten inches long, with a smooth black handle, though it looked as if it'd be more at home in some gourmet chef's kitchen than in the garage. Suddenly Elliot got the feeling he was being watched, and when he looked up the man was staring at him. At least it seemed that way. Sunglasses covered the man's eyes. His hair was swept back, like Elvis in his early days, except it was blonde instead of black. He wore a jacket, fastened at the waist and zippered part way, leaving a V-shaped opening through which showed his chest covered by a white T-shirt. Elliot tossed the knife back into the toolbox and started toward Nick, but before he got there the man turned and walked away. "Who was that?" Elliot asked.

Nick shrugged. "He wanted directions to the peach orchard. I get that all the time around here."

"Peaches are out of season."

"Yeah, I know. They got other things out there, though."

As Elliot looked up, he saw the squatty silhouette of Charlie Johnson blocking the light from the doorway. "I noticed Maggie Caldwell's truck outside," he said. "She doesn't get out much."

"Running a little rough," Nick said. "Told her I'd have a look at it."

Johnson walked around the garage, surveying the premises and stopping when he came to the toolbox. His expression said he saw the knife. He smiled. "Hello, Kenny."

Elliot nodded.

"Sorry I came down on you so hard earlier. Hope you understand." Smiling, he walked toward the exit. "I'll leave you boys to your reminiscing. By the way, Kenny, Carmen asked about you."

Nick waited until Charlie Johnson was gone then turned to Elliot. "You and Carmen belong together. That's never changed."

Elliot thought about Nick's words. He guessed the thought of things being the way they were made sense to him. "I'm not so sure, Nick."

"I guess it's too bad about their marriage then."

"I never figured Anthony Davenport as her type," Elliot said.

"You got that right."

Questioning Nick about Carmen's husband didn't feel right, but Elliot continued anyway. "What kind of guy did he turn out to be?"

"He didn't deserve Carmen, that's for sure."

"Come on, Nick."

"He was going out on her."

"How do you know that?"

"I saw him a couple of times with a woman, and it wasn't Carmen."

"Could've been a friend."

Nick shrugged. "She didn't look like a friend."

"How did she look?"

Nick paused and averted his eyes as if he thought his answer might come across as less than sane. "Like Marcia, only all grown up."

Nick's answer caught Elliot off guard, but it got him to thinking about the case again. Marcia Barnes had more than fit the profile of the killer's victims. She epitomized it. "Speaking of Marcia," Elliot said, "did she ever mention that she thought someone was watching her?"

Nick pulled a grease rag from his pocket and wiped his hands. "Not that I recall. Why?"

"She told me several times. And once when we were at Murphy's Point we both saw someone looking through the car window."

"So what are you trying to say?"

"Maybe Marcia was right."

Nick was silent for a moment. He seemed to be processing the information. "Johnnie used to tell stories like that. Sometimes I think he half believed them; something about a dog-man that roamed the Point, preying on unfortunate lovers."

"Teenagers in parked cars," Elliot said. "They called him the Sandman."

Nick gave Elliot a strange look then shook his head. "All small towns have stories like that. Besides, my dad told me the same story was going around when he was a kid."

Elliot thought it over. Nick had a good point. The tale did have an urban legend flavor. Some versions even had the villain with the features of a dog. "I guess you're right. I wonder how stories like that get started?"

Nick stuffed the rag back into his pocket. "I guess kids in boring little towns have to create excitement somehow."

Elliot looked at his watch. "Hey, I need to be going. I've got work to do."

"Are you coming back?"

Elliot thought about the autographed football he'd found in the back room of Johnson's house and another piece of the puzzle dropped into place. "Do you remember the kid we used to see at the games, the one nobody knew?"

Nick thought for a moment. "Never saw him at school or anything, and you couldn't get close to him or he'd run away?"

"That's the one. Any idea what happened to him?"

"Not really. Whatever made you think about him?"

"Just curious," Elliot said, handing Nick a business card. "I'll see you around, okay?"

Nick examined the card. "You're a cop?"

"That's me."

Nick shook his head. "You never cease to amaze me, Kenny."

Elliot paused, looking through the open garage door. "My mom wasn't all bad," he said. Nick gave him a curious look.

"What we were talking about earlier," Elliot said. "I guess she got to feeling bad about it. Anyway, a few days later I found a picture of some guy, all framed and everything, sitting on the dresser beside my bed. It was even signed with an inscription. I knew it wasn't my father, just some old photo she'd found, but it was the thought that counted...knowing she cared enough to do that, go to all that trouble."

"What did it say?"

Lost in the moment, Elliot looked at Nick, unsure of what he was asking.

"The inscription?"

Elliot nodded. "It said love. Love, Papa Terrance."

Nick smiled. "Hey, before you go I've got something I need to say." He paused, looking for the right words. "I never told you I was sorry."

"Sorry for what?"

"For taking you to Latham's house that night. That's part of it anyway. I didn't know the booze was going to be there, but I shouldn't have taken you, just the same."

Flashes of the bloody crime scene went through Elliot's head. Nick was talking about the party they'd gone to after the game. Johnnie had lost the game, but that wasn't the problem. Marcia Barnes was the reason their voices had risen to the point of attracting attention, and the reason Elliot had taken Johnnie down. The silent staring faces of the shocked fans watching him walk off the field was something Elliot would never forget, but it was the hurt look in Johnnie's eyes that still haunted his dreams. Nick had pulled him off Johnnie and persuaded Elliot to go to Latham's house to cool off and forget about things. It was also the night Johnnie and Marcia were killed. "Don't go blaming yourself for something you didn't do, Nick. None of it was your fault."

"I don't know," he said. "I just keep thinking that maybe none of this would've happened if I'd just left well enough alone."

Elliot wondered if there was any truth to Nick's words. "Don't be silly," he said. He gestured to Maggie Caldwell's truck, the one Charlie had inquired about. "Where's Maggie living these days?"

"Same place she always did," Nick said.

Maggie Caldwell's place didn't look much better than the falling-down structure where Elliot had lived, but the grass was mowed. Taking care of Maggie's lawn had been one of his summer jobs. Her property sat at the intersection of two country roads, and the windows on the side that would get the most traffic were covered with tar paper to keep car lights from shining through. The house was situated next to the property line and the road. The driveway, which was nothing more than beaten-down earth, led to a large metal building that served as a garage and storage area. Maggie's place looked the same as it had nine years ago, when Elliot had last seen it.

As Elliot opened the gate and walked through, he noticed something rather odd in the yard. Blowing in the breeze, like a nostalgic monument to an all but bygone era of suburban life, were blue denim jeans on a clothesline. Blue jeans were not the type of thing Maggie would wear, but he'd often seen them hanging there.

Elliot closed the gate and realized he was in trouble. He'd made a mistake. Maggie had always kept a dog, and the present one sped toward Elliot, slowing as he neared, but not stopping. Inches away, the dog edged closer, a deep growl coming from his throat. His tongue slipped between his bared teeth like a wet serpent. Options of what to do next ran through Elliot's head. He came up with the only solution. He had nowhere to go, and if he turned and ran the confidence afforded the dog by that action would be Elliot's undoing. So he did the only thing he could. He held his ground. Elliot offered the back of his hand to the dog, showing he was friendly, but just as he did the door to the cabin flew open and an old lady, brandishing a baseball bat, came charging out, screaming like a siren. It was Maggie Caldwell.

Elliot visualized Maggie striking him with the bat, cackling like a demented hen over a fresh lay of eggs as the life drooled out of him. She took a swipe, but Elliot jumped to his right, catching the bat near the end of the swing. Keeping his grip, he wrestled it from her and tossed the weapon into the yard. A spew of obscenities followed, causing the dog to gain both anger and confidence. "Maggie," Elliot said. "It's me, Kenny."

She studied Elliot, a grin spreading across her wrinkled face, then she turned to the dog and yelled, "Shut your trap, you old mongrel."

The dog obeyed, dropping his tail between his legs and disappearing behind the house. He had no doubt tasted the wrath of Maggie's bat.

Maggie snorted. "Thought you looked familiar." She turned and walked into the house, stopping after a few feet to turn back and say, "You coming in, or not?"

Elliot followed her through the door. Although he'd seen Maggie's house numerous times, he had never been inside of it until now. The furniture was old and worn, and what looked like sheaves of weeds and clumps of garlic hung from the ceiling.

Maggie went into the kitchen, and when she returned she carried a cup of something, which she handed to Elliot. "Thought you might be hungry."

As Elliot took the cup, thoughts of bat wings and eyes of newt gave his stomach a turn. Like a fool, he asked, "What is it?"

She puffed on a cigarette, the old kind without a filter. "What is it?" she mocked, the cigarette following the movement of her lips as if it were surgically attached. "It's chicken soup. Take more than that to cure what ails you, though."

Elliot took a sip. It was good, and he was hungry. "What do you mean?"

With nicotine-yellowed fingers, she pointed to her head. "Something in here burns you. That's what brought you to Maggie, digging up old bones."

Elliot smiled. "I came to visit, see how you're doing. I also wanted to thank you for looking in on Mom and me the way you did. It meant a lot to me, and to her." Elliot paused. Maggie's statement had piqued his curiosity. "What did you mean by digging up old bones?"

She laughed. "Don't know. Might not mean anything." She squinted, her eyes a hazy brown that looked to be curtained with dingy cellophane. "Might mean everything. Maybe I'm just a nutty old hag." She laughed again, half wheezing. "I suspect you want to know about your unfortunate friends. Everybody needs to know what Maggie knows, but nobody listens."

"I'm listening," Elliot said.

She sat on the couch, patting the adjacent cushion. Elliot sat beside her. She took his hand, the haze lifting briefly from her eyes. "I saw his lights come through the window, so I went to see who it was. He had a young rider with him that night. Something was up, I knew that much, so I followed, sneaking through the meadow beside the road. It wasn't easy, but I stayed with it. I watched him go, saw what he did."

"What did you see, Maggie?"

"Just down from the orchard where the creek runs through, there's a hollow lined with scrub oaks."

Elliot nodded. "Who was it?"

"You go there and you look, and keep looking, 'cause it's there." She laughed. "He was a rebel, he roamed but he couldn't score. He couldn't do it but his sister could." She paused and picked up a framed photograph from the table beside the couch. Showing it to Elliot, she said, "My Bobby's a fine boy, isn't he? Be coming home soon."

It was a picture of her son. Elliot's mother had told him about it. He'd been missing in action in Vietnam and never returned home. Elliot thought about the blue jeans on the clothesline, and suddenly he understood the root of her dementia. Pity waved over him.

Maggie took the nub of a cigarette from her mouth and ground it out in an ashtray. "Small wonder you ended up where you are, hanging around with the likes of Nick Brazleton. You've got other troubles, too. You're in love with that little Mexican girl."

"You mean Carmen?"

She waved her hand. "You're a good boy, Kenny. Maggie should've took you in, got you out of that mess. Maybe then you wouldn't be in such a fix."

Elliot paused a moment. The uncanny clarity at which certain thoughts of Maggie's would cut through the obvious internal noise had begun to amaze him. "Maggie," he asked, "do you know anything about the trouble I got into before I left town?"

She leaned forward and whispered. "The boy isn't right, and he lurches about in the darkness trying to correct it." After that she got up and left the room. When she returned, she handed Elliot a folded piece of paper. "Your mother was in bad shape that day and I knew it." Tears formed in her eyes. "We talked, you know. But she must've known she was going to be too sick. She wrote that up earlier and gave it to me when I came in."

Elliot recognized his mother's handwriting as he slowly unfolded the note and began to read.

> *Terrance showed up again last night. I told him not to ever come back, but he won't listen. He's mean, Maggie. Way down deep mean. I guess it's payback for the life I've lived that he should be the one to leave me with child. It's not all bad, though. That nice man Charlie Johnson has taken an interest in Kenny. He comes over a lot. I can tell he likes me. He's asked me out several times. Can you imagine me going out with a cop? I told him no. He's looking for companionship, but not the kind I can give him. No sense going down a path I can't follow. Hope to feel better on your next visit. Love, Lizzie.*

Elliot held the note in his hand. People had called his mother Lizzie, though her name was Elizabeth. Her words ran through him like a fever. "What's this mean, Maggie? What's she talking about?"

Maggie shook her head. "You stay away from that man, you hear? Don't want nothing to do with him. He's dead anyway, just like everybody else."

"Who's dead?"

"He stepped over the line, and went messing around with the wrong person, went too far. Now he don't do nothing but sit in that car of his, only it's parked in the ravine like I done told you." She turned away and walked into the other room, saying as she went, "Best you be going now. Maggie needs her rest."

As Elliot was leaving, he noticed a riding lawn mower next to the shed. He put it away and oiled the noisy hinges on the shed door, then got in his car and drove away. He knew the area Maggie had talked about, so he drove there to check it out. Elliot stopped at the brick house across the street from the property, and after telling the people inside who he was and what he wanted, he learned that the property owner was out of state. But the homeowners didn't see any problem with his looking around, so he drove up the dirt road across from the house and parked beside the gate to the property.

Elliot walked across the gently sloping meadow until it descended into the hollow. The creek, which didn't see much water anymore except for an occasional rain, ran the length of the property. Maggie hadn't been specific about where he should look so Elliot started next to the roadway and made his way along the rocky bottom, walking deeper into the hollow.

Later Elliot paused to check his watch. He'd been slipping and sliding across the rocks for some time. Nearly an hour had passed. He was deep in the woods, and far enough from civilization to be in a good spot to hide something but so far he hadn't seen anything. Just ahead the ravine disappeared around another bend. Elliot pushed on, but as soon as he rounded the bend he stopped in his tracks. The creek was deep there, the banks being seven or eight feet high, and directly in front of him he saw an obstruction, a large pile of rocks and tree limbs. It looked like a huge beaver dam, except there was no water and Elliot suspected that even if there was, the pile of debris wouldn't hold it. He began to remove the debris, grabbing whatever piece he could get a grip on. He tore away limbs and moved heavy rocks, pausing a few minutes later to observe what he'd uncovered, what was hidden there. He took a step back and stared at the rusted remains of an automobile. But it was what was inside the vehicle that had his attention. Elliot thought about the note Maggie had shown him and the words of his mother splayed across the page.

The driver of the vehicle stared back at Elliot with gaping, hollow eyes.

Chapter Twenty

Elliot knew something wasn't right when he saw the motorcycles parked in front of the open bay door at Nick's garage. He walked through the bay door and everything seemed to stop while everyone turned to look at him. Then Nick resumed his work, his power wrench screaming as before. A couple of bikers stood next to him. Elliot started toward Nick but he'd only taken a few steps when a man wearing a black T-shirt stretching across three hundred pounds of muscle stepped in front of him, blocking his path. The man leaned close, his foul breath lingering heavily. "Don't I know you?"

Elliot recognized the man. His name was Tom Cook. He'd played defense for Porter High.

"Yeah," he said. "This is the one I told you about, boys, the cold-hearted killer."

"I don't want any trouble," Elliot said.

The man grinned. "You're Kenny Elliot all right."

Elliot tried to step around Tom Cook, but a heavy hand gripped his shoulder.

"No way, buddy. I ain't through with you yet."

Elliot shook loose. "I said I didn't want any trouble."

Tom Cook edged closer. "You know what amazes me is the way a sick bastard like you can just go on with his life, like nothing ever happened."

Elliot readied himself. There was no getting out of this. Tom was drunk, which made him dangerous, but it also left him slow and predictable. Elliot saw the right cross coming long before it got there. Stepping toward the big man, he moved left, causing his adversary to miss and leaving him off balance. Before Tom could recover, Elliot stuck a short right into his face then dug a left into his side. He quickly crumpled, catching himself on one knee, panting against the pain.

Elliot shifted his attention to the other two bikers, their facial expressions quickly telling him they weren't sure whether to run or make a stand. Then Nick turned around and Elliot saw his face. He had a cut above his right eye and his nose was busted. Tom and his buddies had roughed him up. They must've heard Elliot was in town and come looking for him. Elliot started toward the two bikers, making their minds up for them. They headed for the bay door, but he cut them off. He went to the nearest bike and shoved it off its kickstand, sending it crashing to the pavement. He waited for a challenge, but didn't get one. "I suggest you clear out," he said. He went back in the garage, stopping beside Tom Cook. "That means you too, fat boy."

When Tom stood, Elliot closed the distance between them, their faces inches apart. "Go ahead," Elliot said. "Make your move."

Tom sneered but turned away. He went to his motorcycle and the other two helped him set it right again. They started their bikes, revved them loudly then peeled out of the lot.

When they were gone, Nick walked over, wiping his nose with a paper shop towel. "Just like old times," he said.

Elliot nodded. "I need a favor."

"You got it, old buddy."

Charlie Johnson's patrol car sat alongside the road that ran next to the property where Elliot told Johnson to meet him. Charlie stood outside his car as Elliot pulled Nick's van off the road and brought it to a stop. He got out and opened the back. After positioning ramps behind it, he backed Nick's all-terrain vehicle out of the van. Charlie gave him a disgusted look. "I hope you don't expect me to ride that thing."

"It's quite a distance from here," Elliot said. He opened the gate and drove onto the property.

Charlie followed, closing the gate behind him, and after a brief hesitation he climbed onto the back of the all-terrain vehicle. "I heard about your fiasco in town with Tom Cook. Seems to me you haven't changed all that much. Trouble still follows you around."

Elliot didn't answer. He just drove slowly, trying not to jostle his passenger any more than necessary. When he reached the place where he'd found the car, he stopped the vehicle. Charlie climbed off, Elliot dismounted, and together they made their way down the embankment to the creek bed. When they reached the bottom, Charlie slowly walked over to the old car that sat there. Elliot had removed the rest of the debris and searched the car before calling Charlie. The driver of the vehicle had a hole in his forehead. He'd been shot. Assassinated, Elliot thought. He showed the hole in the skull to Charlie.

"I see it," he said. He seemed irritated, unhappy this had been forced upon him. "It doesn't take a forensic expert to see something like that."

The car was an old Cadillac, a 1989 or '90, Elliot thought. "Why do you suppose no one ever reported it?"

"Beats me. Most likely nobody ever saw it. And even if they did, an old burned out car sitting in a creek bed isn't all that unusual, even in this day and age."

"Good point," Elliot said, "except they usually don't have skeletons sitting at the wheel. Any idea who it is?"

Charlie gave him a curious look. "How the hell should I know? Looks like he's been here awhile."

"There's something you need to know," Elliot said. "Maggie Caldwell tipped me off about this. I got the impression she thinks it has something to do with Johnnie and Marcia."

Charlie looked as if he wanted to melt into the ground and disappear. "I wouldn't put much stock in what old Maggie says. She's a few bricks shy of a load, if you know what I mean. Anyway, contrary to what you might think, I conducted a thorough investigation of those murders. If this poor sap was connected, I would've known about it."

"I didn't mean it like that. But Maggie saw somebody drive off in here. How else would she have known about it?"

Charlie pulled a handkerchief from his pocket and wiped his forehead. "I don't know. Did she tell you who it was she thought she saw?"

He's mean Maggie. I guess it's payback that he should be the one to leave me with child. "No. Not that I could make sense of anyway. Something's not right here, though. Nobody drives a car without license plates into a creek bed and shoots a bullet through their head. And the car's clean — no tags, no registration, nothing. Whoever put it here went to a lot of trouble to make sure the driver wouldn't be identified if someone did happen to stumble onto it."

Charlie shook his head and sighed. "I'll see what I can do. But I can't promise anything. Like you said, there's not much here to go on."

While Charlie climbed the embankment to get out of the creek bed, Elliot tore a page from his notebook and placed it over a small metal plate on the car, rubbing over the paper with a pencil. Figures began to appear on the paper, and soon Elliot had a halfway legible vehicle identification number. After that, since it was obvious Chief Johnson wasn't going to search the old vehicle, Elliot reached inside the car and took the slug that had done the damage to the car's driver. He'd found it earlier, but left it for Johnson to find.

Once he reached the top, Charlie looked back. "What in blazes were you doing down there?"

"Nothing," Elliot said. "Just taking one last look around."

Chapter Twenty-One

Elliot stood outside Carmen's house, a neatly maintained cottage of light brown. Nick had convinced him of what he already knew; he couldn't leave town without visiting her. He got his courage up and forced himself into action, putting one foot in front of the other to walk across the lawn until he reached the house. When he rang the bell, a young boy, around eight or nine years old, answered the door. He had Carmen's eyes. "Is your mother home?" Elliot asked.

He hesitated then said, "Yes, sir."

Elliot wondered if the boy's father, Anthony Davenport, might be there. "Could I speak with her please?"

The boy darted away and seconds later Carmen appeared, a look somewhere between sadness and disbelief forming on her face as she came to the door and realized who was there.

Elliot paused for a moment, afraid his heart would jump from his chest. Carmen looked worried and she'd been crying, but she was nonetheless as stunningly beautiful as Elliot remembered her to be. He wanted to take her in his arms and pull her close, holding her for as long as he could. Coming here was a mistake. He had known it would be.

"Kenny?"

Elliot smiled, and when he spoke the words sounded strange in his head. "Hello, Carmen."

She wiped her tears. "What on earth are you doing here?"

Feeling awkward and not knowing what else to do, Elliot pulled his badge and showed it to her. "I'm working on a case. I think Chief Johnson might be able to help me with it. While I was in town, I thought I should stop by and say hello."

Carmen didn't say anything. She just stood there, staring.

"May I come in?"

She opened the door and Elliot followed her into the living room where they sat on a love seat. "So, are you and Charlie working together?" she asked.

"Not exactly, but I thought he might have some useful information."

She looked away, biting her lip, and again her eyes began to water.

"I know it's none of my business," Elliot said, "but are you all right?"

Carmen broke down, the way people do when they're under stress and whoever happens to be there is who they turn to. "It's Anthony," she said. "He didn't come home last night."

The look on her face said she immediately realized what she'd done and already regretted it. Elliot guessed the breakup wasn't as far along as Nick thought. At least Carmen seemed to think there was hope. "I'm sure he had good reason," Elliot said.

Carmen wiped her eyes. "I'm sorry. I shouldn't lay my problems on you like that."

The boy came into the room. Giving Elliot a suspicious look, he went to his mother and put his arm around her. "It's okay, Mom. Dad's probably just busy, that's all."

"You'll have to excuse my manners," Carmen said. "This is my son, Wayne. Wayne this is Mr. Elliot, someone I used to know."

"Nice to meet you, Wayne."

The boy nodded, but said nothing.

Wayne seemed like a nice kid. Elliot liked him. He started to speak but the phone rang. He figured it might be Carmen's husband, so he kept silent.

Carmen answered it, listened for a moment, then hung up and nodded, which meant that it was her husband calling. When she sat back on the couch, she buried her face in her hands, crying.

An incredible sadness came over Elliot. He felt singularly responsible for her suffering and he wanted to say many things, but what came out was simply, "I'm sorry, Carmen." It was all he could do to keep from crying along with her. He took her hand and squeezed it, but she recoiled, pulled away.

Wayne walked over, staring at Elliot, his face quivering. "Why did you make my mom cry, mister? I bet you're the reason Dad's mad at us."

"No," Elliot said. "Please don't think that."

"But it's true, isn't it? I hate you. I hate you!"

Suddenly Carmen went to the boy, her face still stained with tears. "No, Wayne. You don't know what you're saying. Please stop this. Please."

Elliot got up and started toward the door. "This is obviously a bad time," he said. "I should go now."

Without looking at Elliot or releasing her grip on the boy, Carmen said, "Don't leave, Kenny. I'm not through with you yet." Using the same serious tone, she added. "Go to your room, Wayne."

Wayne did as he was told, throwing Elliot a pitying look that said: *You're really going to get it now.*

When Wayne was gone, Carmen turned her attention to Elliot.

"I think I should go," he said again.

She shook her head. "It seems to be my lot in life, having men walk out on me. And I've waited too long to ask you this to let it go now. Why, Kenny? Why did you leave me like that?"

Her question caught Elliot off guard. He sat again, and so did Carmen. "I didn't know what else to do. Even my foster parents thought I was guilty. They left town and I was all alone. Coach Sims knew a lot of people. He arranged for me to stay with some friends of his in Stillwater, renting their garage apartment. I finished out the school year there. After that, I started classes at Oklahoma State."

"But why did you leave like that, without saying anything? You hurt me, Kenny. I thought I had done something to upset you."

Elliot took a deep breath, mustering all the willpower he could to keep from breaking down. "Charlie Johnson and Coach Sims convinced me it was the right thing to do. They said it would be bad for you and your family, and that I should go away where I could get my life together and prove I could make something of myself, then come back and make things right. It made sense at the time. Everybody was down on me and going away until things blew over seemed like a good idea."

"And you're just now coming back? I guess things have really blown over by now."

Elliot thought about his fight with Tom Cook. If things had blown over, it certainly didn't seem like it. "I thought I was making the right decision, ridding you of a burden."

"How can you say that? I loved you, Kenny. I would've shared any burden with you."

Elliot closed his eyes. Hearing Carmen say those words should've been nice. Instead, it hurt like hell.

"Why didn't you at least call?" she asked.

"I did. That night. No one answered. I called again the next day but your number had been changed. They wouldn't give me the new one, said it was unlisted. I even tried later, saying it was an emergency but it didn't work. I guess they could tell I was just a kid."

"You could have written."

"Every night for two months. I never heard back."

"I never got your letters," she said, her voice almost a whisper.

"There's more," Elliot said. "When I couldn't reach you I called Nick. He told me you didn't want to talk to me, didn't want anything more to do with me, said you told him to tell me that."

"Nicholas said that?"

"Yeah." Finally allowing himself to look into Carmen's eyes, Elliot saw that they both understood what had happened. Her parents had not only changed the phone number, they had intercepted the letters as well. And Nick. Who knew what was going on with Nick?

Carmen's lips quivered into a smile.

Elliot started to tell her that he'd thought she'd simply come to her senses and really didn't want anything more to do with him, and that if he'd known there was even an ounce of hope he'd have been there in a heartbeat. But then he saw the wedding ring on her finger. "I guess fate had other plans for us," he said.

Carmen shook her head. "This cannot be happening," she whispered.

Elliot wasn't sure what she meant by that, so he remained silent.

After a moment Carmen said, "I talked with Sally Ellis a few days ago. She got a letter from your foster parents. They're living in Iowa now. Did you ever hear from them again?"

"No."

"They're still acting as a foster family. It doesn't seem right after what they did to you, leaving you at such a time."

"Who could blame them? I was quite a problem."

"I saw the news about those women in Tulsa," she said. "The one that was killed in her car, and the other one. Is that what brought you here?"

"That's part of it."

Her face grew solemn. "It has something to do with Johnnie and Marcia, doesn't it?"

Yes, Elliot thought, *it has everything to do with it*, but what he said was, "I'm not sure. It might."

"It does," she said. "I feel it. Will we be haunted by this thing forever?"

"Not if I can help it," Elliot said. "I'll do everything in my power to bring it to a close. One way or another it will be over." He stood. "It's been wonderful seeing you again, Carmen, but I'd better be going." He looked around the room, and said the only thing that seemed safe. "This is a nice place you have here."

"Thanks. It belongs to Charlie Johnson. I think his sister used to live here."

"I didn't know Charlie had any family. He never spoke of them."

She smiled. "I think she left before we were old enough to notice."

Elliot nodded, then turned and walked out of the house. As he neared his car, Carmen called to him. "Kenny?"

He turned, his heart aching as he saw her leaning out the door. "Yes?"

"I promised Wayne I'd take him to the baseball field. Would you like to meet us there?"

"Are you sure that's a good idea?"

They stared at each other for a moment, then she said, "We need to talk some more." After that, she closed the door.

Elliot drove around for awhile trying to make sense of the last few minutes. Finally, he headed for Nick's place. When he got there he found the garage closed. There was no sign saying so, but the doors were locked and Nick's old blue van was nowhere in sight. When he went around back to check Nick's house, he looked up the street and saw Carmen going into the municipal building.

Nick wasn't home, so Elliot left his car at the garage and started off on foot toward Linzy Field, where Carmen said she would be, taking the familiar route that Nick and he had taken on their way to school. As he walked he thought about Nick, and as he rounded the corner and stood on the grounds of the Dairy Mart, an old drive-in restaurant where the kids used to hang out, one incident in particular bobbed to the surface. Nick had seen some sort of video game machine on television and he wanted it badly. He and his father had argued about it. Nick's dad insisted the family couldn't afford it. Elliot couldn't recall money ever bothering Nick until then.

When Elliot met him outside his house that morning, Nick's eyes had been red but Elliot didn't say anything. It happened quite often,

Nick and his old man getting into it. On days like that, he and Elliot didn't talk much. Anyway, they came to the Dairy Mart where a group of older, more well-to-do boys were standing in a circle passing around a cigarette. Elliot heard them mumbling and laughing, but he didn't let it bother him. Johnnie was the only rich kid he ever got along with. But Nick wasn't in the mood for teasing. Elliot had started across the street, hoping Nick would follow him. He did, but they didn't get away fast enough. Elliot heard the words *white trash* come from the circle, and before he could stop him Nick ripped off his coat and tore into one of the boys. Elliot ran back across the street to keep the others off him, but it wasn't necessary. Nick was clearly getting the best of the fellow and his buddies wanted no part of it. In fact, Nick was on the verge of hurting the kid. It was all Elliot could do to pull him off. He'd never seen him like that. Nick tried to break free and go after the kid again, but Elliot held him, shaking his head and telling him to stop. It worked, but Nick still seethed with anger as they made their way to school. The Dairy Mart was gone now; it was just an empty building.

Still mired in thought halfway between past and present, Elliot continued to walk to the school. Once there he went to the ball field, where some kids were playing baseball. With both hands, he grasped the wire cage of the backstop, leaning face first against the fence, wishing he could transport himself back in time and be a part of it again. He felt the fence wiggle and turned. It was Carmen. "Hey," he said.

She nodded.

"Where's Wayne?"

She pointed to the field where the boy had already joined the other kids. Elliot felt a tinge of pride. "He's a good boy. You've done a good job."

"It hasn't been easy," she said. "He's a lot like his father."

"He's lucky to have someone like you."

The corners of her mouth curved into a smile.

"I saw you going into the municipal building. Is everything all right?"

She didn't answer.

Elliot turned back to the ball field. "It used to be me out there, with Nick and Johnnie. In Tulsa it all seems so far away, but standing here with you, it doesn't seem that way at all. I made a lot of bad choices, Carmen."

"Yes," she said, "you did."

"I miss those days, the ones before Marcia. Things began to change after that, but maybe they would have anyway."

"She had a lot of problems."

Carmen's reply piqued Elliot's curiosity. He had always wondered why Marcia behaved the way she did, and more importantly, why the killer had been interested in her. "What kind of problems?"

"I want to blame her for everything," Carmen said, "but I know it wasn't entirely her fault. She was, I think, raised that way."

"What do you mean?"

She shook her head. "She was pretty. Everyone wanted her, even poor Nick. And she liked it that way."

Carmen's comment about Nick surprised Elliot. "Oh come on. Nick mentioned her looks a couple of times, but other than that he never showed any interest."

"He was crazy for her. You know how shy he is, but somehow he got the nerve to ask her out."

This was news to Elliot. "What happened?"

"She laughed at him, called him a low-rent mechanic, a grease monkey."

Elliot shook his head. "I had no idea. But as long as we're on the subject of Nick, why do you suppose he lied to me about you not wanting to see me?"

"Nick's a lonely person. It's hard for him to make friends. After you left, he asked me out. I thought about it, but I could see what it meant to him and I didn't want to lead him on. So I said no. It hurt him. We didn't speak for awhile, but eventually he started to come around, wanting to be friends again. Don't be too hard on him. It hurts to be lonely." She paused then changed the subject. "Why did you do it, Kenny? Why did you go out with Marcia?"

"I wanted to wake Johnnie up, make him see what she was doing to him."

Carmen looked at Elliot, her expression saying she wanted to believe that. "Why was that so important to you?"

"She was all he cared about. Our friendship was slipping away, and I didn't like that."

"Do you think Johnnie killed her?"

"No, I don't."

Carmen didn't seem relieved by that. In fact, she looked concerned. "Do you know who did?"

"Not yet."

Wayne came running over. The other kids were leaving. "My mom talked to the police. Thinks she saw somebody looking in the window."

Carmen shot him a glare. "We don't know that. It could be my imagination."

"Maybe," Elliot said, "but don't take it too lightly. The world is full of reasons to be on your guard."

She nodded. "Charlie said I wasn't the only one. Several people have called in. He says it's just a Peeping Tom and Gladys Smith got a good look at him. Charlie thinks he knows who it is. He said he would step up the drive-by patrols at night."

"If it is a peeper," Elliot said, "that should do the trick."

Wayne tugged at Elliot's arm. "Hey, mister, wanna play some catch?"

Elliot looked at Carmen, and when her stare locked onto his, her eyes were full of emotion. She mouthed, *Okay.*

Elliot went around to the front of the backstop, taking the catcher's spot, but he remained standing.

"I don't have an extra glove," Wayne said.

"That's okay. Just don't burn them in too hard."

Wayne trotted out several feet, about halfway to the pitcher's mound. Elliot thought of Johnnie and the hundreds of times they'd played out the same ritual, on the same field. When Wayne threw the first ball, he eased it in, more like a lob than a pitch. "You can put a little more on it than that," Elliot said.

He grinned and tossed one that snapped against the flesh of Elliot's hands as he pulled it in. The kid had an arm on him.

"By the way," he said, "I know who you are."

Panic shot through Elliot. Had Carmen told him, or were enough rumors still going around for him to draw his own conclusions? He threw the ball back.

Wayne stepped into it, unafraid.

"Is that right?"

He hummed a fastball across the plate. Elliot caught it, taking the sting away by flexing with the ball's momentum.

"My mom showed me your name on some trophies at school. I asked the coach about it."

Elliot threw him a grounder.

He scooped it up with ease. "You're Kenny Elliot."

Elliot nodded. "What's left of him."

Wayne kept the ball, tossing it into his glove and retrieving it to repeat the process. "Most yards in a season. Most points scored in a single game. Hell, you're a legend around here."

"Watch your language."

"Sorry. Anyway, your records still stand. Both of them."

Elliot shrugged.

Wayne threw him a pretty decent curve ball. Elliot snatched it out of the air.

"So, can you teach me?"

"Teach you what?"

He frowned. "To play football."

Elliot wanted to tell him he couldn't think of anything that would make him happier. "Maybe," he said. "But you'll have to clear it with your mom."

Chapter Twenty-One

"How come you know my mom?"

This time Elliot held onto the ball. He wasn't sure how to field the question. "We're old friends," he said. "I knew your mother when I was your age."

He seemed to consider the answer. "Why haven't I seen you before?"

He was intelligent, inquisitive. "I've been away."

He nodded, but he was suspicious.

Elliot walked out to him, a catcher and pitcher conference. "Could I ask you something?"

"Sure."

"What do you know about the prowler your mom saw?"

Wayne glanced at Carmen, who still stood behind the backstop, watching. "I don't know," he said. "I never saw or heard anything. Sometimes I think she's just nervous, or something."

"What about Chief Johnson?"

He shook his head. "He's like…going along with her. I guess he's only trying to help, but I don't know. He said something about Billy Smith's mom seeing somebody too. Billy didn't say anything about it, and he tells me everything."

"I see," Elliot said. "Well, I wouldn't worry too much about it. Chief Johnson knows his business." He handed Wayne the ball. "I need to talk to your mom some more."

"Okay."

"Maybe we can do this again sometime?"

He tossed the ball into the air and caught it. "Sure."

When Elliot was behind the backstop again, Carmen said, "He likes you."

"I like him, too. And I'm concerned about both of you, with this prowler business."

She smiled. "You shouldn't worry. Charlie's taking care of it."

"Will you tell me about it?"

"Is this a professional concern, or a personal one?"

"A little of both, I guess."

After a brief silence, she said, "It happened early this morning. I was awakened by a sound, like someone hitting the side of the house with something heavy. I thought I'd dreamed it, but when a car drove by its lights cast a shadow of someone on the window shade. I screamed and Wayne came running into the room and turned on the lights. He looked but didn't see anything. After he was back in bed, I got up to get a glass of water, and I saw someone walking past the kitchen window. A little later, I called Nick. He came over, but he saw no footprints or any indication that someone had been there."

"That doesn't sound like nothing to worry about," Elliot said. "And you told all of this to Charlie?"

"Yes."

"Did you see well enough to get any details?"

"What do you mean?"

"Was the prowler male or female, tall or short, thin or heavyset?"

"Tall and thin. Other than that, I don't know. But I didn't imagine it."

"I have no doubt about that," Elliot said. "Maybe you should consider staying with friends, or checking into a hotel for a few days." He handed her one of his business cards, showing her his cell phone number on the back as he said, "If you need to get in touch with me."

She took the card and turned it over in her hands a couple of times before putting it in her purse. "I should be going," she said. She called for Wayne, and after saying good-bye they began walking away.

Elliot called after her. "Carmen?"

They both looked back.

At that moment, Elliot knew he wanted to again be part of her life, wanted it more than he'd ever wanted anything, but how could he tell her? "Maybe we could get together again, have dinner or something?"

She nodded, but kept walking.

Chapter Twenty-Two

Elliot watched Carmen and Wayne until they walked out of sight, then he headed back to Nick's where he'd left his car. The place was still closed; no one was home at the small house behind the garage either. Elliot had an uneasy feeling about it. He was still trying to shake off the feeling as he climbed into his car and headed out of town. It was getting late and he had another stop to make on his way back to Tulsa.

A few minutes later, Elliot drove into the town of Coweta, where he pulled into a parking space in front of the local newspaper office. His conversation with Carmen had brought up Charlie Johnson's sister, and it started him to thinking about Maggie Caldwell. He didn't think everything she had said was nonsense. When first poured from the box, a jigsaw puzzle looks insurmountable, but after a few key pieces are put together the picture starts to fall into place. Once inside the building, Elliot saw no one but suspected Bob Crawley, who spent most of his time with the printing press, was around somewhere. Crawley had grown up in Porter, and more importantly, he knew just about everyone around the area. Elliot had met him once during a class field trip.

Elliot surveyed the interior of the old building. It held enough remnants of its past for him to make an educated guess as to its original function; he figured it had been an old dry goods store. After a few moments, Bob Crawley came from the back wearing a rubber apron that covered his shirt and trousers down to his knees, and a hat that looked like it'd been dropped into a vat of dull black shoe polish. He wiped his hands with a rag, but even after the effort he didn't offer to shake hands. Elliot wasn't offended; he knew Crawley did it out of courtesy, keeping the ink to himself. "Mr. Crawley," Elliot said. "I don't know if…"

"Porter Pirates, football star," he said, nodding. "How could I forget? Not much football news since you left."

The odor that came from Crawley's clothes reminded Elliot of strong furniture polish.

"You're Elliot," he said. "Kenny Elliot."

"Guilty as charged."

He laughed. "What brings you to my little corner of the world?"

"I was hoping to get a little information."

"Well you've come to the right place. Got plenty of that around here. Any particular flavor?"

"I understand you know Porter's chief of police?"

"Charlie? I ought to. I went to school with him. How is the old cuss?"

"Mean as ever," Elliot said, glancing around "Do you run this place by yourself?"

"Just about," Crawley said. "My wife, Josie, comes in a couple of days a week and does the accounting. And I have a guy who comes in and helps me with the press when I need it." Crawley's face grew serious. "I reckon you know him pretty well yourself. What is it you want to know?"

"I heard he had a sister."

"Cynthia? Sure, I know her."

"Like you said, I know Charlie pretty well. In fact, he was almost like an uncle to me, but he never mentioned her."

Crawley shrugged. "He doesn't talk much about her."

"Why's that?"

"She married some fruitcake from Tulsa against his wishes. Old Charlie might get a little weird now and then, but he knows people, reads them pretty well. In his line of work, you have to. He didn't like the guy, said he was a real bad apple. But she wouldn't listen and married him anyway. As far as I know, Charlie hasn't spoken to her since." He paused. "This sounds a little like an interview. What's going on?"

Elliot showed his badge. "I'm just checking some old leads."

Crawley studied the badge then looked at Elliot. "Old Charlie's not in any trouble, is he?"

"Nah, nothing like that. I'm just trying to untangle an old knot."

He gave Elliot a curious look. "I think I know what you're getting at," he said, gesturing toward the back of the large room, while walking in that direction.

Elliot followed.

"Most everything's stored off site now, but I keep a lot of the old stuff close by. Probably shouldn't…fire hazard I reckon, but I can't bring myself to get rid of it." He went to an area, far in the back of the building, separated from the rest of the office by distance and a lack of decorating. A row of filing cabinets stood by the wall. Crawley inspected the tags on the cabinets then opened one of the drawers. "I figure you'll find what you want right here."

Elliot looked inside the drawer and thumbed through the old issues. Then he began to understand why Crawley had led him there. He correctly suspected Elliot had come to study the daily papers issued around the time of the murder of Johnnie and Marcia. It made a lot of sense, and showed Crawley's intuition. But Elliot was worried about going through the articles, afraid of what he might find there. "Thanks, Mr. Crawley."

He nodded. "Just between you and me, I never thought you had anything to do with it. I know a lot of people did, but I always figured there was a lot more to that story than was being told." He started toward the front again. "About time somebody looked into it. Good luck, son, you're probably going to need it."

Elliot pulled out a stack of papers and sat down at an old desk to look through them. Stories about the murder-suicide of Johnnie Alexander and Marcia Barnes accounted for the bulk of the daily news for over a week. Things like that just didn't happen in places like Porter. The musty smell of the old newsprint almost soothed Elliot's nerves, but the pungent content of what was written there wouldn't allow it. The abrasive words, insinuating Elliot's involvement, raked open old wounds and suddenly he had a near overpowering urge to find the nearest bar and go inside to dampen the pain.

The fight after the football game was described, recounting the hostility Johnnie and Elliot shared, and he remembered in startling detail the hollow and distant look on Johnnie's face. Elliot had also gotten into a scuffle at the party, beating a kid up pretty badly, and saying, as Nick and Carmen dragged him out of there, that he was going to make Johnnie pay.

To make matters worse, someone had also reported seeing Carmen's car at the Point later that night. Elliot had been with her, or at least someone who looked a lot like him.

Charlie Johnson had stood up for him, that much Elliot knew, but a lump formed in his throat as he read just how far out on a limb the chief of police had actually gone to save his hide. Charlie agreed that Elliot was at the party, and later with Carmen, but he insisted the boy had never gone to the Point that night. Elliot had been at the party all right, but he had left, and he began to wonder if Charlie and Coach Sims had gone to bat for him to defend his innocence or if in reality they'd pulled out all the stops only to save their favorite football star. He copied the articles, then put the papers away and went to find Bob Crawley again.

When Crawley saw Elliot coming, he smiled. "Find what you needed?"

"Some of it," Elliot said. "Thanks for your help. Could I ask another favor?"

"Sure."

"You covered the story. Is there anything I should know that wasn't in those articles?"

He rubbed his chin. "What I know is pretty much there, in the papers you went through."

"The articles mentioned Dr. Lyndon Shriver, the medical examiner during that time. You wouldn't happen to know where I could find him?"

"Charlie's a good man, son. I'd hate to see him get hurt over this."

"So would I, but this is important."

Crawley frowned. "Yeah, I know Shriver. He doesn't live that far from here. He and Charlie go way back, old army buddies. Rumor has it Charlie saved his life in Vietnam." He grabbed a scrap of paper and started writing. "Here's his address. Maybe he can remember something that will help."

"What about this Mr. Beaumont that was mentioned a couple of times?" Elliot asked.

"Old Clarence? He ran a butcher shop in town years ago. Closed down now. I hated to see it go, but there was no one around to run it after Clarence passed away."

"What was his connection?" Elliot asked,

"That Marcia girl, the one that was killed, she dated Clarence's son a few times. Let's see…Philip, yeah, that was the kid's name. Don't know where he is now."

Elliot found Dr. Shriver living on the outskirts of town with his wife, Vivian. When he told him he was investigating the deaths of Johnnie Alexander and Marcia Barnes, Shriver became nervous and told Vivian he and Elliot were going to talk in his office, a spacious room located in the front part of the house.

Shriver closed the door behind them and opened a cabinet made of shiny walnut burl that sat beside the desk. He pulled a glass and a bottle of gin from the cabinet, filling the glass half full and topping it off with lemon-lime soda. "Drink?" he asked.

Elliot sat in a chair of soft brown leather. "No thanks. I just need a little information."

"Well," Shriver said, looking as though he'd been forced to swallow a bitter pill. "What is it, exactly, that you want to know?"

Elliot thought about that for a moment. Shriver was nervous and he hadn't even asked him any questions. He began to suspect Bob Crawley had given him more than just a lead—he was on to something. "I'd like to know the truth, Dr. Shriver."

"What are you talking about?"

"Why don't you tell me what you observed during the autopsy?"

"What's to tell? I'm sure you've read the report."

"I've looked it over," Elliot said. "But I'm having trouble with some inconsistencies." He stretched the truth. He hadn't seen the report.

Shriver took a sip of his drink. "You don't know what you're talking about."

"That may be," Elliot said. "But Johnnie Alexander was probably the best left-handed quarterback to ever attend Porter High."

"So?"

The question sounded genuine enough, but Elliot could tell by the look on Shriver's face that it wasn't. "Why was the .38 found in his right hand?"

"I guess I never gave it much thought."

"I find that hard to believe, Dr. Shriver. In fact, I'd lay odds that someone with your experience could tell by the trajectory of the bullet, and its position in the entry wound that Johnnie didn't pull the trigger, which means he probably didn't inflict the wounds on Marcia Barnes."

"What are you saying?"

"The report stated Marcia Barnes died first, is that correct?"

"I believe so, yes."

"But that's not the way it happened, is it?"

"I'm getting a little tired of this and I don't have to put up with it." He started to rise.

"My guess would be Johnnie was killed first because he wasn't the target. He was simply in the way."

Shriver poured himself another drink. "I could ask you to leave, Detective Elliot."

"But you won't, and I'll tell you why. This thing's been eating away at you for a long time, and you'd like to get it off your chest, set the record straight. It's something I know a little bit about."

Shriver turned away and walked to a bay window that looked over a garden area. For a long time, he stood there, staring through the window in silence. When he finally spoke, his voice cracked under the strain. "So what if the boy didn't take his own life? They were both dead. Nothing was going to bring them back. What was the harm in helping to close the case, putting an end to the whole sordid affair? Anyway, why do you care? You were the one who benefited the most from the murder-suicide verdict."

Elliot shook his head. He couldn't believe what he was hearing. "Did it ever occur to you that someone actually committed the crime, someone your actions helped to set free to kill again?"

He turned back to face Elliot, his face livid. "What do you think?" He asked. "Well, did you, stud? Did you kill again?"

"Only in the line of duty," Elliot said.

A look came over Shriver like his soul had just been condemned to hell.

"I'm the investigating officer on the cases in Tulsa," Elliot said. "Don't you read the papers, Dr. Shriver, or watch the news? There was enough there for someone with your knowledge to draw a conclusion and see the similarities between the recent killing of Michelle Baker and the murder of Marcia Barnes."

Shriver's eyes grew red, and he began to tremble.

"Why did you lie about it?"

"Have you ever been indebted to someone, Detective Elliot?"

Elliot thought about his getting off the hook. "I guess that depends on how you look at it."

Shriver nodded. "Someone saves your life, you owe them." He turned up the glass and finished the drink. "Do you have any idea what it's like wrestling with such a dilemma, and living with sin because of it?"

Again Elliot considered his answer. "Yes, Dr. Shriver, I think I do. But you can put it to rest now."

"I'll deny everything I've told you."

Elliot slowly got out of the chair and walked toward the door. "I'd better be going now. Thanks for your help."

Outside, Elliot climbed into his car. Dr. Shriver had falsified the report because Charlie Johnson, to whom he felt he owed a great deal, had called in his marker. The question was: why had Porter's chief of police felt compelled to do that?

Chapter Twenty-Three

He had the windows rolled down, letting the air rush into the car, and when he reached down and flicked off the headlights, speeding into the dark night surrounding Highway 51B, the exhilaration went to his head and he had to grip the wheel tightly to regain control and reassure himself it was real. Visiting his old haunting grounds had been such a pleasure that he hadn't made it very far before the desire to experience more of the same caused him to turn the car around and head back.

His work wasn't finished there. Things were getting out of hand, spiraling out of control, and it was up to him to take the reins and pull them tight again. He pushed the accelerator harder. It was times like this, when their separation would narrow, bringing them closer—and he embraced it, for she had set his senses clear. It was destiny, and those who meddled in their affairs had to be dealt with.

But the time would come when it came. He had other things to do, and even in the darkness he could feel he had arrived. He pulled off the road and stopped the car. Getting out, he walked along the weedy path until he reached his destination. Porter was just around the bend, but from where he stood, looking across the black fields, it was hard to tell. He'd forgotten how special the place was. It seemed strange that something so fulfilling could have happened there, a place called the

Point, a lover's lane where teens had taken their dates. It was here he'd made the discovery that would set him free.

He walked a few yards up the pathway, stopping beside a tree, and as he stared at the gnarled oak, there was no doubt in his mind he now stood in the exact spot where it had happened. He closed his eyes and breathed in the night air, flashes of that night going through his head. With a shaky hand, he reached out and touched the rough bark of the tree and as he did tears rolled down his face and his legs gave way, bringing him to his knees.

Gathering himself, he stood and walked back to the car and drove back into town, parking behind the school so he could walk the back roads to the garage and not be noticed. He slipped by the house as he put on his gloves, and edged along the outside wall of the garage until he reached the front. Breaking and entering wasn't his forte, but it almost felt that way, being there in the middle of the night. But you couldn't very well break into a place where you had free access. He slid the key into the old padlock, heard it click open, and seconds later stepped inside the office, closing the door behind him.

Cautiously, he walked into the garage area, flipping on the lights as he went. The fluorescent glow spread across the workbench, bringing into view the large red toolbox that sat atop it. Holding his breath, he opened the toolbox and reached inside, sliding his gloved hand around the handle of the knife that was kept there.

Outside again, he refastened the hasp and closed the padlock, then crept into the darkness. Using the dimly lit streets, he made his way. It was a fresh experience, prowling like a common criminal in the streets of the town he knew so well, and when he came to Carmen's house the excitement roiled in his veins. He got to his knees and crawled to the window where he'd seen her before, slowly bringing his eyes to a level with the sill. The sight of her rendered him lightheaded. She was nothing like *her*, but she was beautiful in her own right, creamy brown skin fitting her frame so well, and her black hair shining.

She turned off the light.

He decided to make his move.

Chapter Twenty-Four

Elliot reached for the bottle of aspirin he kept in his desk drawer and downed a couple with a swallow of coffee. He'd gotten in late the night before and slept badly. To top that off, Dombrowski had jumped him as soon as he'd walked in the office, asking him where he'd been, and why he hadn't called in. Elliot was still struggling over their encounter at the restaurant, but his anger had eased since then. Now he was somewhere between determination to see this thing through and total confusion.

He left his desk and went to the forensic lab, stopping at the lab director's office. Eddie York, the director, was bent over his desk and didn't seem to notice Elliot had come in. "Hey, Eddie," Elliot said.

He looked up. "What can I do for you, Detective?"

Elliot held out the piece of paper he'd used to take the rubbing from the rusted car he'd found in the creek bed at Porter and handed it to Eddie York. "I've got a partial vehicle identification number and I was hoping you could help me run it down."

Eddie York took the paper and examined it. Frowning, he said, "You're missing a few numbers."

"Yeah, I know. The plate was damaged. It looked like someone had flattened it with a hammer. I know it's a lot to ask, but I need to know who the vehicle was registered to, if it's possible."

Eddie nodded. "I'll see what I can do, but I'm not promising anything. Speaking of cars, how's that restoration project of yours coming along?"

"It's not. I'm in over my head. You wouldn't happen to know anything about cars, would you?"

"You kidding? I was just curious, that's all. I'll get to work on this."

Elliot met Beaumont in the hallway as he left the lab. He looked sorry-eyed and nervous, like a dog that'd done something wrong. Elliot stepped around him. He was hungry. He had to think to remember the last time he'd eaten: Maggie Caldwell's chicken soup early yesterday.
Elliot drove to Nelson's Buffeteria on Boston Avenue. Once inside, he ordered eggs and hash brown potatoes, then found a place and sat down.

After leaving the café, Elliot went to the county offices. Bob Crawley had given him an approximate date for Cynthia Johnson's exodus, and he wanted to check it out.

Once there, Elliot took the elevator then walked the hallway to a set of glass doors. He pushed the doors open and walked inside, where a multitude of people stood at or near a long counter, behind which were the county workers. Elliot took a place at the counter and finally a man wearing obnoxious checked pants that clashed with his shirt came over and asked how he could help. Elliot told the man what he wanted and the man pointed to a shelf along the wall that held a collection of large, bound books. They were the county marriage records and were there for public use.

The records were arranged alphabetically by date, and it wasn't long until Elliot found what he was looking for: In May of 1976, Cynthia Rebecca Johnson, Charlie Johnson's sister, married a man by the name of Terrance Kincaid.

Elliot left the county office and went back to the department. Once there he checked his voice mail and found he had several messages, but one in particular caught his attention. It was from Rachael, Lagayle Zimmerman's unusual friend. Punching the button, he listened to the recording.

"Detective Elliot. I was hoping to catch you. If you get this, please call me back." There was a pause, then, "I think someone's following me. In fact I'm positive. At first I thought it was my imagination, after talking to you about what happened and all. But he's there all right. I've seen him more than once. Look, I'm scared, okay? I mean what if it's the same guy Lagayle saw? I'm probably just being silly, but if I don't hear from you, I'll call again. Call me, please."

Elliot flipped through his list of numbers and called Rachael's house. Her mother answered and said she wasn't there. She didn't seem all that concerned. Elliot grabbed a phone book and looked up the number of the restaurant where Rachael worked then dialed it, and after interrupting the voice on the other end as it went through a commercial spiel, he asked for Rachael.

"She's not here." It was Joe Bernard, the restaurant manager, and when Elliot identified himself, he said, "Hey, I'm glad you called. I haven't seen Rachael since the day she talked to you. It's probably nothing. We go through more employees in this business than we do apple pies, but I'm worried about her. She was different, or at least I thought she was. Never pulled anything like this before."

Elliot told Mr. Bernard he'd look into it and hung up the phone, a sick feeling seething through his stomach. Rachael Johnson wasn't exactly petite but she wasn't large either, and she fit the rest of the bill quite nicely: she had blonde hair and blue eyes.

Elliot decided to drive over to Rachael's place and have a look around, but halfway there he received a phone call that stopped everything. He put the cell phone to his ear, and nearly lost all concentration as he listened.

"Hello, Detective."

It was the mechanical voice of his attacker at the old schoolhouse. "You're proving to be a real nemesis...always in the way."

"Perhaps if you'd tell me what it is you're trying to accomplish," Elliot said, "I'd sympathize and get out of your way."

He laughed, but it sounded more like an estranged growl. "You wouldn't understand; no one ever does."

"Why don't we stop this little game? I've always preferred face-to-face discussions. Anywhere you like, just pick a time and place."

"I think this is the part where I say, you're going to have to do better than that. But I won't. In fact, I'm going to give you what you want, go out on a limb, help you. After all, we're old friends, aren't we?"

"How did you get my cell phone number?" Elliot asked.

"A mutual friend had it in her possession."

"Are you talking about Rachael Johnson?"

A long silence followed. Elliot began to wonder if the man had disconnected, but then the robot voice came back on line.

"Rachael's quite fond of you, speaks of you often. Pretty fantastic for a dead person, wouldn't you say?"

Elliot's heart sank, and he heard himself ask, "Where's the body?"

"If you insist, my presumptuous friend, then find where the market crosses over 4th Street and go east until you reach a northbound Illinois town. The Depression Bridge is close, but the concentration camp is where you'll catch your prize."

"What's that supposed to mean?"

"Well, if you really want to know who and why, you'll just have to figure it out."

Elliot's thoughts raced. He had to be speaking of a place somewhere in the city. The phone went silent, and Elliot knew the man was gone, but suddenly, he also knew where to go. An image of the area the voice had described had formed in his mind with such clarity that he could almost feel the rough surface of the concrete that formed the overpass where the MKT railroad crossed over 4th Street. The Illinois town was the key, for when Elliot realized his caller was speaking of Peoria Avenue, everything else fell into place. As he headed north and caught a glimpse of 1930 chiseled into the fabric of yet another bridge, he remembered the caller referring to the Depression and his inclination to believe he was on the right track grew stronger. When he saw the deserted manufacturing plant he knew without a doubt that he'd found the place.

Elliot turned onto Latimer Place, brought the car to a stop in an old driveway, and called in to relay his whereabouts. He waited for backup, and a few minutes later Sergeant Conley pulled in. Detective Beaumont was with him.

An uneasy look came over Conley's face as he and Beaumont climbed out of the car to join Elliot. It was a sparsely populated area made up of manufacturing businesses and industrial buildings. A lack of traffic, pedestrian or otherwise, lent a deserted feel to this part of the city. More to the point, it was a good place to hide if someone chose to do so, and Elliot had to admit the hair on his neck was standing on end.

The defunct manufacturing plant, with its high chain-link fence topped with coils of barbed wire, indeed resembled a concentration camp, a wartime prison that had somehow survived an apocalyptic siege. Adding to the effect, a small building that looked like a guard shack stood near the main entrance. It sat on stilts about fifteen feet above the ground. The main building, a massive tin-clad structure with rows of windows running along the top, sat in the middle of a huge concrete parking lot surrounded by the fence.

Elliot found a place where the fence had been cut, leaving a large hole, and he squeezed through, motioning for Conley and Beaumont to follow. With their weapons drawn, the three made their way cautiously across the deserted parking lot toward the building. Elliot realized how vulnerable they were, walking across an empty lot literally surrounded by good hiding places, so he circled around to the east fence line to take the long route with more cover. He didn't like this; he didn't like it one bit. He began to feel as if his actions were being manipulated, as though he were following instructions in a choreographed play. He paused, searching the area, trying to catch a glimpse of anything out of the ordinary. The caller was out there somewhere. Elliot could his feel eyes bearing down on him like a bird of prey.

They continued their journey, heading toward the west end of the building where a doorway large enough to accommodate a tractor-trailer rig led to the interior of the structure. As he drew closer, Elliot noticed that the west end of the complex was open on the sides, with only the roof of the building continuing like a large canopy.

Conley whispered, breaking the silence. "Hey, Elliot, this is a big area, a lot of ground to cover. What the hell we supposed to be looking for, anyway?"

"I'm not sure, exactly."

Conley didn't say anything, but the expression on his face begged for a better answer.

Elliot motioned for the group to pause. "I got a call," he said, "some guy disguising his voice with an electronic device."

"That's it?"

"He said things," Elliot continued, "that caused me to believe he knew something about the murders. I decided to pressure him a little, asked him to meet me somewhere so we could talk about it."

Beaumont raised his eyebrows.

"He told me to come here."

They stood for a moment in the stillness with their weapons drawn, glancing at one another, the only sounds other than their breathing coming from the distant traffic running along Peoria Avenue. Everyone seemed to agree silently, yet unanimously, that their presence there didn't feel right.

Elliot considered turning back, but started toward the huge bay door instead. Conley and Beaumont followed. As he entered the building and began walking across the expansive concrete floor, Elliot surveyed the surroundings and noticed various abandoned pieces of machinery littering the area along with piles of scrap metal. The high ceilings and windows reminded him of a high school gymnasium. Near the door there was an old truck. The fact that it was still there where some worker had left it was amazing in its own right, but Elliot found it even more unbelievable that, other than a few strokes of paint added by a spray can, it looked to be in pretty fair condition.

Elliot paused when he came to the area where the walls ended, then eased out into the open under the canopied area. He swung around looking in all directions, holding the Glock in front of him. Beaumont and Conley were right behind him. The only thing of interest beneath the colossal tin gazebo was an industrial trash bin. Elliot made his way to the trash container and used the heel of his hand to shove one of the massive lids open. It banged loudly against the back of the bin, echoing a metallic sound through the shattered silence. With the lid removed, the bin revealed its contents: nothing. It was empty.

"Maybe we should forget about this and get out of here," Beaumont said. "This place gives me the creeps."

Elliot started to speak but as he turned, he saw a flash and an object—maybe a rifle barrel—sticking over the top of a building across the street; and as the events unfolded, seemingly in slow motion, he watched, helpless, as Conley, unaware of what was happening, stepped in front of him. The sickening sound that followed was a familiar one, for it always sounded the same—like a pound of raw meat slapping the surface of a stainless steel table. Conley collapsed into Elliot's arms, driving them both into the side of the dumpster. Elliot laid him on the ground. Blood covered his shirt. Before he fell unconscious, he grabbed Elliot's lapels and pulled him forward, his eyes full of fear and disbelief.

Another shot rang out, ricocheting off the concrete floor. Elliot scrambled to his feet and dragged Conley behind the trash bin, then opened fire, squeezing off a couple of shots in the direction of the shooter.

Beaumont swore under his breath. He, too, had leaped behind the bin.

Elliot ejected the empty clip in his gun and slapped in a full load. He knew it was little help against a high-powered rifle, but it was better than nothing. Beaumont was staring at him, motionless. "Get an ambulance," Elliot told him, "and call for backup."

The shots had come from a two-story cinder block building across the street. Taking cover along the back edge of the structure, Elliot made his way to the west end of the lot before working his way toward the area. As he neared the entrance to the building, he noticed it was locked and empty with a wooden For Lease sign nailed to a post in the front lawn. He suspected the shooter was gone by now, but he had to check it out. He eased around the building, looking for a way onto the roof. At the rear of the building, a ladder leaned against the wall. Transferring his weapon to his left hand, Elliot climbed the ladder and stopped before cautiously peering over the roofline. He saw nothing. He climbed onto the roof and edged closer to the only hiding place available, an air-conditioning unit. He carefully made his way around it, but again found nothing. The shooter was gone. Using the higher vantage point afforded by the roof, Elliot scanned the area. The only thing he saw was a black and white patrol car coming to a stop in front of the plant across the street. Seconds later, an ambulance showed up.

Elliot climbed down from the roof and started up the street he would've taken if he were trying to make a getaway: the one leading away from the scene. Soon he came to a salvage area where several busted-up city buses were parked. Holding the Glock in front of him, he entered the nearest bus. It smelled of body odor and cheap wine: a lair for the homeless. Elliot walked the aisle, checking behind each seat, hoping the bus was empty of its inhabitants. If one of them was to take the opportunity to poke his head up to see what was going on, in his high-strung condition Elliot might blow it off the poor cuss's shoulders before either of them realized what was happening. Just as Elliot reached the last row, something jumped onto the seat, and it was all he could do to keep from shooting the scruffy alley cat that'd decided he'd had enough of this game of hide and seek. Elliot's heart pounded as the cat jumped through the window. Other than that, the bus was empty.

Elliot searched the other buses—four of them in all—but found nothing. The shooter was gone. As he made his way back to the warehouse, the thought of Conley taking a bullet that was meant for him caused his stomach to burn. He went to Beaumont who was watching the ambulance drive away. "You okay?" he asked.

"I guess so."

"How's Conley?"

Beaumont shook his head. "He lost a lot of blood."

"Where'd they take him?"

"St. Francis. He kept asking for you."

Chapter Twenty-Five

Scrambled thoughts ran through Elliot's head and he wondered if the hollow emptiness that'd started to grow inside would eventually engulf him as he walked through one of the glass portals that separated St. Francis Hospital from the rest of the world. He searched the halls, quizzing various concentrated brains with lab coats and clipboards, until he found the intensive care unit, that part of the hospital with a higher saturation of fears and a bed for David Conley. After winning out over the final spate-of- protests at the nurses' station, Elliot stood in the hallway outside Conley's room, where he saw David's wife, Susan, recognizing her from pictures Conley had shown him. He often talked of his family. Elliot's legs grew weak as he approached her, something that always happened to him when he had to walk the corridors of medicine. He didn't think it was a phobia, exactly, but hospitals and the people who occupied them always reminded him of sickness and death rather than healing. He extended his hand and took a deep breath before saying, "I'm Detective Elliot."

Susan Conley fought to keep her face straight. "You were with David when it happened?"

She looked tired and much older than she was, but she was nicely dressed and graceful in her worry. "Yes," Elliot said, handing her one of his cards. "If there's anything I can do, anything you need…"

"You've done enough already, if you ask me."

It was Conley's son, a fourteen-year-old who was into dark clothing and body piercing. Elliot met his glance for a moment then turned back to Mrs. Conley "I *am* sorry."

The boy sneered and walked away, stopping by the window to stand beside his sister. She was twelve, if Elliot remembered right, but her dress was short and tight, her face painted with makeup. They loved their father, though, and they were worried about him.

Conley's wife gestured for her children to follow her. "It was nice meeting you, Detective. We appreciate your concern."

Elliot watched them walk away then went into Conley's room. He found him awake, though his eyes were glassy and distant as if he were seeing something other than his present surroundings— another time and place perhaps. He looked smaller, robbed of his usual gruffness among the array of life-support equipment, but he seemed to be aware of Elliot's presence.

Elliot stepped up to the bed and Conley looked toward him, a faint smile on his lips. "Wondering if you were going to show up."

It wasn't what Elliot wanted to see. He'd hoped to find Conley well and complaining, asking Elliot when he was going to break him out of this joint. He took his hand, holding it with both of his own. "Saw your family in the hall."

Conley nodded. "Families are nice, especially when you need someone. Have you found Rachael Johnson?"

"No."

His breathing was rough, labored. "I've been thinking about things," he said. "Got time to do that here. Wondering about you, why you live like you do."

"You should spend your time more wisely."

He tried to laugh, which made him cough. He raised his free hand and shook it slightly then lowered it to the bed. "We need to talk. There's something you need to know."

"Don't worry about it," Elliot said. "We can figure it out later."

He shook his head. "Beaumont's been checking up on you, poking around in your past."

"Yeah. I know."

"Dombrowski's behind it."

"I figured as much," Elliot said, "but something puzzles me. What got Dombrowski interested?"

"The way I hear it, he got some anonymous letters."

Elliot thought about that for a moment. Whoever wrote those letters knew quite a bit about the murders. "Any idea who would do such a thing?"

He shook his head. "I wish I did, pal. I'd show him a thing or two. Hey, there's something else I've been meaning to tell you. My being here, Rachael Johnson's disappearance...even the killings in town, none of it has any more to do with you than it does with any other citizen. The world's problems aren't your fault, kid, no matter how much you'd like to take responsibility for them."

"Even when you're sick you talk too much."

Conley smiled and quivered as if he was laughing, but nothing came out. Suddenly his grip tightened around Elliot's hand and when Elliot again saw his eyes they held an unspoken statement: he knew he was dying. Elliot pulled loose from Conley's grip and ran into the hallway, grabbing the first medical person he could find. Together they went back into Conley's room.

"What happened?"

"I don't know," Elliot said. "He stopped breathing."

Someone else appeared and Elliot watched as he filled a syringe with fluid and injected Conley with it.

Before long Conley was breathing again, somewhat stabilized, but Elliot had a bad feeling. Death was close, hanging around and hovering over the bed like a thick fog. It was the worst thing

Conley could've done, responding to Elliot's backup call. If Elliot hadn't known it already, then the events of the last few days had certainly made it clear. He had a bad track record with friends. Hell, he had a bad track record with life.

Conley closed his eyes and faded into a slow, rhythmic sleep. Elliot hated to be the one to have to do it, but he placed a call to Conley's wife, telling her she might not want to stay away too long, then he walked out of the room and left the hospital. His mental faculties were as jumbled as Conley's. He needed to be alone in a place without distractions so he could think. Not knowing where else to go, he found his car and drove home.

A few minutes later, Elliot pulled into his driveway and hit the garage door opener, but he left the car parked outside on the drive beside his pickup. He wanted to work, and he couldn't get to his tools with two cars crowding the garage. He went inside and changed into some old clothes. Returning to the garage, he turned a five-gallon bucket upside down and placed it in front of the Studebaker as a seat and resumed his job of removing the bumper. Earlier he'd soaked the bolted joints with a substance from a spray can that claimed to loosen such things.

The nuts were still tight, but a few busted knuckles later, Elliot pulled the front bumper off and laid it on a tarp he'd spread across the concrete floor. He felt good about it. He'd actually accomplished something. And even though he was taking it apart and not putting it together, it was a start. He moved around to the rear of the car and removed the back bumper.

It wasn't long until Elliot's thoughts fell into a more orderly fashion. He wiped the dust from the side window with a shop towel and pressed his face against the glass, peering into the car's interior. Like the Studebaker, he felt faded and worn, but his instincts kept the spark alive. He was closing in, beginning to unravel the affair, even though it appeared he was getting nowhere. He'd been close to the killer, close enough to see him, though he'd slipped by like smoke in the wind.

Elliot imagined the car restored, with new tires, a tight, level suspension, and a shiny coat of paint. But he didn't want it too perfect. He wasn't the type to sparkle something up only to put it in a glass case and look at it. For him, getting to know the car—feel its ride and hear its engine—was the main attraction. He wanted to drive it.

He wiped his hands and put the shop towel away so he could go inside and shower. After that he changed back into dress clothes and left his house for the department. The way he saw it, if there was a key to figuring this whole mess out, it was Lagayle Zimmerman.

When Elliot arrived at the department, he entered the building through the front door, and as he strode across the lobby he thought he saw someone standing near the elevators. The ball cap, the long hair, and the overalls… it had to be Nick. Just as Elliot started toward the elevators, someone stepped in front of him, and he lost sight of the person who he thought was Nick. When Elliot got there, whoever it had been was gone. Elliot made a quick search of the lobby then rode the elevator up and went to his desk. He'd just sat down when the phone rang. The voice that came through the phone was soft, nearly inaudible. "I need to speak to Detective Kenneth Elliot, please."

Elliot's heart skipped a beat. "Carmen?"

"Kenny, we need to talk. It's important."

Elliot paused. This was almost too good to be true, Carmen calling him. So why did he have a bad feeling about it? "All right."

"Not like this, not over the phone. Could you meet me someplace?"

"Sure. I can wrap things up and be there in a couple of hours."

"That won't be necessary. I've been thinking about this all day. So I decided to drive up. I'm almost there."

A lump formed in Elliot's throat. "In Tulsa?"

"I'm on the highway, the one that 51 turns into."

"The Broken Arrow Expressway?"

"Yes, I think so."

Elliot thought about it for a moment then decided to ask, "Have you seen Nick?"

"No, not since you were here. Chief Johnson asked me about it, too. Is something wrong?"

"It was probably just my imagination, but I thought I saw him in the department lobby just now."

"I hope everything is all right with him."

"I'm sure it is. He probably had some business to attend to and didn't have time to tell anyone."

"Maybe so," she said, "but it isn't like Nick to do that."

Elliot gave Carmen directions to his house and left the station, wondering what it was that she considered important enough to drive all the way to Tulsa to discuss.

Elliot found Carmen sitting in the swing on his front porch, the daylight softly playing across her delicate features. In his presence she stood, and he was helpless to stop himself from closing the distance between them. She offered little resistance as he pulled her close and he immediately felt the warmth of her soft skin radiating through him. Suddenly, better judgment took over and he released her, stepping away. "I'm sorry. I shouldn't have done that."

She smoothed her hair back into place. "It's all right."

Elliot fumbled for his keys and unlocked the door. Once inside he flipped on the light. "Come on in."

Elliot immediately saw how unkempt his house had become over the last few days. He preferred things neat and orderly, feeling nervous and out of sync when they were not. But the case had consumed him, taking all his time and energy. "You'll have to excuse the place," he said. "I've been a little busy. Actually, preoccupied would be closer to the truth."

She glanced around, the clothes scattered across the furniture catching her attention. "It's not that bad."

She was being kind. "Yes it is," Elliot said, straightening the pillows on the couch. "But have a seat anyway."

Carmen looked away, dropping her gaze to the floor as she sat. "How long have you lived here?"

Elliot sat in an adjacent chair. "About three years. I hadn't really planned on buying a house, but one of the guys I work with, his wife's into real estate. She showed it to me. It was some sort of corporate-owned property. I guess they needed a loss and wanted to get rid of it. Anyway, I got a pretty good deal on it."

She nodded. "It's very nice."

Elliot considered asking Carmen what it was she'd come to talk to him about, but before he could, another notion came along and pushed everything else to the side. Here, sitting in front of him, was the person he'd been with that night. Most people go through life thinking that somewhere down deep they have the right stuff, and that no matter what the circumstances or conditions, honor and wisdom would prevail in guiding their actions. But the truth is few people even have a clue as to the real scenario, because not many ever find occasion to have their mettle truly tested. The bottom line was, Elliot had to know for sure about that night and how he fit into it. He had no choice but to ask, though as it came out it was more of a release than a question. "I need to know, Carmen. I have to know what happened that night."

A concerned look crossed her face. "What are you talking about?"

"Johnnie and Marcia. I had something to do with it. I see it in my dreams."

Carmen's eyes grew wet, her face contorted. "I've been wondering when you would put me through this." She paused then continued. "Nick called me to pick you up at the party. You were drunk. I shouldn't have let you drive, but you insisted. I begged you not to go to the Point, but you wouldn't listen. You were out of your head, you were crazy. I had no choice but to go with you. Driving fast and all over the road, it would have been better if we'd just crashed. I prayed Johnnie wouldn't be there, but in my heart I knew that he would be." She paused and pulled a tissue from her purse to wipe the tears that had started to roll down her face. "You jumped out of the car, leaving it running and parked in the middle of the road. I came after you. I didn't know what you would do."

"Then it's true," Elliot said. "I read the old papers. There wasn't enough there for me to have picked it up that way, not the way I remember it. What did I do? You have to tell me."

She shook her head. "It wasn't your fault. When you saw them like that, you went into some kind of shock or something. I had to drag you back to the car. Everyone would think that it was you. I knew that. I had to get you out of there. You didn't have anything to do with it. Yes, we were there, but Johnnie and Marcia were already dead. We found them that way. You know I wouldn't lie to you, especially about something like this."

Elliot sank back into his chair. He felt as though someone had given him a painkiller, relieving the pressure of a nine-year migraine. He felt the words, "thank you," escape his lips.

"There's more," Carmen said, her words trailing off as she spoke. "It's about Wayne."

Elliot sat forward. "Is he all right?"

"Yes. He tries to be strong. I couldn't have made it through all that's happened without him."

"Where is he?"

"I left him with a friend," she said, looking away. When she spoke again, she talked quickly, as if she wanted to get the words out before she changed her mind. "I have something to tell you. I promised myself it would be my secret, but I don't have the right to keep it from you." She paused.

When he could wait no longer, Elliot asked, "What is it?"

Carmen's eyes filled with tears. "Wayne is your son, Kenny. You are his father. I know you were drunk and don't remember, but there it is."

Carmen's words hit Elliot like a load of buckshot and for a moment the room spun. He got up from the chair and stepped closer to her. "My God, Carmen."

She buried her face in her hands and began to cry. Elliot sat next to her, pulling her close, his heart throbbing in his chest. He had destroyed her, the most beautiful person he'd ever known. But that wasn't enough. He'd also created a child with her, only to leave him fatherless.

"I haven't told Wayne," she said. "I don't know how."

"Maybe you shouldn't."

She pulled away. "Why not?"

"Look around you. Look at me. I'm not the same person you remember, Carmen. Hell, I'm not even sure I'm the same person *I* remember."

She looked up, not to speak, but to stare into Elliot's eyes for what seemed an eternity. Finally she said, "Yes you are, Kenny."

Elliot shook his head. "Wayne has enough to worry about without having my weight strapped around his shoulders."

Carmen jumped to her feet then drew her hand back and slapped Elliot across his face. It stung, but what hurt was the fact that she would do it. "You are pathetic. I hoped you would change, but still you have no respect, for yourself or anything else. Always with you it was Johnnie and Marcia, Johnnie and Marcia. Well, I hate to disappoint you, Kenny, but they were not the angels you thought they were. You had them on a damned pedestal so high nobody could reach it."

Elliot had never heard her swear before. In fact, he couldn't recall seeing her angry. It hurt. He was to blame.

"You're a good man, Kenneth Wayne Elliot. I'm not sorry I met you. And I'm not sorry I love you. I'm just sorry that you can't see past your own self-doubt. I shouldn't have come here," she said, turning away. "I'll let myself out."

Elliot followed her, though he knew it would do no good. He wanted her to stay, but he figured it was best if she didn't. She got in her car, and without another word she backed out of the drive and sped away, the rubber of the tires burning against the pavement.

Chapter Twenty-Six

The rifle salute shattered the morning silence, contrasting with the haunting sound of bagpipes that had come before. Beneath a cool and endlessly blue sky, Elliot tried to be a part of the ceremony, but he felt removed from it, as if he were someplace else seeing the event broadcast over closed-circuit television. He hadn't heard from Carmen since she'd stormed out of his house.

Folding chairs had been placed on the cemetery lawn in neat rows, a quasi theater of the dead. The mourners watched as pallbearers carried the casket past then they all sat down in unison, acting on the minister's instructions. Elliot looked across the sea of dark clothing: friends, relatives, and cops. A sharply dressed cadet approached Conley's wife, and when he saluted and handed her the neatly folded flag, she began to cry. Elliot closed his eyes and prayed for God to allow him to trade places with her husband, but of course when he opened them again it hadn't happened. The gravesite service dragged on forever and Elliot concluded the minister didn't have any real knowledge about the life and nature of the man whose misfortune he was trying to exploit to save a few souls. It angered and disgusted him, and he thought that God must see through this charade and know the hearts of the true sinners in his presence.

Later, as the cars were pulling away, Elliot walked over to where Dombrowski was standing. They shook hands then collapsed into an embrace, hugging each other tightly for a few seconds. Elliot's mind raced, trying to come up with a way to express how he felt, but all that came out was, "I'm sorry." Then, for reasons he didn't understand, he added, "I *will* get this guy. He's going down."

Dombrowski glanced at the others then back to Elliot. "If that's supposed to make me feel better, it doesn't. You better watch yourself, Detective." Again he looked away, and after a brief silence he said, "I'll tell you what would make me feel better. It would make me feel better if everyone in the department, especially me, wasn't worried about you."

Elliot turned and walked away.

"Stop being such a renegade, Elliot," Dombrowski called after him. "That act is wearing thin."

Elliot didn't answer. He knew he'd regret it if he did. Carmen was right. It was time he stopped rolling in defeat. A mental reprimand was in order and he wasn't about to show himself any mercy. He had to get a line on things and focus on the facts, throw up the blinders and go forward, and to hell with the rest of the world. He wondered about the message the killer had scribbled on the wall above the body of Michelle Baker—*In your stead, I take the heat of moist breath against my neck.* The thought conjured up images of the killer's other messages. This one was different. It didn't mention silence as the others had. Apparently the idea of silencing his victims held some fascination for the killer.

Elliot drove out of the cemetery and pulled onto the street. He'd only gone a few blocks when his cell phone rang. It was Eddie York from the forensic department. "Yeah," he said. "I think I've finally run down the vehicle identification number you gave me."

Elliot pushed the phone closer to his ear. Maybe things were looking up. "What do you have?"

"I've narrowed it down to three," he said. "Was it a 1985 Buick LeSabre?"

"No."

"1987 Oldsmobile?"

"Nope."

"How about a 1989 Cadillac Seville?"

Elliot squeezed the receiver, an eerie sensation crawling across his skin. "That's the one."

"I was afraid you'd say that. The latest record I could find on the vehicle is about ten years old. It was last registered to a Terrance Henry Kincaid."

Elliot gripped the steering wheel, the phone heavy in his hand, as Eddie York rattled off the last known address for the owner of the car Elliot had found covered with tree limbs at the bottom of a dry creek bed in Porter, Oklahoma. It was Rachael Johnson's address.

Elliot pulled to a stop in front of Rachael's house. He climbed out of his car and started toward the door, but he'd only managed a few steps before he saw Rachael's neighbor, John Eagon, leaning on the fence between the houses.

Elliot walked over to where Eagon was standing. "Have you seen Rachael?"

"Don't reckon I have, not for a few days. That don't mean much, though. Rachael's funny like that, she'll be around for a few weeks then disappear and you don't see her for awhile. If you ask me, the whole family's a bit touched. Small wonder the old man took off like he did, leaving it all behind." He gave Elliot a sly look. "That's the story anyway."

"I need to talk to Mrs. Johnson. Do you think you could get her to come to the door?"

"That won't be necessary. She's on the other side of the house, working in the flowerbeds. I reckon you'll find her there."

Elliot glanced around. "Thanks."

"Wait a second," Eagon said, motioning for Elliot to come closer. "There's something I've been meaning to talk to you about. The wife tells me I should keep my mouth shut concerning things that, as she puts it, I'm not sure about. But the way I see it, I am sure."

"What is it?"

"When Rachael was just a youngster, I used to see two children playing in that backyard. Yep, I'm sure all right. I saw them with my own eyes."

"Why would something like that trouble you?"

John Eagon leaned closer. "'Cause Rachael's an only child. That's the story they gave everybody, anyway."

Elliot thought about that for a moment. "Maybe it was just a friend."

"Maybe, but they looked an awful lot alike."

"It could have been a relative, a cousin perhaps."

"I guess that's possible. But every time it comes to mind, I get a bad feeling about it. Anyway, I just thought you should know."

"Thanks," Elliot said. "I'll keep that in mind."

Elliot found Rachael's mother working in the yard, just like John Eagon said he would. She didn't see him at first, and when he spoke it startled her. "Good morning."

Her expression said it all. She would've preferred being anywhere right then, other than where she was, caught without escape and forced to talk to Elliot.

"Are you Cynthia Johnson?"

Her eyes darted back and forth. "Do I know you?"

Elliot identified himself and showed his badge. "I have some information for you."

She slowly got up from her squatting position and brushed the dirt from her pants. "Information?"

"Yes. It's rather important."

An undeniable mask of fear formed on Cynthia Johnson's face, but she said nothing.

"It might be better if we went inside."

She didn't want to, but she realized she had no choice. She started toward the front of the house. Once there she opened the door and stepped inside, gesturing for Elliot to follow. As soon as Elliot crossed the threshold he was immediately struck with a feeling of despair and grief, as if fear and tension were woven into the house, permeating the fabric of its structure. The house resembled a museum in both smell and decor, with overstuffed chairs embellished with crocheted doilies and hand-carved shelves stuck into corners holding ceramic remembrances.

Nervously she sat down, folding her hands in her lap. "What's this all about?"

It was a stuffy old house, smelling of mothballs and furniture polish. And Elliot feared, unexplainably, that if he stayed too long there, he too would become a part of it, understanding the meek lady in front of him, knowing how she felt as she sat alone in one of the overstuffed chairs playing with the starched white doilies that covered its arms and mumbling "Yes, dear," to a disembodied source of scathing words and commands of obedience. He turned back, taking a moment to clear his head. "It's rather bad news," he said, though he didn't believe she would take it that way. "It's about Terrance Kincaid, your husband. I'm afraid he's dead. We found him in his car at the bottom of a ravine in Porter, Oklahoma."

A curious expression crossed her face. "Dead? Are you sure? You can't be certain, can you?"

The words crossed her lips like a prayer, and at that moment Elliot knew that she was Cynthia Kincaid. After her husband disappeared, she and Rachael had used her maiden name. Elliot started to tell her that no definite answer as to the true identity of the remains in the car had been reached, but he couldn't bring himself to do it. "We're pretty sure it's him."

She leaned back in her chair, putting her hands to her mouth. "I thought he'd left us. All these years, that's what I thought." Her relief lasted only a few seconds then the worried look returned. "It's Charlie, isn't it? He's done something. He never forgave me you know."

Elliot knew Cynthia Kincaid was talking about Charlie Johnson, Porter's chief of police. "Your brother is fine, Mrs. Kincaid. Whatever happened to your husband happened a long time ago."

Cynthia Kincaid's right hand started to clench but settled for twisting the chair doily instead. "Charlie said he wouldn't bother us anymore. But he doesn't know Terrance, not like he thinks he does. Rachael and I didn't take any chances. We got out of here, stayed with my cousin Bernice in Stillwater for awhile. It was nice there. Rachael liked it, but later she wanted to come back here…to come home. I can't imagine why."

Elliot nurtured one of those gut feelings that—like it or not— solves more cases than all the computers and government agents combined. And that feeling was telling him Cynthia Kincaid was deeply concerned about his being there, as if his presence was a threat to her guarded way of life. A photograph on the fireplace mantel drew his attention. He stood and crossed the room for a closer look, recognizing young Rachael with a man whom he also recognized from a picture his mother had given him. He suspected the man was Terrance Kincaid. "Do you know where Rachael is, Mrs. Kincaid?"

Wrinkles creased her forehead. "She left a few days ago. She does that now and then, not keeping in touch when she decides to disappear. I don't blame her. I don't blame her one bit."

"Why do you say that?"

Cynthia Kincaid wadded the chair doily into a ball then tried to straighten it. "My husband was not a nice man, Detective. When he left, Rachael and I tried to get on with our lives but we just couldn't. Too much had happened, too much damage. He abused her and I let it happen. She hates me for that." She paused, taking a deep breath to regain her composure. "And now the bastard has managed to reach up from the grave and slap her one more time. Don't you see? If you hadn't found that old car, Rachael wouldn't even be involved in this."

Elliot wondered about that, Rachael's involvement.

"Do I need to take precautions?" she asked.

"What do you mean?"

"You don't know Terrance, not like you think you do."

"I don't think you need to worry about that," Elliot said, glancing around the room, a strong compulsion to search the house running through him. He noticed an odd looking door along the wall of the hallway. It was different from the others, thicker and heavier, but what caught his attention was the heavy padlock securing it. He turned to Mrs. Kincaid. "Would you open this room, please?"

She shook her head. "We mustn't do that. He doesn't allow it. You don't know him."

Elliot didn't have a warrant, but his compulsion to see what lay beyond the locked door influenced him to ignore that. "I'm afraid I must insist."

Cynthia Kincaid wrung her hands and looked around, as if her husband might suddenly appear, then she seemed to make up her mind. She stood and went to an antique desk in the corner of the room, where she searched through a drawer, pulling out an envelope. When she came back, she handed it to Elliot.

The envelope was sealed and when Elliot tore it open a key tumbled out, falling to the floor. Elliot stared at Mrs. Kincaid for a moment, then scooped the key from the floor and inserted it into the massive lock, twisting the key until the lock popped free. He hesitated for a split second, then removed the lock and pushed the door open.

In contrast with the rest of the house, which was filled with dark, polished furniture, this room was empty. As Elliot stepped into the void, however, he realized it wasn't completely bare. There was a mattress lying on the floor, and a faded poster depicting the movie *East of Eden* tacked to the wall. Then, as his eyes adjusted, he saw that a few broken toys littered the floor beside the mattress. "What is this place?" he asked.

Cynthia Kincaid did not answer, and she had not come into the room, but stood trembling outside the doorway.

Seeing nothing else of interest except rays of sunlight coming through a busted window shade, Elliot turned to leave, but as he walked across the room one of the floorboards popped loose beneath his stride. He knelt down to examine it and when he pulled the board free he saw that something was hidden there. It was a child's jewelry box. When he picked it up, he found that it was also a music box that played a tune once opened, and though it was a pleasant melody—"When You Wish Upon A Star"—it sent a shiver up his spine. The box contained a diamond and emerald necklace with matching earrings, and a tube of red lipstick.

The jewelry reminded Elliot of Rachael, though he couldn't recall seeing her wear it. Something like that would be reserved for special occasions. He remembered what Cynthia Kincaid had said about abuse and a vision of Rachael laying across her bed with the necklace draped around her throat struck Elliot. Suddenly he wanted nothing more than to be out of that room. He walked out, closing the door behind him.

Elliot didn't see Cynthia Kincaid, but the smell of fresh furniture polish that filled the air conjured up images of her sitting in one of the overstuffed chairs knitting another lace doily. He found her in one of the bedrooms sitting on the bed and flipping through the pages of a photo album. She looked up when he came into the room, and the expression on her face said she was ready for a stopping point, a way to finally get off the mad ride that had been all too much her own doing. Elliot sat on the bed next to her.

She smiled. "Musty aren't they? Reminds me of wet cardboard." She pointed to a snapshot of herself with Rachael.

"How old was she then?" Elliot asked.

Cynthia didn't answer, but kept turning the pages, stopping occasionally to explain a particular shot. There were only a few shots of Cynthia alone, and even fewer of her with Rachael. Most of the pictures featured Papa Kincaid and Rachael, and in those shots Rachael wore jewelry, a diamond and emerald necklace with matching earrings and her lips were painted a deep shade of red.

Elliot pointed to one of the pictures of Rachael. "Is that a birthmark on her cheek?"

"Oh, no," Cynthia said. "Terrance wore a ring, a god-awful looking thing." She clinched her hand into a fist. "He hit Rachael, hit her hard."

Elliot put his hand on the shoulder of the reminiscing mother, then got up and walked out of the room. He wasn't sure why, but he went into the kitchen, stopping by the window which was above the sink. It overlooked the backyard. Elliot had seen enough in the photo albums to understand that Papa Terrance Kincaid had not played the ordinary role of fatherhood. He hadn't squashed the cushion of a recliner, reading the paper while the family pet chewed his slippers. Judging from what he'd seen, Elliot suspected Papa Terrance spent most of his time in the kitchen, drinking sour mash whiskey from a coffee mug while his wife sat quietly, hoping to avoid confrontation, and young Rachael tried to remain anonymous, hoping Papa wouldn't get drunk enough this time or, if he did, that he'd have other ways to entertain himself.

Elliot opened the cabinet beneath the sink and squatted to look inside. In a cleared space of its own, separated from the plastic tub of cleaners and brushes, sat a half bottle of whiskey and an aged, cracked ceramic mug. There had been no happiness here. In a place and time where there should have been a house full of laughter, there was only pain, laced with the sounds of scared children huddled in their own very different bedroom corners.

Elliot stood and looked through the window into the backyard. It looked old and unused. Metal lawn chairs, the old style that rock on curved tubular frames and leave faded paint marks on the clothing of anyone brave enough to sit in them, occupied the cracked concrete patio. In the center of the yard, a stone birdbath full of stagnant water stood silent sentry. Beyond that was a broken brick barbecue pit. A chain-link fence surrounded all of this, but what caught Elliot's attention was an area in the corner of the yard where an old oak tree shaded a patch of grass closed off by a black wrought-iron fence—a fence within a fence. Inside the protected area, which was better maintained than the rest of the yard, were flowers and what looked to be a headstone.

Elliot heard a sound and turned to see that Cynthia Kincaid had come into the kitchen. "Tell me something, Mrs. Kincaid. Is that a grave in your backyard?"

Cynthia gathered a few dishes from the kitchen table and put them in the sink. "Yes. We had a dog, a wonderful collie. She was only with us for a precious few years. Such a beautiful girl." Cynthia paused and began to cry. "Terrance buried her out there like yesterday's garbage, wouldn't even let us mark it. 'That would be foolish,' he said. We did, though, Rachael and I, after he was gone. We made it look like it ought to, like a graveyard."

"Take me out there," Elliot said. "I want to see it."

Cynthia shook her head and mumbled something, but did as she was asked, mechanically leading Elliot to the back door and opening it.

Elliot pushed open the screen door and stepped down to the patio. He paused then strode to the enclosed area while Mrs. Kincaid, still mumbling, slowly followed as if pulled along on a leash against her will. The hinges of the tall black gate complained as Elliot pulled the gate open and stepped inside the small enclave. The air seemed thick and depraved, and Elliot had a feeling the small patch of earth inside the wrought-iron fence was less than sacred. In fact, he suspected it was a place of dark sin. The small headstone had no markings other than the birth and death dates: April 23, 1977—June 15, 1988.

"Eleven years is a pretty good life span for a dog," Elliot said. "How did your collie die?"

Cynthia Kincaid looked pale and shook visibly. "Terrance," she said. "Terrance killed her." Tears formed in her eyes and rolled down her cheeks in large drops. "I don't think he meant to. He lost control. He hit her. He hit her with that god-awful ring." She paused, staring at the grave. "Things were never the same after that. What little we had went into the ground that night."

Elliot pulled his cell phone and called the department. From behind him, he heard Cynthia Kincaid say, "Oh, dear God."

The backyard of Cynthia Kincaid's house had become a center of interest, with curious neighbors gathering at the fence to point and whisper. Elliot and Detective Beaumont stood a few feet away from the grave, giving the workers ample room, but staying close enough to observe. Pieces of the dismantled wrought-iron fence lay in a jagged pile while the excavation team dug away the cover of dirt, and as two of the crew members lifted a small pile of bones from the pit an uneasy quiet came over the crowd. One of the onlookers screamed, and a lady, Mrs. Eagon, Elliot thought, fell to her knees while her husband knelt by her side, frantically waving a handkerchief close to her face.

Finally, Eddie York looked up from the bones and shook his head. "These aren't dog bones, Detective. They're human, probably the remains of a child."

Elliot uttered a silent prayer, and while a buzzing array of voices spread through the crowd, he led Cynthia Kincaid away from the homemade cemetery plot and over to one of the uniformed officers. What he had to do next, he didn't want to do. "Cynthia Kincaid," he said, "I'm placing you under arrest for suspicion of murder." He clamped the cuffs around her wrists, and read her rights. Afterward he looked into her eyes. "Do you understand what I'm telling you?"

She leaned close, and into Elliot's ear she whispered, "You don't know him, not like you think you do."

Chapter Twenty-Seven

The air hung lifeless over the area without so much as a leaf moving on a tree, but it matched Elliot's mood as he turned away from the disturbed earth where the child had been buried. A hand holding his arm interrupted his exit. It was Beaumont.

"You look like hell, Detective."

Elliot instinctively reached for his face to feel the beard that must have grown there, for he had not shaved lately, and as he rubbed the stubby growth the thought of his obsession snaked through his mind like a serpent through murky water. The case had taken over. It owned him, controlling his actions with deliberate influence like an evil and possessive spouse. "You're right," he said. "I'll drop by the house and clean up."

Beaumont nodded then asked, "What happened here? Did the lady kill her kid?"

Elliot studied the crew still working in Cynthia Kincaid's yard. "No, I don't think so. That's not the way it happened."

"What do you mean, you don't think so? Why the hell did you arrest her?"

"There's no one else around. Besides, I think she knows what happened."

A confused look came over Beaumont's face. "How in blazes did you stumble on to this, anyway?"

"The person we found in his car in Porter? This was his last known address."

Beaumont shook his head. "You've uncovered some darned unusual things lately, I'll give you that much. But I don't understand how any of it relates to the killings here in Tulsa that we're supposed to be investigating."

Elliot wasn't surprised Beaumont didn't understand. He didn't have all the facts. But to Elliot, the relation was as clear as day. But he no longer trusted Detective Beaumont—and the captain, well, he wasn't ready to understand. So Elliot held back, an ace up his sleeve. "It all ties together," he said.

"Well, I certainly don't see how."

Elliot turned away. "It'll all make sense when I'm through."

"Wait a minute, what's your next step?"

"I need to check some records."

"What kind of records?"

"Birth records," Elliot said, climbing into his car before Beaumont could ask any more questions. As he drove away his mood was uneasy and he felt as though Dombrowski was in the car with him, breathing down his neck.

Elliot went to the county offices, and when he arrived he parked and went inside. Sure, he could've just gone back to his office and logged onto the Internet to find what he needed, but he'd always preferred face-to-face meetings and real-life records over getting lost in virtual hallways. Anyway, it wasn't long until he had the information he was after. On April 23, 1977, Rachael Hannah Kincaid, also known as Rachael Johnson was born in St. John's Hospital, eleven months after her parents, Terrance and Cynthia, were married. Just to be sure, Elliot checked the records under both names, going back one year before the marriage and forward ten years after. He found nothing. The records appeared to support the idea that Rachael was an only child.

Elliot made a few copies and left. He was on his way to St. John's when his phone rang; it was Detective John Cunningham, back from vacation. Elliot and Cunningham had become detectives at the same time. They were also friends. Cunningham sounded nervous, speaking quietly like he feared someone might overhear him. "Where are you?" he asked.

"Not far from Woodward Park," Elliot said, "on 21st Street. Why?"

"Pull over, we need to talk."

"I'm not in the mood for games, Cunningham. What's going on?"

"It's no game. I only wish it were."

Elliot turned into a strip mall, parking between a pickup truck and a van. "All right, I'm off the road. What's up?"

"Dombrowski called me in this morning, asking a lot of questions. Like what did I know about you, and had I noticed any change in your habits."

"What did you tell him?"

"Well I don't know much, do I? Anyway there's more. Dombrowski sent me and Beaumont out to investigate a murder. We just got back."

"A murder?"

"That's right. Some waitress from a dive called Fuzzy's over on 61st. Twenty-two years old, one hundred twenty pounds, blonde hair, blue eyes. Sound familiar?"

"Yeah. Sounds like our man struck again."

"There's more. Dombrowski had us take some pictures and show them around the bar. Pictures of you, Elliot. Several people remembered seeing you in there that night. Some even remembered you talking to the waitress, the victim."

"Yeah, I was there a couple of nights ago. So what?"

"The body was found in an empty building two or three blocks away, some sort of bloody message written on the wall. We also found a knife."

"That's different," Elliot said. "The killer doesn't usually leave the weapon behind."

"Maybe so, but that's what we found. And your fingerprints are all over it."

"My fingerprints?"

"That's right."

Cunningham's words hit Elliot like a sledgehammer. His mind raced for answers, but when he snagged onto the only obvious solution he didn't like what came to the surface. "What did the knife look like?"

"Like expensive cutlery, about ten inches long, with a smooth black handle."

"No," Elliot mumbled.

"What was that?"

"Nothing," Elliot said. But as he watched rain striking the surface of the parking lot, a disturbing notion began to make its way into his thoughts. He wondered if he drove to Nick Brazleton's garage and looked inside his toolbox, would the knife he'd seen still be there, or was it the same one Beaumont and Cunningham had found beside the latest victim? The thought of Nick being somehow involved had crossed his mind on several occasions, but he'd managed to push it aside. He could no longer do that.

The phone grew heavy in Elliot's hand, and his thoughts began to scatter as if a gust of wind had entered his head, throwing his senses across the landscape. He didn't want to be on the wrong side of the law, but he couldn't see the sense of turning himself in either. Dombrowski had evidence against him, and it would take time for the captain to get to the bottom of things and figure out he was innocent. Time was a luxury he couldn't afford. The pattern of the murders indicated the killer had a habit of lying low for awhile, not resurfacing again for as much as a year after each murder. If he disappeared into the woodwork now, their chances of catching him would be nearly nonexistent. And Elliot would look like a much better prospect. He didn't understand it all yet, but he was getting close. He couldn't just let the killer slip away. He gripped the phone. "What should I do?" he asked.

Cunningham took awhile to answer, "How the hell should I know?"

"Surely you don't buy into this, think I'm guilty? It's a setup, Cunningham."

"I don't know what to think. Anyway, I called, didn't I?" The phone went dead, severing the line just as a black and white patrol car pulled into the parking lot. Elliot sank down in the seat, hiding his head. Had Cunningham called just to get his location? Somehow he didn't think so, but he held his breath anyway, praying as the squad car drew near that he wouldn't be discovered. The car pulled alongside and stopped. Elliot's heart pounded. He felt like a teenager who'd just stolen his first car. A few minutes later, he thought he heard the car beside him start rolling again, though he wasn't sure. It felt like he'd been there, crouched down in the seat, for hours. Finally he couldn't wait any longer. He slowly brought his head up and peeked over the steering wheel. The police car was gone. But this was just a precursor of things to come. They would be looking for him, which brought up an interesting question. How was he going to continue his investigation with the entire Tulsa police force breathing down his neck?

The wind picked up, flinging rain against the window as if it were being sprayed at the car through a high-pressure hose. Elliot sat motionless in the front seat, staring through the blurry window. What he was contemplating was pure insanity, yet the more he turned the idea over in his mind the stronger his compulsion to remain free became. He thought about calling Dombrowski to explain his situation, though he dismissed the idea as quickly as it formed. The captain wouldn't understand. And even if he did, what could he do?

Elliot pulled onto the roadway and somewhere in the back of his mind the details of his plan began to form. He was tired, worn down from worry and lack of sleep. He needed to find a place where he could rest, lie low for a while, and do some serious thinking. He had to take care of a few things, though, before he could do any of that. First of all, he needed some cash and banks were out of the question. It was Saturday afternoon and they'd be closed until Monday. He could find an ATM, but that would leave a trail. Then again, if Cunningham could be trusted, they probably didn't know that he knew they were looking for him. Since they wouldn't expect him to be on the run, they wouldn't yet be doing things like checking credit card and ATM usage. He decided to chance it, pulling into the first convenience store he came to and drawing out a few hundred bucks. With that done, he drove toward town. He decided to pay his new friend, Bernie Sykes, a visit.

Sykes wasn't in his office, but Elliot found him in a small apartment upstairs in the same building. Sykes didn't look happy to see him. Elliot guessed a cop should get used to that, and for the most part he had, but he couldn't help wishing someone would smile when they saw him coming.

Sykes stood by the door, holding it open and looking like he'd just been shot. "What the hell do you want?"

He didn't offer to get out of the way, but Elliot pushed him aside and went in anyway. The apartment wasn't much, just a one-room efficiency with an unmade bed in one corner and an old mohair couch in the other. A stack of magazines brought the television up to eye level for anyone sitting on the couch, and beside the bed a turned-up wooden crate served as a nightstand. A coffee mug sat atop it. "Nice place," Elliot said.

Sykes let out a heavy sigh and closed the door. "What do you want, Elliot? And make it quick. I'm kind of busy, in case you didn't notice."

Bernie Sykes was pathetic but the sad part was, when Elliot looked at the overweight private investigator he saw himself in ten years. Like it or not, they had a lot in common. Elliot sat on the couch. "Bernie, old pal, I need a favor."

Chapter Twenty-Seven

"What the hell are you getting at?"

"When we talked the other day, I got the feeling you'd like to get out of town for awhile. What would you say to an all-expenses-paid vacation?"

Sykes sat on the bed. "What kind of crap are you trying to feed me?"

"All right," Elliot said, "let me put it another way. I need your services. I'd like to hire you for a couple of days. I'll pay your going rate and throw in an extra thousand."

Sykes rubbed his chin, contemplating the offer. The prospect of cash was piquing his interest. "Why? You're a pretty good detective. What the hell do you need a PI for?"

"Like I said, I need a favor."

Sykes retrieved a cigarette from a package on the makeshift nightstand. "I think I'm starting to get it now. You're in trouble...in some kind of jam. Something's gone wrong, and now you need old Bernie's help, is that it?"

Elliot nodded. His hunch about Sykes had been correct. Beneath all the layers of self-induced failure the old sot was a pretty decent investigator. "I don't have time for idle chitchat. Are you interested or not?"

"Well that kind of depends on what it is you want me to do."

"Not much really. Just walk in my shoes and be me for a few days."

Sykes' face went blank. "I don't know, Elliot. A guy like you is bound to have a lot of enemies." He paused and shook his head, "It ain't worth it."

"You pull it off, and I'll throw in another five hundred."

"Make it a grand, and maybe I'll think about it."

Elliot stood and walked over to the PI, stuffing a hundred dollar bill into his hand. "It's a deal then. I'll be in touch, Mr. Sykes."

Chapter Twenty-Eight

A squat old man with eyeglasses a quarter of an inch thick sat behind a wire cage, engulfed in tobacco smoke. Elliot followed the deliberate pathway through mounds of junk and stopped at the window. "Hello, Bob." Bob Roderick was a pawnbroker and a pretty fair locksmith. But it wasn't Roderick's legitimate talents Elliot was after.

He looked up, studying Elliot for a moment, but said nothing.

"I've got a job for you," Elliot said, placing his driver's license, along with a photo of Sykes, on the counter in front of Roderick.

With pudgy fingers, the old man fumbled the items into his hands, bringing them close to his face and moving them back and forth as if his eyes were scanning them into his brain. Finally he looked up. "What am I supposed to do with these?"

"Make me a driver's license," Elliot said, "with his picture on it instead of mine."

Roderick put the license and picture on the counter, looking as if he might ask, *what makes you think I could, or would do something like that?* —But he didn't. He simply went back to whatever it was he was working on.

Elliot went to the jewelry counter, placing his hands against the glass. "You got some pretty classy stuff here. I could ask where you got it. Lots of stolen property floating around the city."

Muttering quietly, Roderick relit his pipe and shuffled away, disappearing behind a curtained doorway.

Waiting for him to return, Elliot tapped his fingers against the countertop, taking in the surroundings in the same amazed state that always overtook him when he came into the place. It was a museum, a collection of eccentric oddities. He often thought if the building were to tumble down, Bob Roderick's small part of it would remain unharmed, held in place by its internal stuffing. Elliot shook his head then used his cell phone to book a hotel room on the beach in Panama City, Florida. It was where Sykes wanted to go. After that he called the airport and arranged a flight.

Roderick returned with a metal tray that he placed on the counter. "You're lucky I'm so congenial," he said, gingerly picking up the fake license. He placed Elliot's order in front of him. It was flawless.

"You do good work."

He grunted. "Always knew you were too much like the rest of us. What are you going to use that for?"

"I need to get into a private club."

Roderick nodded then relit his pipe and spoke around the stem, "Should be good enough to get your man past airport security."

Elliot wondered how he knew so much then figured he must've overheard him placing his calls. He wondered what other business went on in the pawnshop, but he knew better than to ask. Roderick was a wealth of hidden talents and Elliot left it at that. "Thanks for your help," he said, then pushed through the door and stepped outside.

Elliot drove back to Sykes's place. When he got there, Sykes was ready with his bags packed. Elliot was thankful for that; time was quickly becoming critical. Sykes followed Elliot to the airport and once there, they left the patrol car in the parking garage.

Elliot climbed into Sykes's car and drove him around to the terminal. Before Sykes got out, Elliot handed him the rest of the cash he'd drawn out of the ATM. He also gave him a thousand he'd borrowed from Bob Roderick. "The rest of it will be waiting for you when you get back," Elliot said.

Sykes stuffed the money away. "See that it is."

"All right, here's what I want you to do. Once you get inside, call the hotel and make a hotel reservation in your own name. When you get to Panama City, put on a pair of sunglasses and a hat then check into the hotel as me. Go to the room and call the Tulsa Police Department, telling whoever answers the phone that you saw a car that looked like a cop car parked in the garage at the airport. You thought that was a little unusual so you figured you'd better call it in and report it. Give them the tag number and hang up. That'll get them started on the trail. Once you've done that, take off the hat and sunglasses and change clothes. Wear something loud and touristy. Then go back to the front desk and check in as yourself. The hotel clerk will be busy and won't make the connection, and the cops will be looking for me, not you. You can spend a few days relaxing in the sun."

Sykes grinned. "Don't worry about a thing. I'm good at this kind of stuff."

"That's what worries me," Elliot said. "Don't let me down."

"Yeah, whatever. Just don't wreck my car. It ain't much, but it's all I've got."

Elliot watched Sykes until he was inside. The old PI could easily drop everything and just go home with an easy thousand. Even worse, he could turn Elliot in, hoping to gain a few favors, even pocket some reward money. Elliot turned onto the roadway. It was a chance he'd have to take.

When Elliot left the airport, it was early afternoon, but he was exhausted. He spotted a bar and turned in, coaxing Sykes's Monte Carlo around to the back of the parking lot. He got out and walked to the front, listening to music leaking through the painted windows as he neared the entrance. When he pushed open the cheap, red vinyl door, he paused, adjusting to the darkness and taking in his surroundings.

It was a slow night. A few couples snuggled in booths while several singles sat at the bar. Behind the counter, a tall man with a neatly trimmed beard busied himself washing glasses and trying to be inconspicuous as he watched a lady who sat on one of the barstools fumbling for a cigarette. As soon as she brought it to her lips, he was there lighting it for her. She'd been attractive once and still was in the dark, but her youth had disappeared. Except for the bartender and a guy who sat beside her, she wasn't drawing much attention. Elliot figured five or six more hard years like the one she was presently living might well be her undoing. He sat down two barstools away and ordered a beer.

A few minutes later, Elliot began to feel the effects of the alcohol. In his present condition, the cold brew hadn't wasted any time. He looked in the lady's direction and nodded; she smiled. The idea of falling asleep in such a dive only to be awakened by the angry prodding of the bartender was even more unappealing than the crazy thoughts running through Elliot's mind. Not knowing what else to do, he let the fantasy win out and smiled back. And even to his own surprise, he didn't stop there. He walked over and sat down beside her. "Buy you a drink?" he asked. She looked him over as he signaled for the bartender. "What'll it be?"

Her smile said she'd heard it all before but was too tired to care. "Whatever you're having, hon."

With his conceptual abilities expanded to their limits, Elliot tried to imagine the encounter as a romantic fling, but he couldn't. Then, like a bad actor in a bad movie, the bartender slapped down their order. "Seven-fifty."

Elliot slammed down a ten, returning the bartender's percussive gesture one better, making the glasses jump.

The lady seemed to enjoy it. She laughed, putting a hand on Elliot's knee. "Don't mind old sourpuss. Sometimes I think he was born that way. What's your name, cutie?"

Elliot thought about his answer for a moment then smiled and said, "Beaumont. Jeremy Beaumont."

She looked him over again. "So, what's your game?"

Her straightforwardness brought a smile out of Elliot. She'd quickly sized him up, seen right through him. As a cop, he appreciated such a talent. He leaned forward and motioned for her to come closer. "I've got a bit of a problem and I need some help."

She drew back a little. "So you came to me? Why? I don't even know you."

"I guess that's the whole point."

She smiled, an I-get-that-all-the-time look forming on her face. "What kind of help are you looking for?"

"There's a hotel just around the corner, the kind that worries about cash and not names."

"And you're all alone and don't want to be, is that it?"

"Not exactly," Elliot said. "I'm not looking to gain your company, not that your company wouldn't be entertaining. But I've got other problems that need to be addressed right now."

"So what *do* you want?"

"I want to check in, but I don't want anyone to know I'm there."

"So what's in it for me?"

"How does fifty dollars sound?"

She shook her head. "Not enough. I'm taking all the risk here. For all I know you could be some kind of pervert or something."

"All right then, a hundred bucks. Final offer."

She raised her glass and drained it, then got up and started toward the door.

Elliot followed. As they were leaving, he heard a mumbling and turned around to get a dirty look from one of the men at the bar.

It wasn't far to the hotel, so they walked. Once there, it wasn't difficult for Elliot to convince his new acquaintance that sleep was really all he needed. He gave her money for the room and told her to make up a name and sign in while he waited outside. A few minutes later, she brought him the key. He paid her the agreed amount, then said good-bye and went inside, walking through the dirty hallway until he found his room. He slid the key into the lock and opened the door to his new home, and as soon as his head hit the pillow he was out.

Chapter Twenty-Nine

The cold downpour drove him beneath the alcove of the Mid-Continent Building where he hunkered against the wall in a corner, water dripping from his clothes. He had no idea how he'd gotten there, though he'd obviously been in the rain for some time. Disjointed memories flew through his head as he fought to regain awareness. The lapses were becoming more frequent—a disconcerting notion—yet there was something unusual beneath the surface of his return and he couldn't quite get a handle on it.

Suddenly he knew why. The thoughts in his head were not entirely his own. And even that didn't go far enough; he had a residual lingering of *her* feelings woven throughout his senses. He had come to realize her presence, a product of becoming stronger, but the revelation did little to console him because he also knew what she'd done, what she'd been doing. His blanking out, losing pieces of time, was the result of her manipulation. She'd learned to spread her tentacles into his brain, making him think her thoughts. The idea ran through him like a fever.

He was on to something, and the more he explored it the worse it got. She wanted him dead. The extent of her deviousness amazed him. She'd been trying to throw him off track, get him to worrying about Kenny when *she* was the real problem. She'd even gone so far as to change her looks…more precisely she'd taken to using other people as she had used him. A terrifying idea, though he had to admit her disguise was a good one. And it had nearly worked. Had he not seen through her with his own eyes he might not have known.

With the exception of the few details he'd managed to hold on to, he knew nothing of the takeover. He suspected it was something like being possessed by a demon, an unseen and unwanted spirit. Of course he never expected her to drag anyone else into their sick little game, especially someone like Carmen Garcia. Other than these reflections—a shadow of her control—he remembered nothing of a big gap of time, a couple of days, perhaps. With that recollection, panic shot through him. He'd been at home with Mother and she wasn't well. She had, in fact, been quite beside herself. That was where he needed to be, at home where he could find solace, renewing his strength for the battle. She was the problem, and he would look through her current persona and deal with her. This time he would do it right, removing all chances of failure. He straightened his clothes and left the protection of the alcove, walking quickly lest he be too late.

Chapter Thirty

Reluctantly Elliot began to come out of the sleep he'd fallen into hours earlier, awakening in a state of confusion. He found his watch. It was 2:00 p.m. He rolled out of bed and started toward the bathroom, his eyes straining to find the unfamiliar path, though as he heard someone pounding at the door, he realized it was that which had interrupted his dreams. He stumbled to the door and opened it just enough to see. The hotel proprietor stood outside the room, waiting impatiently. Elliot struggled into his pants, then opened the door and paid the man for an extra day.

After settling with the manager, Elliot closed the door then jumped into the shower, where he lingered, relishing the cleansing steam until the hot water played out. However, as he twisted the knob to shut off the water, a sensation of desperation shot through him. It was as if someone had tapped into his conscience with a message of doom. It wasn't a premonition, it was a knowing, a fact-based truth that'd somehow been planted in his understanding. And he knew with certainty that it had to do with Carmen. She had called out to him. He toweled off and grabbed his cell phone. The battery was dead. He looked around, but the shabby room had no phone. He'd spent a lot of time arranging his disappearance, but a moment's reflection told him he had no choice. He got dressed and made his way to the office, where he found a pay phone. He fumbled some change into the slot and dialed her number. When she answered on the second ring, the sound of her voice soothed him like a powerful drug. He tried to speak, but nothing came out.

Finally she said, "Kenny?"

"Yeah," Elliot said, wondering how she knew it was him. "Sorry, my throat's a little dry."

After a long pause, she said, "I've been worried. I'm glad you called."

Again desperation threatened Elliot, and a world of emotion swam inside of him. All he managed to say was, "Are you all right?"

"I think so, but I'm scared."

"Has something happened?"

"It's probably nothing, just my imagination. Wayne's been asking about you."

Elliot felt his heart jump. There was more than a conversation happening between them. It was a connection, unspoken but there just the same. "I've been thinking about him, too."

She paused, and when she spoke again the subject was deepened. "I think we should talk about Nick."

A vision of Nick pushing the bill of his cap up with the blade of the knife, the one in the toolbox, rumbled through Elliot's thoughts. The look on Nick's face that day had been unsettling. "Why do you say that?"

"He's still missing. Have you heard from him?"

"Not since I left Porter."

"Sylvia Barton saw him just before he disappeared. She said he was acting strange, wouldn't speak to her. What's going on, Kenny?"

"I don't know. It's probably nothing. He'll show up, eventually." He was sure Carmen saw through his reassurances.

"Maybe you're right. I thought I saw him last night, walking along the street outside my house. I called to him, but he didn't answer. It was dark, perhaps it was someone else."

Disconcerting thoughts danced in Elliot's head. "Maybe it was the prowler again, the Peeping Tom."

"Yes," she said, "I wondered about that too."

"Did you call Chief Johnson?"

"No. Wayne thought it was a bad idea. It might sound strange, but I tend to agree with him."

"What do you mean?"

"Charlie's been acting kind of...well, patronizing."

Elliot gripped the phone. Wayne had said something along those lines while they were playing ball. He'd been concerned about Chief Johnson going along a little too eagerly with his mother over the prowler issue. The thought ran ice water through Elliot's veins. Kids were known for their imaginations, but when an eight-year-old tells his mom not to trust the chief of police, something's not right, especially when that same police officer was as close to the boy as an uncle. "Will you do something for me?" Elliot asked.

"What is it?"

"I want you and Wayne to get out of that house as fast as possible. And whatever you do, don't tell Johnson what you're up to."

After a long pause, Carmen answered, "All right, if you feel that strongly about it."

"I do," Elliot said. And then he heard himself say something that he knew he should not have. He said, "I love you." But as he was hanging up the phone he responded to a feeling that someone was watching him, and as he turned toward the office, he saw the manager back away from the door.

Chapter Thirty-One

As he neared his destination, his fears began to grow and even before he fumbled the key into the lock he knew things were not as they should be. Something was very wrong. He slowly pushed the door open and entered the house where he'd spent his life, but its familiarity had disappeared, melted away and seeped through the cracks in the hardwood to lie in the dank earth below the floor. The furniture was in place, the smell of her cooking lingered, the curtains still shrouded the windows, but it was not his house.

As to why this might have happened, he could only guess. Perhaps he'd stepped through some kind of hidden portal into another dimension where things were just enough out of sync to not be right. Or maybe his world was the one not right, and this the one that should be. The idea made sense.

He walked on through the doppelganger house, making his way into each room, searching for common ground and not finding any, though what he did find was even more disconcerting. Mother was gone. He had yet to check the bathroom, and when he did, what he saw there made his skin crawl. Where disinfected cleanliness once lived, the most intolerable filth now resided. Bobby pins with laminated particles of hair running through their eyelets, and broken pieces of emery board dotted portions of the countertop, becoming permanent parts of the lavatory surface, a demented mosaic creation embedded in the residual stickiness of hair spray.

Now the truth was reflected back at him like a nasty black and white documentary, revolting in its honesty yet captivating in some sick and hypnotic way. Mother, too, had gone wrong, as they all had. It wasn't to have gotten this far. Coming through the portal had changed him, honed his senses beyond their former boundaries. It was then that he understood. Everything—his thinking, his memories, his ability to see—existed for the single purpose of setting things right. Indeed *she* was a monster, and she had come into this house and she had taken Mother.

The success of his mission had acquired new meaning, but it would not be easy. Through her Trojan-horse strategy, she had enlisted the aid of the enemy, gained the protection of Kenny Elliot. Kenny was a hard person to deal with. Who, after all, knew Kenny better than he? No one, he suspected. Not even Carmen. And it wasn't so much that Kenny put a lot of stock into winning. He did not. There was just something about his nature that refused to let him lose.

But he would do it. He had a few tricks left up his sleeve. He left his house and slipped into the outside world.

Chapter Thirty-Two

Elliot hung up the phone and walked to the south end of the counter where he could see into the manager's office. He didn't think enough time had passed for the news media to be flashing his face all over the city, but the manager had already switched off the set and was walking toward him.

"Is there a problem?" the manager asked.

"I don't know. Do you always watch your customers so intently?"

The manager shook his head. "I wasn't watching you. Must have been your imagination."

Elliot turned away. In the corner of the lobby, he saw a vending machine and after shoving some cash into it, he received a toothbrush and a razor. He wasn't sure about the man behind the counter; his face was hard to read. He was used to dealing with trouble. Elliot decided not to take any chances. He went back to the room and gathered up his things, and after leaving the key on the dresser he found Sykes's car at the bar where he'd left it and drove away.

The car responded to Elliot's commands as he guided it to a stop in front of a joint called Casey's.

Casey watched Elliot walk in, not making any visible expression except for changing the ever-present toothpick from one side of his mouth to the other. "I wondered if you were ever coming back."

Casey rented a couple of rooms upstairs. Elliot had stayed there, years ago, when he'd first gotten into town. "Didn't give my room away, did you?"

Casey repositioned the toothpick. "Funny you should ask. Fellow was in here looking for you yesterday."

"Cop?" Elliot asked, pulling out a twenty.

"Looked that way to me."

"Did he give a name?"

Casey operated the cash register. "Nope. Fancy dresser, though."

Beaumont, Elliot thought, as Casey handed him the keys. He left the change on the counter and started toward the back of the room. "It won't be permanent," he said, "just a few days."

In the rear of the room behind the pool table, a hallway covered with graffiti led to a rickety set of stairs. The stairway had its good points, one of which was the distinctive sound it gave forth when supporting the weight of anyone heavier than a Cub Scout. The only way to gain access to the room without sounding an alarm was to come up the fire escape. Elliot climbed the stairs, pausing momentarily on the small landing.

Chapter Thirty-Three

At the door, Elliot dug the keys out of his pocket but paused briefly before keying the lock. He sensed someone was watching him. He spun around, scanning the small hall-like area, and when his gaze fell upon a figure skulking in the shadows of a darkened corner, he pulled his weapon. In response the figure straightened and stepped forward, speaking in a strained but familiar voice. "Hey, old buddy."

Elliot couldn't believe what he was hearing, much less seeing. He stepped back to get a better look, to make sure. It was Nick all right, looking dirty and ragged, like he'd given up his home and taken to living on the streets. Nick studied Elliot's face, his eyes darting back and forth. "We need to talk, Kenny."

"Talk? Where the hell have you been, anyway? Carmen's worried sick."

He didn't answer.

"How did you find me?" Elliot asked.

"I've been following you, trying to get my nerve up. There's something you need to know. It's the reason I'm here."

Elliot unlocked the door and led Nick into the room, closing the door behind them. Nick was shivering and his clothes were damp.

Directing him to the chair beside the window, Elliot stripped a blanket from the bed and wrapped it around him. "Talk to me, Nick. What's going on?"

"It's about Carmen."

"What are you talking about?"

"Nothing's like it used to be… Changed…everything's changed."

Nick didn't smell of liquor, but something was obviously wrong with him. "It's all right," Elliot said. "Just take it easy."

Nick pulled the blanket tighter, tucking it beneath his chin. Elliot suspected Nick's living in the past was giving him trouble coming to terms with the present.

"Why did you lie to me about Carmen, tell me she didn't want to see me?"

"It was Chief Johnson's idea. He told me that if you called I should try and discourage you. He was right, you know. Everybody was mad at you. It was better if you stayed away. And you're not the only one who has feelings for Carmen. I've always loved her. She just doesn't see it. Look, if it makes you feel any better, I've lost a hell of a lot of sleep over it." With that Nick buried his face in his hands and began to sob raggedly, his shoulders moving to accentuate his grief. "I'm sorry, old buddy. I'm so damned sorry."

"Take it easy," Elliot said, "it's all in the past. Too late to worry about it now."

"Can I stay here tonight?" Nick asked. "I'm too tired to go home." He wiped at his tear-stained face, but only succeeded in rubbing the dirt around.

Elliot sat on the edge of the bed. "That's not a good idea."

"Why not?"

Elliot thought for a moment. Was he getting ready to turn the best friend he'd ever had back out onto the streets, or was he about to let the killer loose? "I'm in trouble, Nick. I'm on the run. Being with me will only make things worse for you."

"What am I going to do?"

Nick looked scared and defeated, not the happy, carefree friend Elliot had first met in school at Porter. He'd been reduced to the lowest common denominator of his makeup, and Elliot felt responsible. He got up from the bed. "You must be hungry. Have you eaten?"

Nick shook his head.

Elliot gestured toward the bathroom, such as it was. "Why don't you get cleaned up? We'll go get something. I'm pretty hungry myself."

"No. I don't want to go back out there."

"Then I'll go get us something. What would you like?"

"I don't care," Nick said, "as long as it's hot."

"No problem. I'll lock the door. Don't let anybody in except me."

Elliot closed the door and trotted down the stairs. As he left the bar, he wondered if Casey had seen Nick come in. He didn't have to go far for food. A diner was just down the street. It wasn't the best in the world, but he couldn't afford to be choosy. He ordered cheeseburgers and fries.

When Elliot arrived back at Casey's, he was still wrestling with the idea of letting Nick stay the night, but the problem was resolved for him. He unlocked the door and walked into the room to find it empty. Nick was gone.

Elliot managed to eat part of a hamburger, but his appetite had disappeared. He walked to the window and peered out, wondering if Nick was out there somewhere. He thought about trying to get some sleep, but he worried that as soon as he closed his eyes, cops would bust down the door and come storming into the room. It wasn't likely. Beaumont had come looking for him, but Elliot had not been there at the time and Casey would have been convincing in his telling of the truth that he hadn't seen Elliot. And Nick had only found him there because he'd followed him. Like the zoo animals he'd pitied as a child, Elliot paced his cage and, like they had, he gave up occasionally and sat down, sinking into the prison's discomfort. Again he wondered about Beaumont. He knew far too much. Something wasn't right about it. He remembered Clarence Beaumont, the Coweta man he'd read about in the old papers. He'd had a son who'd dated Marcia.

Elliot strapped on his holster, threw on his jacket, and left the solitude of Casey's little corner behind. He had a lot of ground to cover. He was beginning to get some ideas about who he was looking for, but first he had to pay someone a visit.

Once he arrived at his destination, Elliot pulled into the parking lot of the building. He went inside, keeping his head down as he brushed past the people in the lobby. He took the elevator up to his floor and then roamed the burgundy colored carpet until he found the right apartment. After ringing the bell several times, he knocked but still got no answer. Beaumont was either not at home, or not answering the door.

Elliot started toward the elevator, but when he got there, the door hummed open and a man stepped out, studying Elliot a little too closely as he walked past. Elliot pretended not to notice, but the man and the shoulder holster beneath his coat had his attention. He didn't look like a cop and that worried Elliot, so he stepped onto the elevator but kept it on the floor by holding the open button.

As soon as the stranger rounded the corner, Elliot got out and ducked into the stairwell, leaving the door cracked open. Sure enough, the man came back to see if he'd gotten on the elevator. Whatever he was up to, he didn't want anybody around to witness it. Satisfied that Elliot was gone, the man went back down the hallway. Elliot waited then followed, stopping at the corner to watch.

The man stopped at Beaumont's place and pounded on the door. When he got no answer, he shook his head and leaned against the wall, waiting. His business with Beaumont was obviously important to him.

Chapter Thirty-Three

Elliot didn't like the looks of it. He decided to check it out. He walked casually down the hall toward Beaumont's apartment. By the time he got there, the man had turned away to once again bang on the door, and when Elliot spoke, the man spun around to face him with a surprised look on his face. Then, like a cornered fighter, he lunged forward, swinging wildly.

Elliot feinted left but stepped to the right, and before the man could find him again he reached over the stranger's shoulder, tore back his lapel and stripped his weapon from its holster. He pressed the barrel against the man's temple. "Something I can do for you?"

"You Beaumont?"

"Who wants to know?"

The man didn't answer. Elliot searched inside his jacket but found nothing. "Talk, even if it's a lie."

He shrugged. "The boss wants his money."

Elliot nodded and backed away. "All right, consider the message delivered."

"That's not a good idea."

"Do I look like I care?"

"You made a deal, man. I'm telling you, it ain't worth it."

The hum of the elevator caught Elliot's attention. He tightened his grip on the nine-millimeter, keeping it pointed at the man's midsection while he listened to the carpet-muffled footsteps coming down the hall. Seconds later Beaumont appeared, stopping in his tracks as he saw what was happening.

Elliot winked. "My man here says you owe him some cash."

Beaumont cautiously approached. "This isn't my doing," he said. Reaching inside his coat, he pulled out a stack of bills. "Here, that's the last of it."

Elliot backed away, giving the stranger some room.

He took the cash, stuffing it away while holding the other hand out, signifying he wanted his weapon back.

Elliot ejected the clip, cleared the chamber and tossed the nine-millimeter at the man's feet.

Without another word, he scooped it up and left.

Beaumont waited for the elevator to make its noise then he unlocked the door and went inside. Elliot followed him.

Beaumont slid out of his overcoat and put it away in a closet before tossing his keys onto the granite surface of a table beside the door. After that he sat down in a chair and switched on some music using a remote he'd picked up from the coffee table. It was classical—Bach, Beethoven—that sort of thing.

Elliot wouldn't have expected anything else. He sat on a leather sofa and put his feet on the coffee table, which earned him a disgusted glare. "First drug dealers, and now loan sharks," Elliot said. "I'm starting to think I've misjudged you. Maybe you're not such a bad guy after all."

Beaumont leaned forward, switching off the music. "Coming from you, that's an insult. What the hell are you doing here, anyway?"

Elliot wondered why Beaumont wasn't saying anything about his being in trouble. He suspected he'd been warned not to in case something like this happened. The police still didn't know Elliot knew they were looking for him. They wanted him to come to the department, walk into a trap. "I've been doing a lot of thinking about you," Elliot said, "why you know so much about me…why it means so much to you." Beaumont just stared at him, taking in his words as if they didn't fit the mouth they'd come from.

"You graduated a year ahead of me," Elliot said, "you weren't into sports, and you grew up in Coweta. Your father owned a butcher shop there. So I wouldn't have known you, would I? But you knew me. You dated Marcia. She had a way of getting to a guy, didn't she? It's been you all along, hasn't it, feeding Dombrowski information. When that didn't work you wrote a few anonymous letters to the captain." Beaumont made a move Elliot didn't like so he drew the Glock and aimed it at Beaumont's head.

The look on Beaumont's face was somewhere between fear and disbelief. He showed both hands, letting Elliot know he might have misinterpreted his actions. "Don't like to lose, do you? If ever I had any doubt about that, the past few days have erased it. Yeah, maybe I did those things. But all I did was speed up the process. I didn't kill those girls. And it wasn't me who got careless and left his knife beside the last victim. You did that all by yourself."

"Well I hate to disappoint you, Philip Jeremy Beaumont, but it wasn't me either."

"Why the hell did you pull that little stunt at the airport?"

"I had to buy some time. Our killer has a habit of dropping out of sight when the heat gets too high. If he fades back into the scenery now, we may never catch him. I can't let that happen."

Beaumont's face reflected Elliot's intensity. "How do you explain the knife, and your fingerprints?"

"It's a long story, Beaumont. I doubt you'd understand."

Elliot took a moment to consider the rest of his answer. But how could he express this obsession in words? "I've been tangled up in this guy's web for a long time," he said. "I have to put a stop to it. I've no other choice."

"What makes you think I won't call Dombrowski the minute you walk out of here?"

"I suspect you will, but you look a little ragged out. Getting tough to peddle your wares, is it?"

Beaumont frowned. "No thanks to you. Tremain was…" His words trailed off, letting the sentence die.

Elliot grinned. "I have a knack for knowing the wrong kind of people. It can get a lot worse. I can see to that, if you like."

"A few days ago that might have scared me. But not anymore. You're all washed up, Elliot. You won't get away with this. Sooner or later they'll catch up to you."

Keeping the Glock aimed at Beaumont, Elliot stood. "I'd hoped you would see things differently," he said, finding the phone and smashing it and the base station. After that he searched Beaumont, taking his weapon and his cell phone. "Don't try to follow me. It won't do you any good. And by the time you get to a phone I'll be gone." He cupped his hand around Beaumont's chin. "Don't worry, kid. If I was going to hurt you, you'd already be hurt."

As Elliot walked across the parking lot toward his car, the thought that Beaumont was being a little too cooperative ran through his head. He dismissed it. He had other things to worry about. He wanted to return to Club Gemini for a little chat with Metcalf. But not just yet. He had a few things to take care of first. He made a few stops and went back to Casey's.

A short time later, Elliot looked in the mirror, but the reflection that stared back wasn't right, though it smiled when he smiled and mimicked his every move. The reflection's hair was black, not sandy, and he wore blue denim jeans, sunglasses, and a black leather jacket, clothes Elliot would never have worn. And he already had a few days growth of beard. It was a good disguise.

Elliot drove downtown to Club Gemini, and when he parked and climbed out of the car, a crowd of people milling around the parking lot scurried away, frightened by his sudden arrival. Before he got to the door of the club he took his hand away from the grip of the Glock, telling himself to take it easy, practice some self-restraint. He went inside, glancing at a few familiar faces in the crowd as he made his way to Metcalf's office. Once again, Metcalf came out before Elliot got there, and going against his own warnings, Elliot immediately grabbed him, shoving him against the wall.

The man with the English accent saw what was happening and came rushing over. "Take it easy, mate. There's no need for that."

Rage ran through Elliot like a sickness. Holding Metcalf with one hand, he used the other to stiff-arm the Englishman, stopping him in his tracks. He heard the words, "Not now, pretty boy. I'm not in the mood," escape his lips. The Englishman quietly backed away. Elliot turned his attention back to Metcalf.

"Leave me alone," he said.

Elliot clamped his hand around Metcalf's throat. "I don't want to hurt you, but I don't like being lied to, so I just might. The word *cooperation* comes to mind. It would be in your best interest to embrace it. Do you understand?"

Metcalf nodded, doing his best to stop the noises from gurgling out of his throat. Elliot reminded himself to use restraint, but Metcalf wasn't making it easy. He couldn't stop trembling. It was like holding a frightened puppy. Elliot breathed hard, like an animal ready to pounce. "I'm going to ask you again. The man in the pictures I showed you. You know him, don't you?"

Metcalf didn't want to answer, but when his eyes locked onto Elliot's he nodded.

"I need a name," Elliot said.

Metcalf shook his head. "Please, he'll kill me."

Elliot squeezed harder.

"Ralph," he said. "He calls himself Ralph."

"Ralph who?"

He tried to shrug. "That's all I know. I swear."

Elliot fought to regain his composure. "Why are you so afraid of him?"

He shook his head.

Again Elliot applied pressure to his throat. "Why?"

"He used to hang around here, but not anymore. He's bad news, freaking crazy."

"I need his full name."

Metcalf closed his eyes, and when he reopened them they showed even more fear that before. "That's all I know. But there is something different about him. James Dean. He dresses and acts like James Dean."

At that moment, Elliot's anger crystallized and drained, like sand from a busted hourglass. The dancer at the gentlemen's club where Michelle Baker worked had said the same thing. She'd said someone unusual had been there the night before Michelle disappeared. She said he looked just like James Dean. "Do you know where I can find him?"

Metcalf straightened his clothes. "Try the cemetery. He's a freaking spook if I ever saw one."

Chapter Thirty-Four

It was after 9:00 p.m. when Elliot left Metcalf's club, but he had a few stops to make before calling it a night. He'd convinced one of the clerks at Hillcrest to do a records search, and she'd come up the name and address of the nurse on duty the night Cynthia Kincaid had come in to give birth. He already had the nurse's name from going through the logs, but he wanted to be sure, and the address and phone number were helpful. As he dialed the number, he headed in the direction of the nurse's home. He arrived there with his luck still holding out. Christina Martin answered on the third ring. Elliot explained what he wanted and she agreed. A few minutes later, he was sitting in her living room.

"Thanks for seeing me on such short notice, Ms. Martin, and at this time of night."

"Not a problem," she said. "I wasn't doing anything anyway, except for watching television. What's this all about?"

"Just tying up a few loose ends," Elliot said. He took a sip of the coffee she'd given him then sat it down. "You were on duty the night Cynthia Kincaid came to the hospital and gave birth to her daughter, Rachael?"

"Yes, sir. I was there all right."

Elliot got his notepad and flipped to the correct page. "You made an entry in your log, something about not trusting Mrs. Kincaid's statements?"

"Yes I did. You see, she didn't give birth at Hillcrest."

"Where did the birth occur?"

Christina Martin sat down. She'd been standing until then. "It seems she waited a little too long—not convinced it was really happening was how she put it—before she decided she'd better get herself to the hospital. Her baby was born on the way, before she got there. At least that was her story."

Elliot jotted down the information. "What was it, exactly, that made you doubt what she said?"

Christina Martin sipped her coffee then said, "I worked in the maternity ward, Detective, and had for ten years at the time. Back then, mothers and their babies were my life. I think I would've known a newborn when I saw one."

Elliot leaned forward, his attention piqued by Ms. Martin's last statement. "So what are you trying to say?"

"That baby wasn't born on the way to the hospital that night. She was at least twenty-four hours old, probably more than that, if the truth be known. Anyway, I knew something wasn't right about the whole thing. That's why I logged it in that way. You know how it is with folks filing lawsuits at the drop of a hat. I wanted it on record that I didn't think the mother was telling the whole truth."

"Did anything ever come of it?"

She shook her head. "Not that I'm aware of. But I didn't stop there. I notified the Department of Human Services, too."

"Why did you do that?"

"I don't know. Like I said, something about the whole thing just didn't feel right. Now that I think about it, maybe it was the look on Cynthia Kincaid's face that got me going. She looked scared, like she wanted to cry out for help but was afraid to. I guess I was worried what she might do, in case she was suffering from postpartum depression, or God knows what else."

"So your concern was for the child's safety?"

"I was worried about both of them, the mother and the daughter."

Elliot nodded. "I must say I'm impressed with your memory. It seems to be quite good."

"Why do you say that?"

"More than twenty years have passed since the incident, yet you recall it as if it were yesterday."

She laughed. "Well, I wish I could take credit for that, but I can't. I have a friend who still works at the hospital. She called me right after you came in, told me you were asking around about it. Of course that jogged my memory." She paused then continued, "I did worry about it for a long time, though, wondering if I should have pursued the matter further. Is that why you're here? Did something go wrong? Did something happen?"

Elliot thought about the empty room in Cynthia Kincaid's house where it looked as if someone had been locked away. Images of the suggestive photos he'd seen of young Rachael also ran through his head. The old photographs more than hinted at a history of sexual abuse. He could have said, *Yeah, Ms. Martin, your intuitions weren't screaming at you for nothing the night when Cynthia Kincaid and her new baby came to the hospital,* but he didn't. The way he saw it, Christina Martin had already beaten herself up enough over it through the years. She didn't need any additional guilt hanging over her. What he said was, "Just tying up a few loose ends, Ms. Martin. You've been most helpful."

Elliot walked out of Christina Martin's house wondering about Rachael Kincaid. He'd suspected all along that Lagayle Zimmerman was the key because she was different, didn't fit the profile. And Rachael...well, she knew a lot more about Lagayle than she was saying. That much he was sure of as well.

When Elliot pulled into the parking lot at Casey's, he saw a black and white patrol car driving through. He tried to act casual, turning into the first empty space he came to, but the squad car didn't leave as it should have. Instead the driver wheeled the vehicle around and came back, heading in Elliot's direction. Elliot didn't know whether to stay put or get out and walk toward the building as if the cop car being there meant nothing to him. He decided on the latter, waving a friendly hello as the squad car drew near, the driver having chosen to cruise up the very lane in which he'd parked. Elliot kept walking, but as the black and white passed by, the officer's face seemed as big as a billboard and he was staring right at Elliot, flashing a grin that said, *we gotcha now, boy*. But the car didn't stop, it just kept on rolling, finally leaving the lot altogether. The disguise was working.

When Elliot walked in, Casey glanced up. "What the hell's going on, Elliot? Squad cars have been patrolling the parking lot."

"Yeah, I noticed."

Casey sat a beer in front of Elliot. "That's not the whole of it. A Captain Dombrowski called, wanting to know if I'd seen you or if you had contacted me. They're obviously looking for you."

Elliot sipped the cold beer. "What did you tell Dombrowski?"

Casey looked hurt by that. "If I'd told him anything other than a lie, then somebody would be here, wouldn't they?"

"Sorry. It just seemed like a question that needed asking."

"What the hell's going on, Elliot?"

"I'm in a jam, Casey. I'll get it straightened out, though."

"What are you going to do?"

Elliot didn't want to say he didn't know because that wasn't completely true, and even though he wasn't sure, he didn't want to sound that way. "I just need a little more time," he said.

Casey leaned forward. "Give it to me straight, son. Have you done something you shouldn't have?"

They stared at each other for a moment, during which Elliot thought he saw a bead of sweat trickle down Casey's forehead. "It's all a big mix-up, Casey. I need to get some rest. Is it okay if I sleep on the sofa in your office?"

Chapter Thirty-Five

Elliot tried to find a comfortable spot but he couldn't, and when he could no longer tolerate lying there, he sat up on the leather sofa and took in the darkness of Casey's office. The liquid crystal display of the clock said it was 6:00 a.m. Casey was already there. Elliot could hear him in the bar.

Elliot took the opportunity to slip out of the office, avoiding any further discussion. Stepping outside, he walked across the parking lot until he reached the space where he'd left Sykes's car. The morning world seemed serene and unreal, and Elliot felt even more detached from it than usual. He saw no patrol cars as he climbed into the car and drove away.

Being victims of time, the schools that Rachael Kincaid would have attended—Longfellow, Horace Mann, and Central High—were either gone or being used for something other than their original function. Elliot wondered if any of the students who'd roamed the halls of those educational palaces ever dreamed that their school would end up a hospital for Native Americans, a medium security correctional facility, or the administrative offices for a utility company. Somehow he didn't think so. Anyway, he figured he could get the information he needed at the district administration office.

The lady behind the desk said her name was Sandra Lee. It fit her. She was attractive, not in a flirty or ostentatious way, but rather in a wholesome, motherly way.

She smiled. "Now, young man,"—She called him that even though Elliot had identified himself as a police detective—"What can I do for you?"

"I need some information," Elliot said, "on Rachael Hannah Kincaid. I'd like to know if she got her education in Tulsa, and which schools she attended. She would have started around 1983, and my guess is she would have attended Longfellow. I'm looking for confirmation, as well as anything out of the ordinary...not that there would be, but just in case."

"I see. Well, make yourself comfortable. This could take awhile."

Elliot thanked Ms. Lee then asked her where he might find a cup of coffee. She gave him directions to the break room, and when he got back she was sitting at her desk, smiling, with her hands folded together.

"Any luck?" Elliot asked.

She nodded. "You were right on both accounts, about the date and the school."

Elliot thought about Ms. Lee's answer then asked, "Did she continue on through middle and high school?"

She smiled. "I wasn't always in administration, Mr. Elliot. I used to teach. I would've been pleased to have you as a student. You're perceptive, and that's a rare quality in people these days. Rachael attended school through the fifth grade. However, she didn't continue after that. Her mother decided that home schooling would be better and pulled her out." She shook her head. "I hate to see that. I realize parents usually have good intentions, but they can't begin to give their children the education we can. They're doing them a huge disservice."

Elliot stood, extending his hand for Ms. Lee to shake. "Thank you," he said. "You've been most helpful."

With a much clearer picture of what he had to do, Elliot drove back to Casey's place. Along the way, he called Nick's garage. He didn't know if he expected anyone to answer, but someone did. Whoever it was didn't speak, but Elliot could hear breathing. "Nick," he said, "what's going on?"

The breather didn't answer.

"Why did you leave without saying anything? That makes twice you've done that. Come on, buddy; talk to me."

The breathing continued for a few seconds, but no words came over the phone, only a clicking sound as the person on the other end disconnected.

Elliot pulled into the parking lot at Casey's. He realized he was ignoring the voice inside his head that told him he should be more careful. He could only guess how long his internal alarm had been going off, but as he entered the building it began to get through. The hair on the back of his neck felt like cactus needles, and he realized his more cautious nature had been lulled to sleep by the combined forces of raw emotions and exhaustion.

Elliot slowed to a casual walk as he surveyed the area. Near the bar he saw Detective Cunningham and someone who looked like Mendez at a pool table. Elliot pleaded with his survival instinct to accept his apology for ignorance and come forward and tell him what to do next, but all it would say was, *I told you so.* Elliot figured tipping his hand now, letting them know he was aware of their presence, would only make matters worse and drastically cut any time he may have for evasive maneuvers. Glancing over his shoulder, he saw no other officers waiting outside of the front door. They had not staked out the building. It was just the two detectives.

When the heavyset man at the pool table turned around and started toward him—not a direct approach, but a casual slanted cantor—Elliot saw that it was indeed Detective Mendez.

Mendez, though, had a look of bewilderment on his face. He wasn't sure if it was Elliot or not: The disguise. Elliot kept walking. The fact that they had him was obvious, rendering any resisting efforts as tantamount to lunacy, though admittedly he leaned that way at times.

Mendez called after him, "Excuse me, sir. I need to ask you some questions."

The moment was a lifetime, those few seconds while Elliot saw the events of the murders flash before his eyes. He knew there was a killer out there and that he could not let his arrest put a grinding stop to the wheels of justice, but he also thought of Carmen and his son Wayne going on with their lives without knowing how Elliot truly felt about them. Suddenly, he knew he could not let that happen. He would get free somehow and go to Carmen, tell her he loved her more than life, and he was sorry for the suffering he had put her through. After that, fate could take its course. It was then that Elliot's cell phone rang. He wanted to ignore the ring, but then thought better of it. He should act natural: business as usual. He waved, just a minute, to Mendez then pulled the phone, "Yeah?"

"Hey, Mister, is that you?"

"Who is this?" Elliot asked. But the small, frightened voice sounded familiar. "Wayne?"

"Ma-mom said I should call… if something happened."

"What's up, buddy?"

"I don't know. Someone's at the house. I gotta go."

The phone went dead. Elliot moved quickly, slamming Mendez into the wall, the impact dazing him into a momentary state of incoherence. Elliot darted up the back stairs.

As anticipated, Mendez recovered quickly and Elliot could hear him coming up the stairs behind him. Elliot turned and kicked the oncoming detective in the face. The action worked well, knocking Mendez down the stairs. In almost the same fluid motion, Elliot spun around and unlocked the door to the apartment. He ran across the floor and dove through the glass of the window, rolling onto the fire escape.

When Elliot dropped to the ground, Cunningham was coming around the corner of the building. "Give it up, Elliot. If you're innocent, it'll all work out. Come on, pal."

Mendez was coming down the fire escape. Elliot raised his hands as if surrendering. Cunningham smiled and holstered his weapon. But when he approached Elliot to retrieve his weapon, Elliot grabbed him and slung him into Mendez. Then Elliot turned and ran, jumping into Sykes's car when he reached the vehicle. He jammed the key into the ignition and fired the car to life, tearing out of the parking lot in a full tilt run.

Chapter Thirty-Six

Elliot knew he wouldn't get far in an identified car. Options flew through his head like distorted images in a carnival house of mirrors. He drove down Cincinnati Avenue until he reached the expressway then headed east. It was the route they would expect him to take, but he sped onto the highway nonetheless, flooring the Monte Carlo. Seconds later, a black and white unit heading west took the next exit, its lights flashing. The driver had caught sight of Elliot's fast moving vehicle. Another one appeared in his rearview mirror, some distance behind. Desperation and regret flowed through Elliot's veins like a torrent, and with no choices other than to keep running he mashed the accelerator pedal to the floor, burying the speedometer needle to the right.

Elliot began to gain on his adversaries, putting a couple of miles between himself and the patrol cars. In a near-reflexive action, he pulled the gear selector down into a lower gear, aiding the brakes in slowing the vehicle as he took the next exit. Even with that the car's momentum outweighed the action and the vehicle skidded hard into the curb as Elliot fought to maintain control. With the tires protesting against the pavement, he turned onto the access road, taking the first stop sign to the right. He passed the busy convenience store that had grabbed his attention and caused him to pull off the expressway.

Elliot drove deep into the neighborhood he'd entered until he found a suitable spot. When he found a stopping place, he pulled to the curb and parked, leaving Sykes's car behind as he got out and walked back to the convenience store. He went inside and purchased a ball cap.

Elliot walked outside after ditching the sunglasses and putting on the cap and waited beside the corner of the building until someone came along and left their car running. The prize was a little unexpected, a low-slung Honda with tinted windows and loud music pouring from the interior. He'd hoped for something less conspicuous, but it was pretty much a take-what-you-could-get situation.

As soon as the driver ducked into the store, Elliot jumped into the vehicle and backed out, straightening the car quickly as he left the parking lot. He drove back to the expressway and pulled onto the entrance ramp, the urgent sensation that he needed to get to Carmen growing stronger by the minute. It was as if a channel between them had been opened, instigated by his feelings for her that he had secreted away, only to be released and awakened by their recent reconnection. He suspected the path he'd taken would surely end in disaster, but Carmen was all that mattered now, she and Wayne.

As Elliot drew near the outskirts of Porter, he knew the radical car he was driving would draw attention. It couldn't be helped. He held the wheel tightly and drove to Carmen's house. When he arrived, he pulled off the road and parked on the grassy shoulder, thoughts of what he might encounter swirling through his head.

The dull sound of metal clanking together behind Elliot told him he'd gotten out of the car, and the increasing size of the front door said he was moving in that direction, though his feet didn't feel the ground. Then something that made his blood run cold caught his attention, gripping his heart with fear. No one answered his banging on the door or his stabbing of the bell. No one answered because no one was there, and no one was there because *it* was there: the same cursed message that'd been on the window of Johnnie's car. It wasn't a *Johnnie Boy was here*, or even a *Johnnie Boy*, but an interrupted, scribbled-in-paint *Johnnie B.* But it was there and it was enough.

Elliot tried the door but it was locked. He took a step back and delivered a hard kick, but it held fast. It'd been dead-bolted. He reached for the Glock and he saw his hand take aim as the blast busted the lock, taking part of the door with it.

Walls flew past Elliot's field of vision, walls of pictures and family things, but no real family came with them. They were gone. He'd taken them. Elliot continued through the house, calling for anyone, but he received no answer. Defeated, he slowly retraced his steps. As he was about to leave, he heard a muffled cry coming from the closet by the front door. He readied his weapon and flung the door open, but what he saw there was not an intruder. It was Wayne, huddling in the corner, frightened to tears.

"Please don't hurt me, mister."

Elliot holstered the weapon and brought Wayne to his feet, pulling him close, the boy's head falling against his stomach. "It's okay," Elliot said softly. "I won't hurt you." Seconds later, he asked, "Do you know where your mother is?"

Wayne shook his head. "Someone was at the house. I was riding my bike, and as I came down the street I saw a car. It looked like they were fighting and she was trying to make my mom get in the car. I rode real fast, but by the time I got there, the car was pulling away. I tried to follow them but I couldn't keep up. I went back to the house but no one was there. Mom was gone. When I heard you at the front door, I thought they'd come back for me so I hid in the closet." Wayne began sobbing again.

"It's all right. You did the best you could." Elliot said, pausing to stoke the soft hair of Wayne's head. "Did you see who it was?"

The boy shook his head. "Just some lady."

"What kind of car was it?"

"I don't know. A brown one, I think."

Elliot let go of his son, thinking about what the boy had said, and as Elliot reached into his coat pocket and pulled out the folded piece of paper Rachael Kincaid had given him with her phone number on it, bringing the note to his face and taking in the sweet smell of perfume that lingered there, it all fell into place. A suspicion that'd been forming for some time solidified into an understanding. "All right," he said. "You did good. Is there a friend or someone you could stay with? I have to go find your mother."

Wayne shook his head. "No, I want to go with you."

"That's not a good idea."

"Please, Mr. Elliot? I don't want to go to anybody's house. I'm scared. I want to go with you."

Against his better judgment, Elliot agreed. To be honest, he wasn't crazy about the idea of letting the boy out of his sight, anyway.

Elliot drove into town, pulling into the parking lot of Nick's garage. Leaving Wayne in the car, he started toward the office door. It was padlocked. Pressing his face against the glass, he peered inside but saw only darkness. As he turned away, walking toward the garage bay doors, he heard the sound of another car pulling into the lot, and when he turned back he saw Chief Johnson walking toward him with his weapon drawn and ready. Johnson paused directly in front of him, and Elliot saw something familiar in the chief's eyes. They showed fear and anger, but they also reflected concern. "What are you doing here, Kenny?"

When Elliot spoke, his voice was ragged. "Carmen's gone. Wayne saw someone take her. You have to help me find her."

Johnson stepped closer, his eyes watering as he reached inside Elliot's jacket and took the Glock. "You need to come with me."

Charlie was old and slow, and Elliot could easily have broken away, but he suspected the old police officer knew where Carmen was and the only way he was going to find out for sure was to cooperate. "Sure," he said, "just give me a minute."

Elliot walked over to the car where Wayne was. Speaking softly, he said, "Will you do me a favor?"

Wayne nodded.

"Something's not right here."

"You got that right."

"Yeah," Elliot said. "Here's what I want you to do. I'm going to get in the car with Chief Johnson. After we've gone, go to the police station and wait for me there. If I'm not back in one hour, tell Deputy Stanton everything that's happened. But not until then, okay?"

"This is about my mom, isn't it? Something bad has happened to her. Why do things like this have to happen?"

"I don't know," Elliot said. "There are a lot of bad people out there. But there are a lot of good ones, too. And as long as we have people like your mom around, it's still worth fighting for."

"Is my mom going to be okay?"

"I'll find her," Elliot said.

Johnson stood beside his car, waiting, and when Elliot got there the chief put him in the backseat behind the security cage. "The word's out," Johnson said. "You're a wanted man. I have to take you in."

"All right," Elliot said, "but first tell me where Carmen is."

"What makes you think I know?"

"Your boy left his calling card on her door."

"Don't worry, she's safe. She called and told me about seeing the prowler again. I told her she could stay at my place for awhile until things blew over."

"She's at your house?"

Johnson didn't answer.

"I need to see her, Charlie. I need to know she's safe. Then you can take me in."

Charlie Johnson put the car in gear and backed out of the parking lot. "I wish I could help you, Kenny, but it's kind of out of my hands now." Then he whispered, almost to himself, "It's gone too far."

Elliot didn't like the sound of Charlie's voice, and a heavy sinking sensation came over him. "Why don't you let me go, tell them I got away?"

Johnson seemed to think it over then shook his head. "It's too late for that. Where would you go? Where would you hide?"

"Maybe I won't have to. Come on, Charlie. We both know you can prove I'm innocent."

Charlie didn't stop at the municipal building, but kept on driving, pulling off the main road to circle around the back way, and when

Charlie turned onto Dixieland Avenue, Elliot's suspicion of bad things to come increased tenfold. "Where are you taking me?" he asked.

"You said you wanted to see Carmen."

"This isn't the way to your place."

"I know. Just be patient."

Elliot saw where they were going, and when Charlie Johnson pulled to the side of the road, stopping the car in front of the old house where Elliot had lived as a child, a knot formed in his stomach. "Why are we stopping here?"

"It's a good place to hide, don't you think?"

Elliot began to wonder if Charlie had reconsidered his plea and was still willing to help him. Somehow he didn't think so.

Charlie got out of the car, opened the back door, and stepped back. Porter's chief of police might have been slow, but he wasn't stupid, and Elliot knew for a fact that he was deadly accurate with the .38 he was aiming at Elliot's head. He gestured for Elliot to walk toward the house, and as they tramped through the weeds, finally reaching the front door, Elliot suspected he'd better start buying some time. Trouble was ahead, even more than the usual trouble that blew like dust through the streets of Porter.

"Open the door," Charlie said, "and step inside."

Elliot did as he was told. Charlie came in behind him and closed the door.

"I know more about this than you think, Charlie."

"What the hell are you talking about?"

"Your sister, Cynthia," Elliot said. "She married someone you didn't like very much, a man named Terrance Kincaid. Looks like you were right about him all along. Together he and your sister turned out some pretty disturbed children. By the way, I had a little chat with your friend, Bob Crawley, the newspaper editor. He said you were quite the hero, saved a few people from becoming prisoners of war. One of them was Lyndon Shriver. I had a little chat with him, too. He feels indebted to you, even after he falsified the autopsy reports."

Johnson's eyes darted back and forth. "So maybe it all ends here."

"Maybe," Elliot said, "but you can't be sure. Perhaps I told someone else what I know. Maybe I even wrote it down somewhere, just in case something like this happened."

The look on Charlie's face was that of a caged animal. "You're lying, trying to save your skin."

"Why don't you tell me where Carmen is?"

"Turn around and face the wall," Charlie said.

Again Elliot did as he was told. "There's been a lot of killing, Charlie. It's time to put a stop to it."

"The time for talk is over, son."

"I know about your nephew. I always wondered about that little back room on your house. I had a look around in there while you were getting dressed after I came to visit. I saw the autographed football. It was your nephew's. He stayed there, didn't he? You can't protect him forever."

Charlie didn't answer.

Elliot waited a few seconds then slowly turned around, but Charlie Johnson was gone. Elliot was alone. He started for the door, but a sharp pain across the back of his head brought him to his knees. For a moment he couldn't see. It was all he could do to hold onto consciousness. Then someone grabbed his hand and began to cuff him, but whoever it was, Elliot could tell they didn't have experience. He let the stranger find his left wrist, but when he felt the touch of metal on his right one he moved his hand, creating a maligned position. It hurt like hell as the binding clamped shut just below his knuckles, but with effort he thought he could wiggle free.

Once secured, Elliot was led into the back bedroom where blankets had been put over the windows, and when Elliot's captor closed the door, darkness enclosed the room. Someone else was in the room as well. Elliot could hear him breathing. He took a guess. "You don't want to do this, Charlie. You're in enough trouble already."

"You're the one that's in trouble. Everybody thinks you're guilty. It'll look like just another one of your murders, a lover's spat gone bad. Since they'll find you here and know they already have their man, it'll blow over in a few months and everything will be fine."

"No it won't, Charlie. The killing won't stop. If you think it will, you're fooling yourself. How many lives have to be wasted before you wake up?"

Johnson stabbed a gun barrel into Elliot's head. "Shut up."

Thoughts of rushing the aging police officer and throwing him to the ground went through Elliot's mind, but a strong hand on his shoulder followed by another gun against his head put his escape attempt on hold. And then a battery powered lamp was turned on, and when the light crept across the room, Elliot saw Carmen, fastened to the wall, her eyes half-closed as if she'd been drugged, with only the binding chains keeping her from falling to the floor. But that wasn't all the light revealed. It also showed the identity of their true captor, the one who held the other gun to Elliot's head.

She laughed, then strode across the room and sat on a tall swivel chair, her long legs crossing. In one hand she held a cigarette, but the other toted a Glock handgun, probably, Elliot suspected, the one Charlie had taken from him. It was Rachael Johnson—or more correctly Rachael Kincaid. "Hello, Kenny," she said. "I should've killed you a long time ago. It certainly would've simplified things. But I just couldn't bring myself to do it. You see, we have a kinship of sorts, a metaphysical snafu that tangled up our destinies." She paused and smiled, pain showing in her eyes. "Now it seems we've come full circle. You should've left well enough alone. But you want to know what bothers me the most about this? I was really starting to like you. We could've had something special together." She stopped and looked at Carmen. "I just love Hispanic women, Kenny. They're so sexy. You two will have plenty of time to get reacquainted. It'll take awhile for anyone to find you here, and even when they do, it'll be like my uncle said: a lover's spat gone bad. You simply got mad and killed your little girlfriend. Then, out of remorse, you took your own life."

"Why don't you let her go?" Elliot asked. "It's me you want, isn't it?"

Chapter Thirty-Six

"Well, I just can't do that. Too many loose ends, and all here for the tying."

Elliot took several deep breaths, but his throbbing hand refused to relax. He had to hurry. Swelling would soon set in, and if that happened he could kiss freedom good-bye. He began to pull, not a yank like a thorn removal, but a slow pressure that sent shards of pain through his hand. "I know why you do what you do," he said, "killing those beautiful women. Why don't we talk about it?"

She glared at Elliot. "You've got it all wrong. I'm not your killer."

"But you did murder Lagayle Zimmerman."

Rachael shook her head. "I had to," she said, getting off the chair and walking toward Carmen. "She would've ruined everything. Just like your little girlfriend here."

Elliot had to distract Rachael, keep her occupied. "Let's not forget my friend, Officer David Conley."

"I didn't mean to kill him."

"But you did. You're just as bad as your brother. In fact, you're just like him. After all, you are twins, aren't you, Ralph?"

In a voice that had already become louder and deeper, Rachael said, "Don't call me that. I'm not Ralph. Ralph's dead."

"No," Elliot said, "you are. I found your grave in your backyard."

In an instant, Rachael's face went from ice to fire, and her jaw twitched as she took off the wig, letting it drop to the floor like a dead rat. Then she paused, as if she hadn't caught up with herself, the transition being much more than a simple charade. Her presence actually seemed to change as she shook off her well-worn femininity, but when she removed her contact lenses, lowering her head and dropping them one by one into her cupped hand, it was then that Elliot saw the little boy who'd lived like he wasn't there, locked away and hidden from the world as if he were no more than a thought in someone's mind. And once again, Elliot found himself looking into those eyes, the ones that had peered through the car window at him and Marcia Barnes that night, and at that moment he came to realize he was standing face to face with Rachael's brother. He was looking into the disturbed, hazel eyes of

Ralph Kincaid. It was the strangest thing Elliot had ever witnessed, and had he not seen it with his own eyes, he would not have believed it.

Elliot glanced at Charlie Johnson, who looked completely dazed. "I know all about you, Ralph. We used to see you walking through Miller's field and sitting in the stands at the football games. And let's not forget, peeking through the windows of parked cars at the Point."

Ralph Kincaid lowered the Glock then pulled a knife from the purse he carried, a black-handled knife. "You should've quit while you were ahead, cop. Now I'm going to do your girlfriend, fix her up real nice. And you get to watch."

Elliot continued his verbal assault. "Marcia Barnes was your first, wasn't she, Ralph? You killed her because she reminded you of Rachael. But more to the point, she reminded you of yourself, what you'd become."

The distraction began to work. Ralph Kincaid came toward Elliot, away from Carmen. "Your father is to blame," Elliot said. "He made you what you are. It's kind of funny, isn't it? I spent most of my life wishing I could meet my father, and now I 'm glad I didn't. He wasn't a very nice person, was he?"

In a flash of movement, Ralph made the distance from his side of the room to Elliot's, dropping the knife and grasping Elliot's throat with his free hand. "You shut the hell up."

Charlie Johnson spoke, "Don't do this, Ralph. Please don't."

"Papa Terrance made you do it," Elliot said, "forced you to pretend to be Rachael whenever the need arose to cover her murder."

Ralph's eyes grew wet. "She torments me, screams at me from her grave. I have to shut her up."

"But she loves you, looks out for you, killing those who would harm you."

"Don't kid yourself. She's no angel, our Rachael. Looking out for number one, that's what she's doing. I resurrected her. If I die, she dies."

With a collage of razor sharp pains, Elliot tore his hand free of the cuff. "But it didn't stop there, did it, Ralph? Once Papa saw how well you carried out the performance, he made you become your sister more often. He made you become sweet Rachael just for him, to satisfy his longing for her at night."

Ralph's lips quivered, his eyes shining with moisture, and it was then that Elliot made his move. He spun loose from his captor's grip and caught him square on the chin with a hard right. Ralph stumbled, dropped the Glock, then came at Elliot. Elliot didn't have time to pick up the fallen weapon. He sidestepped and dug his left fist into Ralph's solar plexus. But still he came, and then he was on top of Elliot, those burning eyes glaring like hot coals.

Ralph Kincaid was incredibly powerful, running on adrenaline, and Elliot couldn't match his strength, but he could take his mobility. Lowering his left shoulder, Elliot plowed into his attacker, lifting him from his feet. Once he had him, he continued the forward motion, running him into the wall. When Elliot released him, Ralph fell to the floor.

Elliot couldn't find the Glock, but the knife was there. He scooped it up and spun around behind Ralph, putting the blade to his throat. "Capital T for Papa Terrance, Ralphie."

Coming from the wall where she was chained, Elliot heard the weak but distinctive voice of Carmen. "Kenny?"

With Elliot's attention loosened, Ralph made a grunting noise, like that of an animal, and suddenly their roles were reversed. Elliot lay on the floor with his arms splayed out, and stared at the angry man hovering over him, holding the Glock in his face. Elliot knew it was over, and that his recently acquired understanding would die right there in the house where it had all started, though the touch of cold steel against his hand brought a glimmer of hope. A flash belched from the barrel of the Glock followed by a deafening blast. At the same time, maybe a little before and even as Elliot's soul prepared for his executioner's prevailing effort, his flesh reacted to the chance it had been given. He fired one well-placed shot from the .38 Chief Johnson had slipped into his hand. Elliot waited to feel the pain of the bullet tearing through his chest but it never came. Ralph Kincaid crumpled to the floor with blood drooling from the hole in his head.

Carmen was sobbing pitifully.

Charlie Johnson dropped to his knees and he too began to cry, lifting his nephew's head from the floor to cradle it in his arms while blood trickled down the dead man's face and stained the chief's shirt. With sorrow and tenderness befitting the love of a father, the kind of father Ralph Kincaid never had, Charlie held the boy and cried. It was as painful to watch as it was to hear. "He loved going to the games," Charlie said, "watching you and Johnnie play. To be like you and Johnnie was all he ever wanted."

Tears rolled down Charlie's cheeks, falling onto the face of Ralph Kincaid, the tiny swells of saltwater diluting the blood in those areas where they mixed. "He lived in shame, afraid those who might look him in the eye would see what he was, what he'd done."

Emotion settled over Elliot like a heavy fog as he watched Deputy Stanton walk into the room, going quickly to the side of Chief Johnson. Stanton picked up the Glock that lay beside Ralph Kincaid then, gesturing toward Carmen, asked Charlie for the keys. Stanton in turn gave them to Elliot.

Elliot turned away from the sadness and went to the wall where Carmen was shackled. Cautiously he unlocked the bindings, and like a rag doll she melted into his arms. She was barely conscious as Elliot helped her out of the house, but still he could hear her words as she mumbled them, for she said that she loved him. They were powerful, heartfelt words.

Chapter Thirty-Seven

Elliot noticed the glow from the neighbors' security light scattering dimly across his room as he leaned back against the headboard. He wasn't concerned about the light. It was so easily set off it almost didn't matter, and at times like this he actually found it comforting. He'd dreamed of Carmen. She'd come to him in the middle of the night, tiptoeing into his room and taking his hand to place upon her rounded stomach. "He lives," she'd said. "I carried your child, now I carry his."

With that Carmen began to laugh, though it wasn't the soft laughter of the woman Elliot loved, but the harsh and heavy breathing of a man, and when she leaned closer, bringing her face into the glow of the moonlight, it wasn't Carmen that Elliot saw, but the ugly and distorted face of Terrance Kincaid.

Elliot had sat up in a cold sweat, breathing hard until he had realized it was a dream and had fallen against the headboard where he now lay. It was the third night this week the nightmare had brought him out of his sleep. He could only attribute it to the thoughts of unfinished business that crawled around inside his head. It was Carmen. Elliot had tried to arrange dinner with her, to talk things out and see where they stood. But Carmen was still uncertain about her marriage.

Once again Elliot owed his freedom and his life to Charlie Johnson, who'd made sure Deputy Stanton knew Elliot had nothing to do with what was going on in that room, and that he would not have been there in the first place had he not been brought against his will. Charlie told Stanton everything—the whole story, beginning with his finding out about the existence of his nephew. Elliot had asked Johnson why he hadn't done something earlier, stepped forward to help Ralph, but Charlie had only confirmed what was already obvious. He'd said he hadn't known about the boy, until it was too late. No one had. Terrance Kincaid had kept his son locked away in a boarded-up part of the house. The only child the family—or anyone else for that matter—had ever known about was Rachael.

Charlie blamed himself, claiming responsibility for everything, though his only crime was in doing the world a favor by putting a bullet between the eyes of his sister's husband. Then Charlie Johnson had told his deputy he had some things to take care of before turning himself in. God only knows what was going through his mind. Anyway he took one last walk through his house, the one he'd loved and maintained with a fresh coat of paint every year, then went outside and leaned against one of the old oak trees in his backyard, put his service revolver in his mouth, and pulled the trigger.

Time had passed since the ordeal. Dombrowski had given Elliot a thirty-day suspension and it was nearly over. The black-handled knife with Elliot's fingerprints would have been tough to explain had Nick not corroborated the fact that Ralph Kincaid had come into his garage that day, pretending to ask for directions. Kincaid had seen Elliot handling the knife, and had broken into the garage and stolen it. Nick also confirmed the break-in, and the missing knife. Kincaid knew the body of his sister, Rachael—actually Suzie Miller, the waitress he'd murdered—had not been discovered, so he returned to the scene and left the knife there, hoping the effort would throw the police off his trail. It had nearly worked.

Nick was back in Porter, spending his days at the garage and working on cars. Maybe it all turned out best for him. He'd kept to himself mostly, and no one had understood the depth of his problems. As it turned out, seeing Elliot again had plunged Nick a little too deeply into the reality of his fantasy world. He was seeing a therapist now and doing much better.

As for Detective Beaumont, his little problem took care of itself without any help from Elliot. Beaumont was no longer with the department.

Elliot had sent Wayne a football and one of his old Porter Pirates jerseys. Carmen said he loved it. She'd agreed that he and Wayne should spend some time together, get to know one another. But Carmen was the one who tortured Elliot. Seeing her again after all those years had done more than rekindle the old flame. He got out of bed. Perhaps he would call her today and tell her how he felt. He went to the window and pressed his face against the cool glass and looked out over the yard, but somehow the old view just didn't look the same. He suspected it never would.

Acknowledgments

I would like to thank my editor, Susan Koopmans, whose expert guidance helped turn my manuscript into a novel; Allan Macpherson for his help along the way; Jan Judd for answering my marketing questions; Bonnie S. Darrington for the copy editing; and Jana Rade for the wonderful cover art. I would also like to express my appreciation to the Tulsa Nightwriters and the Crossroads Writers for offering inspiration, encouragement, and appropriate criticism; and to the Tulsa Police Department, and Cpl. Tom Vallely, for graciously answering my questions.

About the Author

Bob Avey is the author of several short stories, and various nonfiction articles. He lives with his wife and son in Broken Arrow, Oklahoma, where he works as an accountant in the petroleum industry. When he's not writing, reading, or researching crime and crime scene investigation, he spends his time roaming through small towns, ghost towns, and Civil War battlefields, searching for echoes from the past. Through his writing, which he describes as a blend of literary and genre, he explores the intricacies and extremities of human nature.